AND THEN THERE WAS THE ONE

ALSO BY MARTHA WATERS

Christmas Is All Around

THE REGENCY VOWS SERIES

To Have and to Hoax
To Love and to Loathe
To Marry and to Meddle
To Swoon and to Spar
To Woo and to Wed

AND THEN THERE WAS THE ONE

A Novel

MARTHA WATERS

ATRIA PAPERBACK
NEW YORK AMSTERDAM/ANTWERP LONDON
TORONTO SYDNEY/MELBOURNE NEW DELHI

ATRIA
PAPERBACK

An Imprint of Simon & Schuster, LLC
1230 Avenue of the Americas
New York, NY 10020

For more than 100 years, Simon & Schuster has championed authors and the stories they create. By respecting the copyright of an author's intellectual property, you enable Simon & Schuster and the author to continue publishing exceptional books for years to come. We thank you for supporting the author's copyright by purchasing an authorized edition of this book.

No amount of this book may be reproduced or stored in any format, nor may it be uploaded to any website, database, language-learning model, or other repository, retrieval, or artificial intelligence system without express permission. All rights reserved. Inquiries may be directed to Simon & Schuster, 1230 Avenue of the Americas, New York, NY 10020 or permissions@simonandschuster.com.

This book is a work of fiction. Any references to historical events, real people, or real places are used fictitiously. Other names, characters, places, and events are products of the author's imagination, and any resemblance to actual events or places or persons, living or dead, is entirely coincidental.

Copyright © 2025 by Martha Waters

All rights reserved, including the right to reproduce this book or portions thereof in any form whatsoever. For information, address Atria Books Subsidiary Rights Department, 1230 Avenue of the Americas, New York, NY 10020.

First Atria Paperback edition October 2025

ATRIA PAPERBACK and colophon are trademarks of Simon & Schuster, LLC

Simon & Schuster strongly believes in freedom of expression and stands against censorship in all its forms. For more information, visit BooksBelong.com.

For information about special discounts for bulk purchases, please contact Simon & Schuster Special Sales at 1-866-506-1949 or business@simonandschuster.com.

The Simon & Schuster Speakers Bureau can bring authors to your live event. For more information or to book an event, contact the Simon & Schuster Speakers Bureau at 1-866-248-3049 or visit our website at www.simonspeakers.com.

Interior design by Kyoko Watanabe

Manufactured in the United States of America

1 3 5 7 9 10 8 6 4 2

Library of Congress Control Number: 2025005589

ISBN 978-1-6680-6957-8
ISBN 978-1-6680-6958-5 (ebook)

For Laura, my reading soulmate.

And for Meg, of course.

In an English village, you turn over a stone and have no idea what will crawl out.
—Agatha Christie, *A Murder Is Announced*

It has been said, by myself and others, that a love-interest is only an intrusion upon a detective story. But to the characters involved, the detective-interest might well seem an irritating intrusion upon their love-story.
—Dorothy Sayers, *Busman's Honeymoon*

AND THEN THERE WAS THE ONE

CHAPTER ONE

Georgie wasn't hysterical by nature, but four seemed like an awful lot of homicides.

"Don't you think it's becoming rather odd?" she asked Arthur as they stood amidst a small cluster of villagers outside Mr. Marble's shop, watching as Constable Lexington led Mrs. Marble away. It was a sunny morning in May, the air mild and a bit damp from last night's rain. The storefront bearing a hand-painted wooden sign reading the Marbled Cheese and a display of several wheels of Double Gloucester did not appear the likely location of a murder. There was a fair amount of shocked murmuring among the crowd, combined with the occasional dark mutter about always having suspected something was *odd* about Mr. Marble's wife.

Arthur, who was watching the proceedings while jotting down notes on the pad he'd fished out of the pocket of his trousers, glanced over at her with a frown. "What is?"

"Four murders in a year!" Georgie said in an undertone, but further discussion of this oddity was forestalled by Arthur choosing that precise moment to weave his way through the crowd, soliciting interviews; one person, a very pretty woman about Georgie's age with brown hair and a smattering of freckles across her nose, looked exceptionally eager to speak to him. Georgie was fairly sure the woman was a Murder Tourist—she thought she recognized her from a previous visit to the village that winter—and wondered whether it was her ghoulish interest in violent crimes in quaint settings or Arthur's own particular charms that made her *quite* so happy to speak to a member of the press. Arthur was a reporter for *The Woolly Register*, and Georgie supposed he did have a professional obligation to report on the resolution of a murder investigation, so she waited patiently for him to finish his work.

At last, Arthur pocketed his notepad and returned to her side. "What were you saying?"

"Ten minutes ago," Georgie said acerbically, but then relented. "Buncombe-upon-Woolly is small. Even a single murder should be the event of the year—of the decade!"

"And it was," Arthur reminded her as they turned away from the Marbled Cheese to continue their progress down the high street, nodding to everyone but avoiding being trapped in conversation. (This was always a hazard in a village the size of Buncombe-upon-Woolly, especially when one was a Radcliffe of Radcliffe Hall. And Georgie, for better or worse, could lay claim to that surname.) "I thought the entire village would collectively perish from excitement when the vicar was poisoned—do you know we sold more papers that week than we did in the entire previous *month?*"

Georgie personally thought Arthur might try a bit harder to sound less gleeful about murder-induced profits, but the recent crime spree in Buncombe-upon-Woolly had undoubtedly proved to be a promising development for his career.

"But then Mr. and Mrs. Fieldstone were poisoned only a couple of months later!" Georgie pointed out. "And then there was the Christmas murder at Radcliffe Hall—"

"The readers *loved* that one," Arthur said fondly. "I thought the 'Murder Under the Mistletoe' headline was one of my best."

Georgie cut him a scathing look. "It was at *my house.*"

"I know," Arthur agreed with a solemn shake of his head. "Which is unfortunate in terms of Christmas memories, I expect, but it was dashed convenient for me, in terms of access to the crime scene. *The Deathly Dispatch* only *wishes* they'd had their reporter on the ground for that one!"

Georgie rolled her eyes; *The Deathly Dispatch* was an anonymously published broadsheet that had begun circulating solely in response to Buncombe-upon-Woolly's crime spree, and it was more or less the bane of Arthur's existence, obsessed as he was with getting scoops before its unnamed reporter, who went by the nom de plume Agent Arsenic.

"But this one makes four," Georgie said, refusing to allow herself to be drawn into yet another discussion of small-town newspaper rivalries. She cast a glance over her shoulder at the Marbled Cheese crowd, where Mr. Vincent—the owner and editor in chief of *The Woolly Register*, and therefore Arthur's employer and, given the size of the village, his only coworker—

was still busy taking photographs of the exterior of the Marbles' shop. "I wouldn't have thought Mrs. Marble capable of murder. She's always been very kind."

"You're just annoyed you weren't the one to catch her," Arthur said slyly, nodding at Mrs. Penbaker, the wife of the village council chairman, in passing. Her husband, Mr. Penbaker, had been blustering in his usual fashion outside the Marbles' shop, loudly proclaiming to all assembled that the streets of Buncombe-upon-Woolly were safe once more now that the murderous cheesemonger was soon to be behind bars. Arthur had got a lengthy quote from him on the dangers of bitter wives with easy access to arsenic, and Georgie, who had only listened to approximately a third of his speech before beginning to mentally catalogue the plants in the greenhouse at Radcliffe Hall, had been hard-pressed not to roll her eyes.

Georgie huffed out an irritated breath as they came to a stop before the library, which was an almost offensively charming building of honey-colored stone with ivy creeping up its walls in the very heart of the village. "I didn't *ask* to help solve those murders, you know," she said as Arthur stepped forward to open the door for her. "It's not my fault that no one else in this village seems capable of identifying common poisons."

"Some of us, George, have better things to do than spend our days studying every weed we spot growing along the riverbanks," Arthur said, and Georgie had to exercise great restraint to stop herself from elbowing him in the stomach. She was twenty-five now, and while that had not been an uncommon habit when she and Arthur were younger, she thought vaguely that she should perhaps attempt to be a bit more dignified in her advanced age.

"Being able to identify a bouquet of lily of the valley in a woman's kitchen, when the vicar's symptoms *perfectly* matched those associated with that particular poison, is just common sense," Georgie said in an annoyed whisper. "And yet the police were too stupid to manage even that basic level of investigation."

"See? You're irritated that they didn't consult you." Arthur sounded smug, as he so often did lately, pushing his tortoiseshell glasses up on his nose; his articles for the *Register* had garnered regional interest, and a few had even been picked up by some of the London papers. She could tell he was daydreaming about the glamorous life he would lead in London once he managed to secure a reporting job there instead; he was already dressing the part, she thought, casting a thoughtful glance at the herringbone trousers and carefully pressed shirt he was wearing. He made her feel rather dowdy by comparison, in her serviceable brown dress and woolly cardigan—but, she thought philosophically, she'd spent her entire life not caring much about how she looked, so there was no reason to start now, just because Arthur was looking a bit . . . well, dashing. (At least, she noted with satisfaction, his curly dark hair was as unruly as ever.) No doubt he intended to abandon Buncombe-upon-Woolly for a fast-paced life of nightclubs and cocktails, and would conduct love affairs with half the women in London (and half the men, too, Georgie didn't doubt), and she'd only see him once a year at Christmas. She felt a bit gloomy at the thought.

"I'm perfectly fine, thank you," she said stiffly, and then promptly abandoned him to make a beeline for the botany section, while Arthur headed off to consult the library's collection of other archived Gloucestershire newspapers, to compare historical crime statistics to those of the past year. For all he might tease her about her interest in the recent spate of murders, he was just as curious.

Georgie set about amassing a stack of books to take home with her—many of which, admittedly, she'd already read—and, after some minutes spent browsing, approached the desk where Miss Halifax, the librarian, was seated. She was perhaps fifteen years Georgie's senior, with dark hair that was pinned loosely back from her face; she wore a blue day dress with a white collar and, per the laws of librarianship, a cardigan. She had an Agatha Christie novel in hand and was scribbling away in a notebook as Georgie set her books down before her. Georgie spotted a page labeled *Book club questions*, and she shook her head darkly. The book club, as she understood it, had formed in the wake of the village's recent murder spree, and solely read crime novels.

"Any chance we might see you at the next Book Clue Crew meeting, Miss Radcliffe?" Miss Halifax asked, looking up as Georgie produced her library card from her dress pocket.

Georgie did not snort, but she was tempted. "No, thank you," she said. "I think that there are quite enough murders in my day-to-day life without seeking out fictional ones. In fact," she added, "I should be very happy to not think about murder ever again."

"I think there are many readers who would disagree with

you, Miss Radcliffe." Miss Halifax handed back her library card.

"Well," Georgie said, watching as Miss Halifax set about stamping her books, "I can assure you that I've better things to do than worry about the opinions of *mystery* readers."

"Georgie!"

Georgie, her arms full of books, was attempting to scrape mud off the sides of her oxford shoes so that Mrs. Fawcett did not murder her in her sleep for mucking up her clean floors. She paused at the sound of her sister's voice, and turned to see Abigail standing dramatically on the stairs in . . .

"What on earth have you got on?" Georgie asked, setting the books down on the floor next to her as she unlaced her shoes.

"A Victorian nightgown," Abigail said, in a tone that implied that this should have been obvious—and that, moreover, there was nothing else that she possibly could have been expected to be wearing at—Georgie consulted the antique clock above the empty fireplace in the entrance hall—three-fifteen on a Monday afternoon.

Georgie retrieved her books, straightened, and cast her sister an inquiring look. "Are you unwell?" Abigail appeared to be positively blooming with good health and cheer, as always.

"No," Abigail said slowly. "Only, well." She paused, adopting an expression of martyred suffering that Georgie found a bit much to swallow from someone who routinely slept until ten in the morning. "I'm a bit fatigued." She sighed, rubbing at her eyes—which, Georgie noted, displayed no telltale dark circles or lines or any other hint of exhaustion. "Perhaps we ought to summon Dr. Severin."

Georgie's eyes narrowed. "Indeed? You feel that poorly?"

"Well, you never know. One ought to be cautious with one's health, Georgie."

"I suppose if Dr. Severin were not *quite* so young and handsome, your desire to summon him would remain unchanged?" Georgie asked with a skeptical lift of one brow.

"*Georgie!*" Abigail clapped a dramatic hand to her breast; Georgie was unmoved.

"You're perfectly fine," she informed her sister shortly as she made her way up the stairs past her in her stockinged feet, clutching her armful of books. "And they've arrested Mrs. Marble for her husband's murder," she tossed over her shoulder in passing, relishing the slightly shocked expression on Abigail's face.

"But she always made the most delicious cheese tart for the village fete!" Abigail said mournfully. "I can't believe anyone who makes cheese tarts could be a murderess!"

"I will inform the constabulary of this logical objection at once," Georgie called, before continuing up the second flight of stairs to the top floor of the house. Here, she made her way to the far end of the hallway, opened the door to her bedroom, and shut it behind herself with perhaps more force than was strictly necessary.

"*Sisters*," she muttered to Egg, her elderly beagle, who raised her head inquiringly from the battered blue-and-green tartan pillow she had, until moments earlier, been slumbering upon.

AND THEN THERE WAS THE ONE

Egg twitched an ear in Georgie's direction, which Georgie took to be a gesture of sympathetic commiseration, and after depositing her library books in an untidy pile upon her desk, she settled herself on the floor, reaching out to stroke Egg's soft ears. Egg let out a satisfied sigh, allowing her head to sink back down atop her cushion. Ordinarily, Egg would have accompanied Georgie on her excursion, but Miss Halifax had made it clear to Georgie that under no circumstances whatsoever was she to bring her dog into the library.

Georgie looked around the room, her fingers still rubbing an absent-minded pattern on Egg's ear: Radcliffe Hall, the ramshackle estate that had been home to her family for three hundred years, had certainly seen better days, but it *did* have turrets on either end, and Georgie had resided in one of these turrets since she'd been old enough to be moved out of the nursery. Her walls were painted a deep forest green and decorated with a number of framed botanical prints; the four-poster was pushed against one wall opposite a window so that she could lie in bed and take in views of the rolling hills that surrounded Buncombe-upon-Woolly. There were books and empty teacups scattered haphazardly upon nearly every available surface; a record player sat atop her dresser, a teetering pile of records stacked next to it; her favorite tweed jacket was tossed upon a particularly comfortable armchair; the entire room smelled faintly, but not unpleasantly, of dog.

Georgie leaned down to press a quick kiss to Egg's head. She stretched out her legs before her, wiggling her toes in her stockings which, annoyingly, seemed to be forming a hole over one toe yet again. Mrs. Fawcett truly *was* going to murder her—

although Georgie had the faint, dissatisfied feeling that perhaps she ought to stop speaking *quite* so flippantly of murder, given recent events.

It was irritating. The entire past *year* had been irritating, in fact; her thoughts returned to her conversation with Arthur earlier. One murder in a village of this size was a shocking tragedy; two was an unpleasant coincidence; but three—and now *four?* Georgie was a creature of science, of reason, and she simply did not think it normal. Of all the villages in England, why did *hers* have to be the one that had suddenly become a hotbed of murder—and, possibly even worse, a hotbed of Murder Tourists? The Murder Tourists—who had flooded the village over the course of the past year, drawn by lurid headlines and eager to visit the scenes of Buncombe-upon-Woolly's various crimes—had quickly become the bane of Georgie's existence.

There was a tap at the door, interrupting these dissatisfying thoughts. "Come in," she called absently, not moving from her spot on the floor; the door opened and her father poked his head in. Egg thumped her tail several times in greeting.

"Georgie, love, you haven't seen my spectacles, have you?" Papa asked, looking vaguely harried. "I can't seem to find them, and I just received my copy of this year's *Archaeological Journal.*" He rubbed his hands together at the thought of this promised treat.

"Check the tea tray in your study, Papa," Georgie said. "If Mrs. Fawcett brought you your usual three o'clock cup of tea, you might have left them beside the pot." A fact she knew because he did this precise thing at least once a week. (He was also in the habit of losing them atop his head.)

"Of course, of course," Papa said absently, squinting down at the envelopes in his hand; evidently the afternoon post had arrived. "Any news from the village?"

"They've arrested Mrs. Marble for her husband's murder."

"Have they?" Papa asked, still staring at the letter in his hand. "Never thought her capable of murder. Too short."

"I do not believe height is a prerequisite for homicide, Papa."

"I suppose not," he said, looking up at her at last. "You'd know more about it than I would, love." He waved vaguely before retreating; as soon as she heard his footsteps on the stairs, Georgie flopped back onto the floor. She stared up at the ceiling as Egg offered her a politely inquiring tilt of the head.

"Is no one else in this village capable of rational thought?" she asked Egg, stroking a gentle finger down her snout.

She should be glad, she knew, that the police had managed to make an arrest without her assistance this time. And yet, she could not stop the niggling worry that had been present at the back of her mind since the moment she and Arthur had witnessed Mrs. Marble's arrest a few hours earlier. She didn't *want* to solve another mystery and she wasn't going to involve herself in a case that seemed to have been resolved, whatever her misgivings.

She turned her head on the Turkish rug—one that, from this vantage point, quite clearly needed a good beating; she resolutely ignored this fact—and stared into Egg's mournful eyes.

"I didn't *ask* to become an amateur sleuth, you know."

Egg whined sympathetically.

"And it's about time the police started doing their jobs without me."

Egg's tail thumped encouragingly on the floor.

She crossed her arms over her chest, noticing that a small hole was forming in the sleeve of her brown wool cardigan; that would be another project for Mrs. Fawcett, as Georgie's mending skills could be charitably described as limited. "Even if the—the *council chairman*, of all people, were to keel over, that would be none of my concern."

Egg blinked at her. Georgie decided to take this as a show of emotional support, and reached out to pat her head.

Beagles, Georgie thought, were much better company than humans.

CHAPTER TWO

Two weeks later, the council chairman did, in fact, keel over.

"I really don't think this is normal," Georgie said to Arthur as they sat in the Shorn Sheep, Georgie's favorite pub—of, admittedly, only two—in Buncombe-upon-Woolly. News of Mr. Penbaker's death had spread the afternoon before, when his wife had returned home to find him complaining of chest pains; by the time Dr. Severin had arrived, he was dead. Mr. Penbaker had always seemed quite energetic, as evidenced by the amount of time he spent working up elaborate and increasingly unwieldy schemes to draw tourists to the village; everyone appeared shocked by his sudden demise.

This evening, the pub was packed with locals and tourists alike, and Mr. Penbaker's death was the topic of most of the conversations around Georgie. She and Arthur were seated at the bar, nursing a cider (Georgie) and a ginger beer (Arthur, who had sworn off strong drink in the wake of a particularly ill-advised night of revelry a couple of years earlier).

"What isn't?" Arthur asked, casting an interested glance at Harry, the barman; Georgie had her own suspicions as to why, precisely, her teetotaling friend was so eager to continue patronizing the local pub. Harry had been a few years ahead of them in school, and had taken over the day-to-day operations of the Shorn Sheep after his father's health began to decline. He was a man of few words but particularly fine forearms—a fact that Georgie was fairly certain Arthur had noted.

"Mr. Penbaker's death!" Georgie said impatiently. "He wasn't that old!"

"He died in his own bed of an apparent heart attack," Arthur said. "That's hardly unheard of."

"He'd never so much as taken a sick day before," Georgie insisted.

"Have you become so obsessed with murder that you can't see a death from natural causes and not suspect some sort of foul play?"

"I'm not *obsessed*," she protested. "But after this many murders, I can't help but think that the unexpected death of a member of local government might be due a second look."

"I agree, Miss Radcliffe," said a voice from behind her. She turned in time to see Constable Lexington, the only member of the county constabulary with whom she had a remotely positive relationship, set down a pint glass on the bar next to her and take a seat. He was in his early thirties, with reddish-brown hair that he kept combed neatly back from his face. He always had a vaguely melancholy air about him; he'd also never been anything other than scrupulously polite to Georgie, unlike certain other members of the county police force. As the village bobby, he'd been involved in rounding up the suspects in all of the murder cases over the past year, though these efforts had been hampered by the hapless detective inspector he'd had to work with, a man named Harriday from the neighboring village of Bramble-in-the-Vale.

"See!" Georgie said triumphantly to Arthur, before turning back to Constable Lexington. "Do the police intend to investigate, then?"

"Ah." Lexington cleared his throat. "No. You'll note that I said *I* agree, singular. *We*, as in the Gloucestershire constabulary more generally, do not."

"Whyever not?" Georgie demanded. "Have they all suffered head injuries?"

"I couldn't say," Lexington said diplomatically, causing a fleeting grin to flash across Arthur's face.

"You agree with Georgie's paranoia then, Lexington?" Arthur asked, a slightly eager note in his voice; no doubt, Georgie thought uncharitably, he was considering how many more articles he could write if Mr. Penbaker had, in fact, been murdered.

"I do not believe it is paranoia," Lexington said a bit stiffly. His and Arthur's relationship was somewhat strained, in large part due to Arthur's less-than-charitable articles focusing on the police's efforts to solve the various murders, despite the fact that Lexington himself had never been mentioned by name. "I'll admit that I see nothing unusual in Penbaker's death on the surface, but after so many recent murders . . . it might be worth investigating."

"Well," Georgie said decisively, "what are we going to do about it, then?"

Lexington blanched. "I don't know that there's much we *can* do, Miss Radcliffe. Chief Constable Humphreys—"

Georgie ground her teeth at the sound of the chief constable's name; Humphreys had been barely tolerant of her involvement in three of the past year's murder cases, so she could not imagine that he would welcome any perceived interference from her in a matter that he didn't even consider to *be* a case.

"Regardless of the chief constable's feelings on the matter," she said determinedly, "I cannot sit idly by and watch a possible murder go unsolved in *my* village." She paused for a moment, wistfully contemplating her resolution, just two weeks earlier, to stop involving herself in murder investigations. "The Radcliffes of Radcliffe Hall have lived in Buncombe-upon-Woolly for over three hundred years," she added. "It is nothing less than my duty to ensure that the village doesn't gain a reputation for anything . . . unsavory."

"I think it's too late for that," Arthur murmured, casting a glance toward a corner booth, where a group of men and women who looked to be approximately Georgie's age—none of whom Georgie had ever seen before, and all of whom were stylishly clad and well-coiffed—were conferring eagerly over a round of drinks. They had a broadsheet spread on the table before them, and Georgie would have bet money that it was the latest issue of *The Deathly Dispatch*. Even though it had been more than a fortnight since Mrs. Marble's arrest, the broadsheet was continuing to publish multiple issues a week offering grisly details on the nature of her husband's death (a poisoned bottle of wine) and wild theories about her mental instability, citing unnamed sources.

Georgie frowned. "Not again."

"Again," Arthur confirmed, handing his empty bottle to Harry, who whisked it away and, moments later, replaced it with a fresh bottle of ginger beer. "Nothing like a jolly little holiday to the scene of a crime."

The tourists had begun to arrive in earnest at Christmas. By that time, there had been two murders in Buncombe-upon-Woolly in a six-month window of time—an unusual enough occurrence to catch the attention of the London papers. *The Times* had run a lengthy article on the odd series of events (making heavy use of Arthur's reporting, as he would remind anyone who sat still long enough); the article had noted the village's many charms that seemed so at odds with cold-blooded murder, which had excited no small amount of pride among its residents—the prevailing sentiment seemed to be that if they had to have a skyrocketing crime rate, they might at least be appreciated for their finer qualities, too. When the third murder took place at Radcliffe Hall on Christmas Eve, while the initial crop of Murder Tourists were present in the village, it had turned the stream of visitors into a proper rush. They came clutching copies of popular crime novels and were prone to loud discussions of the merits of the police investigations.

On a couple of occasions, they'd made it to Radcliffe Hall, only to have Mrs. Fawcett meet them at the door with a steely gleam in her eye and an evidently convincing threat to lob a frying pan at their heads.

"Agatha Christie has a lot to answer for," Georgie said darkly, still gazing at the group in the corner.

"Have you ever read one of her novels?" Arthur asked.

"Of course not," Georgie huffed, crossing her arms. "Why should I need to read about a fictional cozy village full of homicidal maniacs when I am already inhabiting one?"

"They're rather good," Lexington said quietly, and quickly buried his face in his glass.

Georgie cast him a disgusted look. "I would think you get quite enough of that sort of thing in your professional life, Constable."

"Well." Lexington lowered his glass. "It's just, it's nice to read about them being so tidily resolved."

"*I* have been tidily resolving them," Georgie said through clenched teeth. "Should I expect you to take pen to paper and start fictionalizing my exploits?"

"Not really my line of work," Lexington said, draining his glass. "Shame we can't summon one of her detectives to come help us—that Poirot fellow would sort this out in a heartbeat."

Arthur snapped his fingers, a gleam in his eye. "That's it!"

"What is?" Georgie asked suspiciously; she had known Arthur since he was five years old, and long experience had taught her to be wary when he looked this excited.

"A detective—a *professional* one."

"What—hire one?" Lexington asked, a bit doubtful. "I don't know how much Vincent is paying you to churn out your sensationalist tripe—"

"*Excuse me*," Arthur began, outraged, but Lexington continued before he could work himself into a proper indignant fury.

"—but I don't personally have so much extra coin lying around that I fancy paying a private detective's fees."

"I wonder if we could convince someone to come for the sake of an interesting case," Georgie said thoughtfully. "One who didn't necessarily need the money, whose interest we might be able to pique. Someone established in their career."

"What, are we just going to write to Delacey Fitzgibbons and ask him if he fancies a holiday in the Cotswolds?" Arthur asked.

A moment of silence fell as all three of them contemplated this—mad, unworkable, entirely unlikely to succeed—idea. Delacey Fitzgibbons was a legend—the most famous private detective in all of England. He'd been a police officer long ago but had abandoned Scotland Yard after a public falling-out with the police commissioner, and had struck out on his own, solving one high-profile case after another. The man himself was as famous as his detective feats—he was known to always wear the same tweed jacket and cap, no matter the season or the weather, and had a monocle that he was very fond of holding up to one eye to stare at whichever witness he was interrogating. He also had a very bushy mustache, and no hair on his head at all. He was curt and impatient, but undeniably brilliant. There was no chance, none whatsoever, that *Delacey Fitzgibbons* would come to Buncombe-upon-Woolly.

"Worth a shot?" Lexington asked, after several seconds more of thoughtful silence had elapsed.

"Why not!" Arthur said cheerfully, knocking back his ginger beer.

Georgie cast another irate glance at the table of Murder Tourists, who were now laughing uproariously at something in the latest issue of *The Deathly Dispatch*.

"Come on, George," Arthur wheedled. "Think how good it would be for the *Register* if we found out something spectacular and I had the scoop. It would be nice to remind everyone that the *Register* is a real paper employing actual journalists covering legitimate news, and worth considerably more than some anonymously authored vehicle for conspiracy theories."

Georgie pressed her lips together, and then Lexington said, without looking up from his glass, "I expect if there *is* something to be uncovered here, and we were able to prove that Penbaker was murdered, Chief Constable Humphreys would be absolutely humiliated."

This, ultimately, was all the convincing Georgie needed. "All right," she said, draining the last of her cider. "I'll write to Fitzgibbons as soon as I get home tonight, inviting him to come stay at Radcliffe Hall—but," she added, raising a hand, "I think it's best not to get our hopes up. What could we possibly have to offer someone as famous as Fitzgibbons?"

"Murders in a cozy setting," Arthur said wisely. "People *love* when murders feel cozy, you know. He won't be able to resist."

Annoyingly, Arthur was right.

"I *told* you," he said triumphantly. "I *told* you that no one can resist the allure of a grisly crime in a cozy village setting!"

"Yes, yes," Georgie muttered, returning her gaze to the letter in her hand, as if the contents would have changed at some point in the past thirty seconds. The neatly typed words on the page remained the same, however:

> Russell Square, Bloomsbury
> 7 June
>
> Dear Miss Radcliffe,
>
> I was pleased to receive your letter detailing the unusual circumstances in your village—I had read one of the Times articles on the subject some months back—and appreciate your invitation to come investigate the untimely death of your village council chairman. Unfortunately, my own caseload at this juncture is so full that I am unable to manage a visit to Gloucestershire, but my assistant, Mr. Sebastian Fletcher-Ford, would be delighted to travel in my stead, and to keep me apprised of any developments. Mr. Fletcher-Ford has my utmost trust, and you may confide in him as you would in me personally.
>   He's arranged to arrive on the noon train on Thursday the 14th, and looks forward to meeting you at that time.
>
> Best wishes,
> Delacey Fitzgibbons

"I can't believe he responded," she said, shaking her head at Arthur, who was looking so pleased with himself that it was practically . . . well, criminal. "*Don't* say 'I told you so' again, or I'll personally see to it that *you* are the next homicide in the village."

"Perhaps we should be investigating you, then," Arthur shot back; just then, there was a dramatic clearing of the throat, and they glanced up in unison, recalled from the exciting contents of their letter to their current surroundings. They were seated on a blanket on the village green, where the locals had gathered for the monthly fete. This event, which—rather ambitiously (or at least damply)—took place rain or shine, was organized by the ladies' club at St. Drogo's, the village church, to raise funds for local families in need; it was considered the height of entertainment in Buncombe-upon-Woolly. Georgie couldn't precisely argue with this assessment of the program, though she often thought that the *sort* of entertainment she and Arthur derived from it was not precisely what the organizers intended.

She hadn't been certain it would take place this month, given recent events, but the prevailing attitude seemed to be that nothing—not even the untimely demise of the council chairman—should stand in the way of the monthly fete. They were the only village in the county with such an event—all the other municipalities contented themselves with a more traditional annual summer fair, and nothing more frequent than that—and so they could not allow anything to get in the way of this tradition. They had carried on during the war, after all; there was no reason that the death of one man should disrupt their plans. Georgie couldn't decide whether she found this attitude to be admirably stoic, unsettlingly grim, or both.

Mrs. Pennywhistle, the head of the ladies' club, was standing before the benches at the edge of the green, which was the closest thing the fete had to a stage. She was a sweet-faced woman in her sixties who was fond of brightly colored cardigans. "This month's fete," she said, in a loud, carrying voice, "will be commenced by Miss Abigail Radcliffe, who will be regaling us with"—she consulted her notes—"a poem."

This was uttered the way someone might have announced an intent to entertain the assembled crowd with a spot of pornography; Georgie suspected that, to Mrs. Pennywhistle, poetry and pornography were not dissimilar. There was a round of enthusiastic applause as Abigail rose to her feet from her spot on a blanket with some of her friends; she was wearing a tea dress of white cotton gauze, and her golden hair curled around her shoulders in careful waves, a slender white headband keeping it swept away from her lovely face. Abigail was popular among the villagers and always had been—the girls' mother had died when Abigail was very young, which had inspired a great deal of sympathetic tut-tutting among the matrons of Buncombe-upon-Woolly, who regarded her with a maternal, protective eye. She was pretty enough that she'd always attracted her fair share of admirers among the village boys, and she'd had a wide circle of friends at school. Georgie, who—while she knew she was admired and respected by the villagers, and who had always had a loyal friend in Arthur—had never inspired the widespread adoration that Abigail received, always watched her sister waft about the village, getting whatever she wished merely by producing one of her angelic smiles, with something bordering on bemusement.

Abigail gave an absurd little curtsy upon taking her place

before the crowd, and then announced, "I am going to recite 'The Lady of Shalott.'"

Next to Georgie, Arthur stifled a groan. "Not *that* one."

"She loves Tennyson," Georgie said gloomily. "She's been practicing for the past three days—it's enough to make me never want to get into a boat again."

"It's rather maudlin, don't you think?" Arthur said; Georgie personally found this a bit rich from a man she had personally witnessed shed a tear while reading "O Captain! My Captain!"—when he wasn't even *American*.

"On either side the river lie," Abigail began, clapping a dramatic hand to her breast; Georgie, gazing idly around at the assembled crowd to distract herself from having to listen to this yet again, frowned slightly when she noticed Dr. Severin watching Abigail with a rapt expression. He was, she thought consideringly, extremely handsome—it was no wonder Abigail was so taken with him. He was about Georgie's age, newly arrived in the village as of last autumn, having just finished medical school in Edinburgh. The way he was gazing at Abigail made Georgie vaguely uneasy—Abigail's infatuation would surely fade, especially once Georgie had convinced her to accept their aunt's invitation to come for a lengthy stay in London this summer, but if there was any reciprocal feeling on Dr. Severin's part, this would undoubtedly make matters more difficult.

Georgie added this to her ongoing mental list of worries—between repeated homicides, a lovestruck sister, and an aging dog who had, somewhat alarmingly, vomited twice this week (though Georgie suspected this was simply because of Egg's fondness for drinking the cream from the tea service when no one was looking), this list was growing long indeed—and refocused on the performance before her, which Abigail was just wrapping up with a dramatic, "Draw near and fear not, this is I, the Lady of Shalott."

Georgie and Arthur joined in the hearty applause, though Georgie's was largely the relieved clapping of someone who never had to hear that poem ever again. No sooner had Abigail returned to her seat—with a last, delighted wave to her fellow villagers—than Harry the barman shuffled to the front of the crowd and produced a concertina.

"I'd no idea he could play the concertina," Georgie said as he commenced a surprisingly rollicking sea shanty. "Not much opportunity for it, I suppose, when he's always behind the bar," she added, nodding her head in time. She glanced sideways at Arthur. "You might try to look a *bit* less openly lustful, you know," she said slyly, and was rewarded with a scornful look on Arthur's part.

"I'm not lustful," he objected. "I'm ... appreciative."

"If that's what you want to call it," Georgie said doubtfully, and then broke off, noticing that Constable Lexington was weaving his way through the crowds in their direction, murmuring apologies as he went. "Hello," she said. "It's good you stopped by."

"Why's that?" he asked, lowering himself to the edge of their blanket. He was not wearing his police uniform, but instead had on a pair of carefully pressed trousers and a shirt and tie.

"We heard back from Fitzgibbons," she said, and handed him the letter, which he quickly scanned.

"Interesting," he said, returning the missive to Georgie.

"Bit disappointing we couldn't get Fitzgibbons himself," Arthur said. "Think of the articles I could have written!"

"But perhaps for the best," Lexington said, and Georgie looked at him curiously.

"Why?"

He cleared his throat, looking uncomfortable. "The county police are, er, quite pleased with themselves, at the resolution of the Marble murder."

"Of course they are," she muttered with some disgust.

"I believe"—and here, his voice took on a vaguely apologetic tone—"that they are particularly pleased to have solved it without your assistance, Miss Radcliffe, and are eager to bask in the glory for a bit, so they've . . ." He trailed off, looking at Arthur.

"What?" Arthur asked suspiciously.

"Well," Lexington said, "they've arranged for some sort of interview with *The Deathly Dispatch*."

"What!" Arthur demanded, sitting up straighter. "How the devil are they going to do that? No one even knows who *writes* the *Dispatch*."

"I believe the interview is going to be conducted via the post."

"That's not *real journalism*," Arthur balked.

"I don't know if the man who recently wrote a two-page feature on Ernest the village sheep *really* ought to be casting stones about 'real journalism,'" Georgie noted, nodding at the ram in question, who was munching contentedly on a patch of grass at the edge of the green.

"The point is," Lexington continued, "I don't think they'd

take kindly to any rumors of unsanctioned detective work . . . so it's probably for the best that Fitzgibbons himself isn't coming. It would put Chief Constable Humphreys in a terrible mood, so if you could try to keep this assistant of Fitzgibbons's from drawing too much attention, it would certainly make my job easier."

Georgie shook her head. "This is probably going to make us seem like rank amateurs; it will be a miracle if this Fletcher-Ford doesn't hop on the next train back to London."

"Please," Arthur said, waving a dismissive hand. "This is an assistant to *Delacey Fitzgibbons*—his protégé! He's not going to turn away from an intriguing case. I bet he'll have things sorted in a trice."

"I don't know," Georgie said dubiously. "It's going to be fairly difficult to investigate a crime that may or may not have happened, with a man whom no one is meant to realize is here."

"You worry too much," Arthur said. "Trust me, Georgie—this time on Thursday, you'll be prostrate at my feet with gratitude for my insistence that you send that letter."

"Somehow, I doubt that," Georgie muttered.

And, as it happened, she was entirely correct.

CHAPTER THREE

*T*hursday was an exceptionally lovely day, which Georgie found exceptionally irritating.

"Look at it," she explained to Arthur under her breath as they approached the train station. "The sun shining—the flowers blooming along the lane—the *ivy*." She gestured at the absurdly picturesque station.

"Er," said Arthur. "What about the ivy, precisely?"

"It looks very *charming*," Georgie said. "No wonder we have Murder Tourists!"

"An absolute plague of them," Arthur muttered, eyeing a flock of young men of university age who were murmuring excitedly to each other, several of whom appeared to be clutching—Georgie groaned internally—magnifying glasses.

Georgie had, on numerous occasions over the past few months, been stopped on the street while trying to do something entirely ordinary, like return a library book or pick up an order at the butcher's for Mrs. Fawcett, and subjected to the breathless inquiries of Murder Tourists who recognized her as *the* Miss Radcliffe, amateur sleuth. She had gone through a phase in the spring when she'd taken to wearing exceedingly large hats by way of disguise, until Abigail finally pointed out that she might actually be drawing *more* attention to herself that way.

"My point is," she said, ignoring the Murder Tourists and instead gazing darkly at the quaint, two-platform train station before them, the Woolly River twinkling in the sunlight as it curved behind the station, "this man from London is going to swoop in here and think that Mr. Penbaker dropped dead of natural causes. Who would murder the leader of a village that looks like this?"

Arthur glanced around surreptitiously. "Keep your voice down. We have no idea who's behind *The Deathly Dispatch*—they could have ears everywhere, and I'm not going to let them scoop me, on the off chance there actually *is* a story here."

Georgie shook her head. "This is becoming a fixation."

"They're poaching my readers! All of this hubbub about the murders won't do me any good if the *Register*'s entire readership abandons us for the *Dispatch*."

"You're starting to sound a bit hysterical."

"Rich, coming from the woman who's convinced that an elderly man who died of a heart attack was actually murdered by some secretive village cabal." He visibly brightened at this prospect, and Georgie could practically see the wheels of his mind turning as he pondered cabal-related headlines.

"I have never claimed there was a cabal," Georgie said severely. "And he was only sixty-five—that's how old my father is!" Papa had been more than a decade older than her mother, as it had evidently taken quite some time for someone interesting enough to come along to catch his eye, given how preoccupied he'd been by the Woolly Hoard, his one and only claim to archaeological glory.

"Hmmm." Arthur made a skeptical noise, one that Georgie would absolutely have protested further had she not been distracted at that very moment by a train whistle. She and Arthur climbed the steps to the station, crossing to the edge of the platform just as the train crawled to a halt before them.

"Do you think we'll be able to recognize him?" Georgie asked Arthur a bit uncertainly.

"What, do you think he'll be wearing a cap and monocle, like Fitzgibbons?" Arthur asked; Georgie noted that he was wearing his favorite blue jumper, and that his unruly curls were a bit more tamed than usual. She, too, had dressed with particular care this morning, donning a green skirt and carefully pressed white blouse that Abigail had once informed her was almost stylish, and she'd even taken the time to wipe a bit of the dust and mud off her brown oxford shoes before hopping on her bicycle to meet Arthur outside his small flat on the high street.

"Perhaps it's a prerequisite of the job," she said to Arthur.

She scrutinized the passengers disembarking from the train. There was a harassed-looking mother surrounded by three young children, being greeted by an elderly couple; a pair of middle-aged women dressed in colorful cotton dresses and matching hats, looking around eagerly (Murder Tourists); and then—

Well, quite simply, the most handsome man Georgie had ever seen descended to the platform.

Given the small size of Buncombe-upon-Woolly, she supposed this wasn't saying much—how many men *had* she seen, in her entire life, in total? However, she was fairly certain that this man would cause a stir even in London, where beautiful creatures of every gender must surely waltz about the streets. He was tall and lean, with hair of a golden hue akin to perfectly ripened wheat; it was combed back from his face in an impeccable wave, not a single curl daring to break ranks and spoil the impression of well-coiffed perfection. His eyes: the blue of the summer sky. His attire: linen trousers, and the most immaculately fitted forest-green jumper Georgie had ever seen. His luggage: a leather hand-case that likely cost more than the entire contents of Georgie's wardrobe.

She frowned. Surely a man such as this hadn't arrived for a visit with a single hand-case?

"Ah!" the man said brightly, watching the porter struggle down the train step behind him with two enormous suitcases. "Just there," he added, nodding to a spot about ten feet away. "No doubt I can summon a cab to take me the rest of the way."

Georgie wondered—even as she, to her great disgust, realized that she was still staring, as though hypnotized, at the wave of his hair—what business such a man had in Buncombe-upon-Woolly. He didn't strike her as a Murder Tourist, but perhaps he, too, wanted to be part of the excitement of a quaint place in the grip of a grisly crime spree. He could tell his sophisticated friends in London about it—for, not for a single second, did she doubt that this man was from the capital. The shine of his shoes alone was enough to inform her of this fact—no one who resided in the country had shoes that clean. It was physically impossible.

"Although." Here, the man frowned, a wrinkle appearing in his brow. The expression looked odd on him, as though he'd had precious little cause to make it in his life.

"I would have thought," he continued, seemingly oblivious to the porter's struggles behind him, "that someone would have come to meet me? I'm here at their invitation, after all—what was the name of the lady who wrote?" He patted futilely at his pockets, as though expecting a letter to suddenly materialize from one of them.

"I couldn't say, sir," the porter said, panting a bit after depositing the evidently heavy suitcases on the platform. "Have a good afternoon," he added with clear relief, springing back onto the train as the final "all aboard!" was called. The handsome man, meanwhile, glanced about the platform, his gaze landing on Georgie, who made no attempt to disguise her stare. He brightened at the sight of her.

"I say!" he called with a jaunty little wave of his hand. "You wouldn't be here from—er—" Once again, he patted at his pockets.

"Radcliffe Hall?" Georgie managed, finding her voice at last.

"Just so!" he said cheerfully. "I expect you're a housemaid? I hope you're stronger than you look," he added, sizing her up with an experienced eye. "These trunks are quite heavy—

though I'd be happy to give you a hand." He beamed at her. "Ladies do enjoy my occasional displays of physical strength."

Georgie only narrowly avoided gaping at him, so gripped was she by incredulous horror. *This* was the man Delacey Fitzgibbons had sent to investigate the murders in Buncombe-upon-Woolly? *Him?*

The *him* in question had thrust one hand into his pocket and was continuing to beam at her in an expectant sort of way. Arthur—who, Georgie noticed, had visibly brightened at the prospect of a display of manly strength—stepped forward and extended his hand.

"You must be Mr. Fletcher-Ford."

The gentleman in question reached out to shake Arthur's hand enthusiastically. "Sebastian Fletcher-Ford—were you sent by Miss . . . er. I'm afraid I've forgotten her name, the one who wrote." He smiled sheepishly; Arthur appeared momentarily blinded.

"That would be Miss Radcliffe," Arthur said, recovering after a moment, nodding over his shoulder at Georgie.

"Ah." Fletcher-Ford had the grace to look a bit sheepish. "Not a housemaid, then?"

"Not the last time I checked." Georgie's tone was cold enough to freeze a puddle, but Fletcher-Ford's smile didn't waver at the sound. She took several cautious steps toward him, and he reached for her hand, which he kissed before she could stop him, as if it were 1834, rather than 1934. She wrenched her hand back.

"And I'm Arthur Crawley," Arthur said, apparently sensing—correctly—that Georgie was too discombobulated by this interaction to perform any introductions herself. "And there's Constable Lexington, of course." Georgie, startled, glanced over her shoulder to find that Lexington had indeed materialized behind her and was observing this interaction with a faintly puzzled expression.

"Delighted," Fletcher-Ford said, his tone entirely amiable. He tilted his head, surveying his surroundings. "What a charming part of the country. Do you know, I saw a positively adorable herd of veal wobbling around a meadow on the train ride here?"

"A herd of—do you mean *calves*?" Georgie asked, blinking.

Fletcher-Ford snapped his fingers. "That's the one! Can never keep the two words straight—don't you think it's odd that a lamb is a lamb, no matter whether we're about to eat it or not, but a cow isn't?"

Georgie, Arthur, and Lexington stared at him for a long moment.

"I can't say it had ever occurred to me," Lexington said at last.

Fletcher-Ford winked at him. "That's why I'm here, old sport. Someone's got to think about these things!"

They continued to stare at him, veering precariously close to gaping, before Georgie decided that a bit of diplomacy was called for.

"We are intrigued to make your acquaintance," she said, which she supposed wasn't an inaccurate assessment of the situation. "And though the letter came from me, it was really a collective effort, from Mr. Crawley and Constable Lexington and myself."

Fletcher-Ford gave Georgie a winning smile. "I can't tell you how disappointed I am to hear it, Miss Radcliffe. I do so *love* to receive letters from enchanting young ladies."

Georgie frowned; Arthur coughed.

"So," Fletcher-Ford said, rubbing his hands together eagerly. "I hear you've a spot of murder?"

"Rather," Georgie said. "Four in the past year—but I suspect it might be five."

"Well, I suppose that's what I'm here to investigate, isn't it?" Fletcher-Ford said brightly. "Not, of course," he amended, "that I would presume to fault your work, Constable."

"It's Miss Radcliffe's work, in truth," Lexington said, which caused Georgie's feelings toward him to warm appreciably. She'd never disliked Lexington—he was vastly less frustrating to deal with than every other member of the constabulary, and particularly Detective Inspector Harriday—but she had not thought him the sort of man to openly credit the efforts of an amateur detective over his own. An amateur *lady* detective, at that. It made her wonder, a trifle uncomfortably, if she didn't entirely know what sort of man he was at all.

"Except for the latest case," Georgie corrected. "Mr. Marble, who owned the cheese shop, was poisoned, and the police have arrested his wife—I had nothing to do with that."

"Nor did I," Lexington said in an undertone, looking distinctly discomfited. Before she could pursue this, however, Fletcher-Ford jumped in.

"Well, I'm happy to assist both of you in whatever way I can—I know I'm not old Fitzy, but I expect I can sniff out a murderer in a pinch."

AND THEN THERE WAS THE ONE

Georgie and Lexington both stared at Fletcher-Ford in astonished silence for a moment—the reference to "old Fitzy" had taken a second to process—before Georgie nodded. "We . . . appreciate your willingness to visit." This was uttered a bit reluctantly, but Fletcher-Ford merely offered her an easy smile and a wave of the hand.

"I rather leaped at the chance," he said. "Haven't been to Somerset in positively ages."

"You're in Gloucestershire," Georgie said stonily.

"Potato, tomato," Fletcher-Ford said with an airy wave of the hand. "Rolling hills, sheep, cheese! All rather the same, what?"

"I wouldn't say that too loudly," Arthur advised.

"Just so!" Fletcher-Ford said, laughing heartily. "Wouldn't want to offend the locals, I expect—might see fit to make me their next victim!"

Georgie cleared her throat, attempting to steer this conversation back on track. "We would appreciate your, well . . . discretion, if you wouldn't mind. The local police—other than Constable Lexington, obviously—don't know that we're investigating."

"I am the soul of discretion," Fletcher-Ford said, his expression suddenly solemn. "You cannot *imagine* the number of ladies in London whose reputations are only intact because of that virtue."

"I believe I *can* imagine," Georgie muttered.

"I do admire a woman with a good imagination," Fletcher-Ford offered with a smile. Georgie did not return it.

Arthur, perhaps sensing danger, said hastily, "Perhaps we ought to discuss the investigation, then?"

"Don't suppose we could do so over a bite to eat?" Fletcher-Ford asked, looking around excitedly. "I ate on the train, but I do find that travel causes one to work up a terrible appetite, don't you?"

"I suppose," Georgie began, already weary after three minutes' conversation with this man, and he beamed.

"Capital!"

"We could go and see if there's a room at the Sleepy Hedgehog as well," Georgie said, naming one of the village inns, owned by her school friend Iris and her husband, Henry.

Fletcher-Ford frowned. "But I thought I was to stay at—er—Radcliffe Hall, was it?" He fixed a guileless gaze upon her. "It's what you said in your letter to old Fitzy, after all."

Georgie bit her lip to prevent a curse from escaping. Inviting a middle-aged, eminently respectable, and renowned detective to stay at Radcliffe Hall was one thing; inviting *this* creature was something else entirely. She could not *imagine* Abigail's reaction if she showed up with Fletcher-Ford in tow.

"Er," Georgie said, thinking quickly.

"I do love a nice sojourn on a country estate," Fletcher-Ford continued, oblivious to her distress. "I brought my tennis racquet and my riding boots!"

"Radcliffe Hall is entirely lacking in both tennis courts and horses," Georgie informed him, and he seemed unfazed.

"Don't fret, Miss Radcliffe," he said in a consoling sort of way. "I expect it has plenty else to recommend it, even if its entertainments are less obvious."

Georgie opened her mouth to reply, but Fletcher-Ford continued blithely, "Now, come, Miss Radcliffe—food must come first, I always say! What's the point of a trip to a delightful, albeit dangerous village if it doesn't begin with a nice cream tea?" Before Georgie could work out how to respond to this, he was bounding athletically toward his luggage, which he hoisted effortlessly over his shoulder before positively leaping toward the ticket office to store it temporarily. In no time at all he was back, beaming at them.

"Now," he said cheerfully, "let us find this oh-so-delightful hamlet's finest cup of tea, shall we?" He began to stride toward the station exit, obviously entirely confident that the rest of them would follow.

And, to Georgie's very great annoyance, they did.

CHAPTER FOUR

*T*hey briefed Fletcher-Ford over an indecent quantity of baked goods.

"You wouldn't happen to have another slice of that excellent Victoria sponge, would you, madam?" Fletcher-Ford asked Mrs. Chester, the middle-aged widow who ran the Scrumptious Scone, a tearoom at one end of Buncombe-upon-Woolly's high street; it had a cozy, lived-in feel to it, with mismatched seat cushions and cups and saucers featuring the occasional chip.

"I certainly would, my dear," Mrs. Chester said in reply to his cake-related query, beaming down at him; he met her smile with one of his own. He was seated directly opposite Georgie at the small table, reclining in his seat as though he owned the place. He had, upon sitting down, rolled up the sleeves of that expensive-looking jumper, displaying golden forearms that Georgie was avoiding looking at, for reasons that she was choosing not to examine.

Mrs. Chester vanished into the kitchen and reappeared within ninety seconds bearing a positively enormous slice of Victoria sponge—an astonishing sight from a woman who, while undoubtedly a skilled baker, was known village-wide to be a bit stingy with her portions.

Fletcher-Ford smiled at her in gratitude, and she blushed.

Georgie cleared her throat loudly, and Fletcher-Ford—with one last wink (wink!) at Mrs. Chester—redirected his attention to his dining companions, offering Georgie a polite smile across the table.

"Now that we've procured enough baked goods to supply an entire army, perhaps we might turn our attention to the matter at hand." She knew she sounded ill-humored, but she also didn't care whether this blond, shiny-shoed, jumper-wearing creature from London found her rude. A few tables away, a pair of young Murder Tourists—including the pretty brunette with freckles whom Georgie had noticed a couple of weeks earlier, on the day Mrs. Marble was arrested—were sharing a pot of tea; did none of these people have anything better to do with their summers than idle them away, hoping someone dropped dead?

"You've never attended a boys' school, Miss Radcliffe," Fletcher-Ford said amiably, pouring himself a fresh cup of tea, "if you think this sufficient to supply an army. This would barely have been a midnight snack for my roommate and myself at Harrow."

Georgie didn't doubt this, given the amount of food she had just witnessed him consume, but she refused to be sidetracked. "Mr. Fitzgibbons seemed quite confident in your astute observational abilities, so I'm eager to hear how you think we ought to approach this investigation." That she herself had the gravest doubts about these alleged abilities went unspoken.

Fletcher-Ford took a sip of tea, and then another, his brow furrowing. "The councillor died last week?"

Georgie nodded. "The day before I wrote to Fitzgibbons. The village doctor ruled it a heart attack, and nothing more has been said about it."

"I see," said Fletcher-Ford, which Georgie somehow doubted. "And it's the fifth sudden death in the village in the past year?"

Constable Lexington cleared his throat. "Last summer was the first murder—the vicar was poisoned by a parishioner. Turned out he'd been blackmailing her about a clandestine love affair."

"And Miss Radcliffe, I understand, solved that case?" Fletcher-Ford asked, gazing down into his teacup.

"I did," Georgie said, unable to suppress a faint note of pride. "I spotted the poisonous plant used in the aforementioned parishioner's kitchen."

Fletcher-Ford nodded, his eyes still downcast, and then asked, "And after that, it was . . . ?"

"The baker and his wife," Arthur supplied. "Killed by their son—he poisoned them but made it look like a boating accident—he'd learned they'd changed their will to leave the bakery to his estranged daughter instead of him. Georgie here spotted an invasive plant in their garden and worked out that it had been planted to hide something that had recently been buried, which turned out to be the revised will."

Fletcher-Ford nodded again and glanced up at Georgie. "Fond of plants, are you, Miss Radcliffe?"

Georgie shrugged, using her teaspoon to scrape the crumbs on her plate into a tidy pile. "I enjoy a bit of gardening." More than *enjoyed*, actually, but Sebastian Fletcher-Ford was not the sort of man in whom she'd be confiding her closest-held hopes and dreams anytime soon.

"And the third murder took place at your home, I believe?" Fletcher-Ford continued, still looking at her. His voice had grown a bit less casual as he continued this line of questioning, and Georgie, for a wild moment, wondered if he was perhaps not *quite* as flighty as he appeared at first glance.

"At Christmas," she confirmed. "A distant cousin of my father's, Lady Tunbridge, was visiting us without her lady's maid, so a woman in the village was hired to help her; turns out, she had recently learned that Lady Tunbridge was the mother who'd abandoned her in an orphanage as a baby. She stabbed her in her bed one night."

"How astonishing," he murmured.

"It is," she agreed, feeling gratified. "To think that *three* murders should take place within the span of six months, in a village of this size—"

"Oh." Fletcher-Ford raised a hand to stop her. "That too, I suppose. But I primarily find it astonishing that you have been so intimately involved in all of them, Miss Radcliffe." He blinked at her inquiringly. "Frightful bad luck, don't you think?"

Georgie narrowed her eyes at him. "Indeed," she said through gritted teeth. "I can assure you that I vastly preferred the first twenty-four years of my life, in which there were precisely zero murders in Buncombe-upon-Woolly, rather than the last one."

Fletcher-Ford nodded thoughtfully. "It's very odd," he said, taking a generous bite of Victoria sponge while still managing to make the gesture look elegant somehow. This was ridiculous. What were they teaching them at Harrow?

"Perhaps," he added, setting down his fork, "you might consider giving me a tour of the village?"

Georgie blinked. "A tour?"

Fletcher-Ford smiled brightly, as though he were a simple holidaymaker. "A tour," he agreed. "It would be nice to get the lay of the land, so to speak. Learn who the possible suspects are. Meet the village characters. Perhaps we could arrange some lunches."

"Lunches," Georgie repeated.

"Dinners might seem a bit too romantic," he explained. "Wouldn't want to give the wrong impression—unless it was the *right* impression, of course." He winked. "But old Fitzy never turned down an invitation to a leisurely lunch, I can promise you."

Georgie stared at him, incredulous. "You want to go out to *lunch* to conduct a murder investigation?" Surely, *surely* this was not all that a trusted associate of the much-lauded Delacey Fitzgibbons could contribute to their investigation.

"Well," Fletcher-Ford said, taking a sip of tea, "we did pass another tearoom on the walk here, and it might be nice to taste their biscuits, to compare them to Mrs. Chester's."

A brief, stunned silence fell at this; seeing that Georgie was temporarily at a loss for words, Arthur attempted to come to her aid.

"I was thinking," he said, "that I might write about your investigation, Fletcher-Ford. Offer an inside look at how a famous detective—or, rather, his assistant—does his work."

"You're a reporter?" Fletcher-Ford asked, appearing intrigued.

"For *The Woolly Register*," Arthur confirmed. "It's a, er, local outlet, but with a growing readership." He paused expectantly, as if the young detective would immediately spring forward with more sensible suggestions for what to investigate first, but instead, Fletcher-Ford merely smiled.

"I don't think you'll want to be too obvious, Crawley. If we're meant to be keeping our heads down, it might seem a bit strange to have a reporter dogging our heels."

Arthur cleared his throat. "Naturally, I plan to be discreet. Nothing will be revealed until I publish my article."

"Capital." Fletcher-Ford's smile widened. "Then perhaps in the meantime we might make it seem as though Miss Radcliffe invited me personally to visit, rather than writing to old Fitzy? And now I'm here, it simply transpires that I happen to have a certain expertise—"

Georgie snorted.

"—and am willing to assist an old family friend?"

"We *aren't* friends," Georgie said, nettled.

"But you're a Radcliffe of Radcliffe Hall," Lexington pointed out; Arthur grinned, clearly enjoying himself. "Your father went to *Cambridge*. Surely Mr. Fletcher-Ford is the sort of person your family would rub elbows with."

This tended to be how Georgie's family was spoken of among the villagers. It was the reason she had found herself involved in the first murder to begin with—people trusted the Radcliffes with their problems, as they'd been the local landed gentry for as long as anyone could remember, even though none of the villagers were their tenants any longer. And Georgie was undoubtedly the most useful of the current crop of Radcliffes to consult in a crisis. (There were, admittedly, only three of them, so it wasn't saying much.)

"I'm a Cambridge man myself," Fletcher-Ford said cheerfully. Of course he was. She could just picture him rowing in the Oxford-Cambridge race, or cycling across an ancient college lawn, or doing something else similarly athletic and English. "As are all the men of my family. It's the perfect solution."

"I don't think . . ." Georgie began, but Arthur tapped his chin thoughtfully.

"It does make a certain amount of sense, Georgie," he said. "If we put it about that you and Fletcher-Ford have some sort of personal connection, no one will find it odd to see you together, or think that you're up to anything beyond poking around the village."

"But as soon as we start asking questions, surely they'll realize?" Georgie pointed out.

"Well, since Mr. Fletcher-Ford isn't himself a famous detective"—here, Arthur offered Fletcher-Ford a vaguely apologetic look, as though worried this would cause offense, but the man in question was too busy consuming an enormous piece of shortbread in methodical fashion to take any notice—"then

I hardly think the police are likely to pay much attention to what you get up to. It's not as though they've taken you very seriously in the past, after all."

This, annoyingly, was true—it was only Lexington who had listened to Georgie's concerns about the plant in the bakers' garden, and had insisted that it be dug up. They might not have solved that case, had it not been for him—Detective Inspector Harriday had certainly not been very good-humored about the matter. It had been incredibly irritating at the time, but why not take advantage of this now, to conduct an investigation without ruffling any feathers?

Though Mr. Fletcher-Ford was hardly the sort of ally she'd had in mind.

Fletcher-Ford, for his part, had polished off the shortbread and was surveying the plate before him, debating his next selection. "And if I'm to take you up on your invitation to stay at—Radcliffe Hall, was it?—then it will seem all the cozier." He flashed a smile at her.

Georgie scowled. "The invitation was for *Fitzgibbons*," she said.

"But," Fletcher-Ford said sunnily, "I'm afraid I'm all you have, old bean."

Georgie rolled her eyes heavenward, but unfortunately, he was correct. However, while Papa and Abigail had seemed intrigued by the notion of a celebrity detective coming to visit, she wasn't at all certain how they'd react to the stylish, almost impossibly handsome specimen that she'd be presenting to them instead.

"All right," she said, her mind racing. "Er, I'll need to head home this afternoon, to, um, prepare my father and sister. I don't think you are... quite what they were expecting."

"Just so," Fletcher-Ford agreed cheerfully. "A sister, is it?" he added, looking intrigued. "Is she anything like you?"

Georgie glanced down at her serviceable clothing, worn shoes, and the barely controlled frizz of her dark hair, then thought of lovely, golden Abigail, with her pretty dresses, wide eyes, and romantic tendencies.

"Yes, she's exactly like me," she said definitively, despite knowing that this ruse would crumble the moment he actually met Abigail. Next to her, Arthur buried a smile in his teacup.

Instead of looking disinterested, however, Fletcher-Ford gave her a slow, lethal smile. "I can't tell you how delighted I am to hear it," he said, and then leaned forward to pluck a ham sandwich off the platter before him, leaving Georgie so flustered that she attempted to add another lump of sugar to her already too-sweet tea.

"Perhaps, Miss Radcliffe," Fletcher-Ford said, swallowing a mouthful of sandwich and leaning back in his seat, "you could speak to your family after lunch, and then you might see your way to giving me that tour this afternoon?" The way he said this, Georgie thought irately, made it quite clear that he could not imagine a world in which a woman would *not* jump at the opportunity to spend time with him. She was sorely tempted to tell him that she could think of few things she'd less like to do, but—

Well, she needed him. So instead, she merely offered him her tightest, most awful smile and said, "Certainly."

Radcliffe Hall was in a state of excited agitation upon her arrival half an hour later; Dr. Severin had evidently been summoned for Abigail, and he had somehow been induced to stay for lunch, which was just finishing when Georgie walked in, clutching a stack of letters she'd retrieved from the postbox at the end of the long, winding driveway that led to the house.

"Oh," she said, startled, upon spotting Dr. Severin, who was deep in conversation with Papa as Mrs. Fawcett cleared away the plates. Abigail was reclining elegantly in a chair directly opposite Dr. Severin, wearing the silk dressing gown Papa had bought her for her birthday earlier that spring. (Georgie, naturally, had been the one to select the specific dressing gown from a catalogue and remind her father to make the purchase.) "I didn't realize we had company."

"I was just leaving, actually," Dr. Severin said, rising as she entered the room. "But Mr. Radcliffe, I appreciate the invitation. And Miss Abigail"—here, he glanced across the table at Georgie's sister, his expression softening in a way that caused warning bells to chime in Georgie's mind—"don't hesitate to phone me if you are still feeling unwell tomorrow. Or if you need anything else." He turned to Georgie and raised both eyebrows at whatever he saw in her face. Georgie hastily schooled her expression into something more neutral—or at least less openly hostile. "Miss Radcliffe." He gave her an uncertain smile before departing.

No sooner had the front door closed behind him than Abigail rose from her chair, all previous signs of delicate convalescence mysteriously absent. "Georgie, you didn't have to *scowl* at him!"

Georgie set the stack of letters down in front of Papa, who was still lingering over a final cup of tea, and crossed her arms as she faced her sister. "Are you feeling better? I can't help but notice you grow mysteriously healthier as soon as Dr. Severin leaves the room. How astonishing! Some sort of medical miracle, no doubt?"

Papa frowned, glancing up from his teacup. "Georgie, love, that's not a kind thing to accuse your sister of."

"Does it count as an accusation if it's *true*?" Georgie gestured at her allegedly convalescent sister, who was standing with her hands on her hips, watching Georgie with narrowed eyes.

"I'll have you know, Georgie, that I ran into Dr. Severin at the post office yesterday and mentioned that my hay fever has been particularly severe this year—" This, at least, was true; every spring, Abigail turned into a sniffling, wheezing mess for weeks on end. "—and he volunteered to pay us a visit. He seemed *very* eager." There was a trace of smugness to Abigail's voice at this, and Georgie inhaled sharply in an attempt to keep her temper in check.

"Aunt Georgiana phoned the other day," she said, and both Abigail and Papa blinked at this apparent non sequitur. "She wants to know if you still wish to come stay in July." Aunt Georgiana was their mother's younger sister, who lived in an extremely elegant flat in Pimlico. Now that Abigail, at nineteen, was out of school and more or less at loose ends, there had been discussion of sending her to London for an extended stay with her aunt. Given recent developments with Dr. Severin, Georgie thought that this invitation could not come at a better time.

"I . . . don't know," Abigail said, worrying at the sleeve of her dressing gown. "I'd been speaking to Mrs. Chester about helping at the tearoom, actually."

Georgie blinked. "Since when?"

Abigail met her gaze. "Since she tasted the treacle tart I brought to the fete last month."

Abigail undoubtedly had a way with desserts. Her mince pies were popular village-wide at Christmas, and she made a Victoria sponge for Georgie's birthday each year that Georgie looked forward to for weeks in advance. But still, to consider giving up a summer in London solely to . . . prepare tea cakes for the villagers, and whatever tourists would descend upon them this year? It was absurd.

"I don't think the Scrumptious Scone is going anywhere," Georgie said shortly. "There's no reason you can't help Mrs. Chester once you come back." By which point surely Abigail's attention would have moved on from Dr. Severin.

"Aunt Georgiana isn't going anywhere either," Abigail tossed back, crossing her arms.

"I wouldn't be so certain," Georgie said. "What if she gets married again, to an Argentine polo player, and this is your only chance to stay with her before she abandons us for South America?" This was not, given their aunt's romantic history, as unlikely a scenario as it might have seemed.

"Why don't *you* go, then, Georgie, if it matters so much to you?"

Papa blinked up from his teacup. "Did you wish to go to London, love? If Abigail doesn't want to go, there's no reason you shouldn't."

"I can't *leave!*" Georgie said indignantly. Did no one realize this house—this entire absurd village—would fall apart without her? "I have a *murder* to solve!"

Abigail gave an exasperated shake of her head. "If this is about that detective you invited to stay—"

"Well," Georgie said, would-be casual. "It's interesting you should mention that. Do you recall that I mentioned that Fitzgibbons was sending an associate instead?"

Abigail eyed her watchfully. "Yes."

"Well." Georgie cleared her throat. "This associate—his assistant, really—he is . . . not quite what I expected."

"How so?" Abigail asked suspiciously.

"Well. He's from London."

"Obviously," Abigail said. "If he works for a detective *in London.*"

"And, er," Georgie hedged, "he's somewhat . . . younger than Fitzgibbons."

"How much younger?" Abigail demanded.

"A bit." Georgie hesitated, then added. "Quite a bit, actually."

"Well, how old is he?"

"I'm not any good at estimating those sorts of things," Georgie said cagily.

"Take a wild guess." Abigail's tone was not the sort that would brook any refusal.

"Perhaps . . . thirty? A bit younger?"

Abigail looked mildly incredulous. "And yet I'm the one who's at fault for asking Dr. Severin to treat my hay fever?"

"Well, *I* have no romantic designs on Mr. Fletcher-Ford," Georgie shot back. "Which is more than I can say for you and Dr. Severin."

"Fletcher-Ford, Fletcher-Ford," Papa murmured. "Why does that sound familiar . . . ?"

"He went to Cambridge," Georgie said. "Perhaps you knew his father?"

"I wonder if he's any relation to Alastair Fletcher-Ford," Papa said thoughtfully. "He's a classicist, and if I recall has an interest in radical politics. His wife was a suffragette."

Georgie considered the man of the blinding smile and expensive knitwear she'd met earlier that day, and shook her head skeptically. "I'm not certain it's the same family, Papa . . ."

"Ah, well, we'll find out soon enough!" Papa said brightly. "If he's a Cambridge man, then of course he must stay with us—it's the only decent thing to do! I wonder which college?"

"I couldn't say," Georgie said a bit wearily.

"Nothing like a bit of masculine company to liven things up," Papa said, reaching for the heavily thumbed paperback sitting next to him on the table.

"Unbelievable," Abigail said, throwing her hands up. "A young man from London with a double-barrel surname is coming to stay at Georgie's invitation, and that's that? Does he drive a Rolls-Royce? Is he going to seduce the housemaids?"

"We don't have any housemaids," Georgie said, privately reflecting that, given Fletcher-Ford's charms, that was rather a blessing. "And you can meet him later this evening. Perhaps in the meantime you can consider Aunt Georgiana's offer some more." Georgie did not like the stubborn set of her sister's mouth, though, and suspected she might need to enlist reinforcements in this battle—not, she thought with an internal sigh, that she could expect much help from either Papa or Mrs. Fawcett, who both babied Abigail something dreadful, and would no doubt be appalled by the notion of her being away from home for any duration. She'd need to look farther afield for allies.

"Where are you off to, love?" Papa asked, as Georgie made as if to leave the room. "You just got home."

"I'm just here to fetch Egg," Georgie called over her shoulder. "I'm giving Mr. Fletcher-Ford a tour of the village this afternoon."

"How professional," Abigail said sweetly, and Georgie shot her a venomous look. "I cannot *wait* to meet him, Georgie."

"Neither can I, love," Papa added, patting at his head, once again engaged in a futile search for his reading glasses.

And Georgie—who suddenly wanted nothing more than to delay that meeting for as long as humanly possible—decided that Mr. Fletcher-Ford was going to get the world's most thorough tour.

CHAPTER FIVE

*M*r. Fletcher-Ford was waiting for Georgie by the time she and Egg made their way back into the village. He was lounging against the low stone wall outside the Sleepy Hedgehog, which was directly opposite the Scrumptious Scone, his arms crossed over his chest, nodding at passersby and offering flirtatious smiles to every woman he saw, regardless of age.

"Miss Radcliffe," he called, straightening as she approached. She didn't know what to make of the fact that *she* was not the recipient of one of these smiles; she should probably be gratified and take it as a sign that he respected her as a colleague and an equal. So she insisted to herself, at least.

"And who is this?" he asked, an expression of unalloyed delight crossing his face at the sight of Egg, who trotted next to Georgie with a spring in her step. Despite her age, Egg enjoyed outings, so long as it wasn't too rainy ... or warm ... or muddy... or snowy... or cold. So, on approximately one day out of every fortnight, she was absolutely overjoyed to be at Georgie's side. Her tail wagged enthusiastically at the sight of Fletcher-Ford, who crouched down with open arms to make her acquaintance.

"This is Egg," Georgie said, watching as dog and man greeted each other like long-lost relations. Egg licked Fletcher-Ford's face. He stroked her ears. She barked once in joyful greeting. He rubbed her side, in just the spot that made her lean against him and seem to temporarily lose all strength in her legs.

So much for loyalty, Georgie thought, watching her dog topple onto her side in the middle of the road, her adoring gaze fixed upon Fletcher-Ford.

"The finest of all breakfast foods," Fletcher-Ford said, continuing to massage Egg's side as she stared at him lovingly. "And the finest of all dogs."

"Aren't you worried about muddying your trousers?" Georgie asked with some acidity.

"I send my laundry out," Fletcher-Ford said absently, giving Egg one last hearty pat before rising to his feet. He was a good half foot taller than Georgie, which annoyed her. *Everything* about this man annoyed her.

"Of course you do," she muttered. No doubt he had a live-in cook, too—or perhaps he took all of his meals at restaurants? She couldn't imagine him preparing so much as a piece of toast for himself.

"What was that?" he asked cheerfully, and Georgie narrowed her eyes, unable to tell whether he genuinely hadn't heard, or was merely pretending not to have done. She had the vague sense that the answer to this question would tell her something about the man before her.

"Nothing," she said, before adding, "Egg, get up." Egg made her leisurely way to her feet, quirking her ears at Georgie in the manner she was so fond of.

"Shall we embark on our tour of your fair village?" Fletcher-Ford asked, offering Georgie his arm. She looked pointedly down at it as though he'd just extended a venomous snake toward her, and he lowered it again, looking unperturbed. "An independent woman, I see—my favorite sort!" He stuck both hands in his pockets instead, looking unbothered by the waves of hostility fairly radiating off Georgie's person.

Georgie clucked her tongue at Egg, who immediately fell into step beside her, and they set off down the lane. The Sleepy Hedgehog was situated at the far end of the village high street; if they turned, they'd have a view of the gently rolling hills that surrounded them, the green hillsides neatly broken up by tidy stone walls, the grassy slopes dotted with sheep. Ahead of them, the narrow cobblestoned street gently curved, with honey-colored stone cottages set on either side. Ivy crept up several of the cottages' walls, and the happy sound of children at play emanated from the open windows of one house. A calico cat crossed the street in leisurely fashion, briefly exciting Egg, who offered an inquisitive bark; upon receiving a disdainful look from the cat, accompanied by a sudden puffing-up of its already-bushy tail, Egg sensibly subsided, and the cat continued its progress across the street unmolested.

Fletcher-Ford was looking around him with all appearances of great delight, but Georgie supposed that something more than a silent presence with a dog at her heels was likely expected of her. "This is the high street," she offered. *Very helpful*, she thought with some disgust.

Fletcher-Ford, however, merely smiled. "It's lovely. How old did you say the village is?"

"I didn't. And it depends on what you mean by the question."

"How so?"

"Well," Georgie said, "there's evidence of settlements in this spot dating back to the Romans. Some Roman coins were found here a few decades ago." She pointedly did *not* mention that the so-called Woolly Hoard had been discovered by none other than the village's one and only archaeology enthusiast (her father), or that it had consisted of precisely three coins in total. The British Museum hadn't bothered to send someone out to examine them for months.

"We're in the Domesday Book," she added, "but most of the buildings only date back to the seventeenth century or so. Part of the church is a few hundred years older, though." She felt a bit appalled by the note of faint pride that she detected in her voice at this last addition—she'd never had cause to previously consider whether she was proud of Buncombe-upon-Woolly or not. It had been home for her entire life; her family's history was intertwined with that of the village itself. She didn't leave very often, either, and something about Mr. Fletcher-Ford—with his tasteful jumpers and improbably well-coiffed hair and expensive wristwatch—made her suddenly feel terribly provincial.

"That's the church there?" he asked as they passed St. Drogo's.

"The one and only," she confirmed.

"Site of the first murder, correct?"

"Yes. The vicar."

"The blackmailing vicar," he corrected cheerfully, which Georgie found somewhat distasteful, though if pressed she did not think she would have been able to definitively state what tone was appropriate for discussing blackmailing that eventually led to the homicide of a member of the clergy.

"And then this must be the bakery where the next murder took place!" he added, inclining his head toward the recently renamed Crawford's. The Crawfords were a young couple who had moved to the village from Norwich during the winter and had taken over the premises. Their bread was not as good as Mr. Fieldstone's had been, though Georgie had felt a bit disloyal to discover at Easter that their hot cross buns were vastly superior. "Nice of them all to cluster together so conveniently, isn't it?" Fletcher-Ford asked.

"Have you noted the size of this village? *Everything* is clustered together."

"Just so, just so," Fletcher-Ford agreed, his gaze alighting on Mary Montague, a young widow about Georgie's age who was leaving the bakery with a loaf of bread tucked under one arm, with some interest. "I don't suppose you'd offer an introduction, Miss Radcliffe?"

"For what purpose?" Georgie asked suspiciously.

"I just like to meet the locals," he said, offering her a look of wide-eyed sincerity. "Especially the attractive ones. Present company included."

Georgie cut him a narrow look, certain that he must be

joking, but he was amiably nodding at Mrs. Montague as she passed and didn't seem to notice Georgie's glare. Mrs. Montague gave him a flirtatious smile in return. *Good lord,* Georgie thought; she needed to get this matter wrapped up before Fletcher-Ford attempted to seduce half the village. She did not think the eligible women of Buncombe-upon-Woolly would be able to muster much resistance in the face of his jumpers. And his forearms.

Fortunately, the work at hand recalled itself to them at that precise moment, as they approached the Marbled Cheese. "The most recent murder took place there," she said in an undertone, and Fletcher-Ford followed her gaze. "Mr. and Mrs. Marble live in a flat above their shop—well, *lived*, I suppose. He drank poisoned wine, and his wife has been arrested."

"I see," Fletcher-Ford said neutrally, casting a quick glance in her direction. "Did you solve that one, too?"

"No. The police made the arrest . . . quite expediently."

"And didn't ask for any help from you?"

"They've never asked for any help from me," she said, and out of the corner of her eye, she saw his eyebrows raise at the curt note in her voice. She took a breath and attempted a less openly hostile tone. "The police—except for Constable Lexington—have never viewed my contributions with much gratitude."

"That seems rich, considering, as I understand it, you solved a couple of cases for them." His tone was mild, his expression the same one of bland appreciation that it had been a moment before, but Georgie stumbled a bit at this unexpected word of support. He reached out to steady her with a quick hand to the elbow, but despite his seeming inability to see a woman without flirting with her, his touch didn't linger.

"Detective Inspector Harriday remains very insistent that my contributions were just interferences," she said. They'd stopped walking after her stumble, and now stood before the Marbled Cheese, facing each other. Georgie watched a pair of Murder Tourists—two women her age, attired stylishly— approach and proceed to do a very poor job of pretending that they weren't ogling Fletcher-Ford. She pressed her lips together into a thin line.

"In his telling," she continued, attempting to ignore the women, "he was minutes away from solving each crime himself, until I came along and stole his glory."

"Well," Fletcher-Ford said, his tone still pleasant, "he sounds like a right wanker, so I don't think we need worry much about what he thinks." He inclined his head and added, "Shall we?" and Georgie, who was mildly flabbergasted, allowed him to lead her down the road.

They continued to make steady progress down the high street. It became more crowded as they approached the heart of the village, which boasted a post office, the Shorn Sheep and its rival pub, the Fleecy Lamb (there was a decades-long dispute over which pub had been inspired by the other's name), the stationer, the butcher, and a few other shops. The village school must have just let out, for a gaggle of children of various ages came careening toward them, shouting like banshees. Georgie suppressed the urge to shudder; she greatly preferred children when they didn't travel in packs.

"You've lived here all your life?" Fletcher-Ford asked as they hopped to the side to avoid being trampled by eight-year-olds.

Georgie nodded. "I was sent to Bath to a girls' school for a few years—my sister was, too—but then I came home again as soon as I'd finished."

"And you never wanted to leave? Other than for school, I mean?"

There was nothing in his tone beyond faint curiosity, but Georgie stiffened all the same. "It's very nice here," she said a bit haughtily.

"Undoubtedly," he agreed. "So many cottages. So many lovely young wives. Dare I ask if there's some special treatment in the water here, to produce such fine female specimens?"

Georgie stopped in her tracks. "Mr. Fletcher-Ford—"

"I think you ought to call me Sebastian," he said. "If we're to be giving the impression that I'm an old family friend."

"I've no intention of doing any such thing," she said, sounding a bit like a Regency damsel making her debut on the marriage mart. Which was ridiculous—they were in the middle of Gloucestershire. Buncombe-upon-Woolly was hardly a village that was rigorous in terms of its forms of social address—it would be hard to be when the patriarch of the local landed gentry was commonly spotted wandering around in his Wellington boots with a newspaper held before his face, receiving alarmed shouts of warning from his fellow villagers if he came close to stepping in front of a bicycle or the occasional motorcar.

(Georgie had had a stern conversation with her father on this matter on multiple occasions, but that had not prevented things from progressing to the point that he had walked directly into a postbox a month earlier.)

"All right," he said easily. "I shall be calling you Georgiana, then."

"*No one* calls me Georgiana." At least not if they wanted to escape without bodily injury. She'd been named after her aunt, who was endlessly elegant and had been married three times, to increasingly wealthy (though decreasingly handsome) men. *She* was Georgiana.

Georgie was . . . Georgie.

"No one but me." He offered her what he clearly considered to be a winning smile.

"If I call you Sebastian, will you call me Georgie?" she asked reluctantly.

"Or Miss Radcliffe," he offered, all innocence. "Whichever you prefer, really—though the former is probably best for the purposes of our ruse."

"I would *prefer* to push you into the river," she said through gritted teeth.

"Then shall we continue our tour, so that we might approach the mighty Woolly and give you just the opportunity your heart desires?"

"My aunt has been married three times and never committed homicide," Georgie informed him as they resumed their meandering pace down the high street. "I never appreciated what a remarkable feat that was until this moment."

"That's the spirit, Georgie! That's the spirit!"

By the time Georgie had shown Mr. Fletcher-Ford—*Sebastian*—the school, the chocolate shop, the post office, the butcher's, the grocer's, and the Dozing Dragonfly, the village's only other inn, he professed to have worked up a powerful thirst.

"You drank an entire pot of tea three hours ago," she informed him stonily as they made their way toward the Shorn Sheep, which was beckoning them invitingly as the afternoon turned chilly, gray clouds scuttling across the sky on a cold breeze. June in England could be annoyingly tempestuous.

"Precisely," he said, holding the door to the pub open for her. "That's far too long to go without a drink."

Georgie considered a retort, but in this case, she, too, had worked up a thirst, and so swept past him into the pub and seated herself in a cozy corner booth. "You may buy me a cider," she informed Sebastian, like a queen granting a favor to a subject, and he looked precisely as delighted as she might have expected.

"Usually I have to work a bit harder than that to get a pretty girl to let me buy her a drink," he said, and bounded off toward the bar, Georgie glaring daggers at his retreating back. She thought back to just the week before when she had sat in this very pub, thinking hopefully of the promise of a famous detective coming to help her investigation. She had expected someone who could leap in and take matters in hand, full of brilliant theories, a keen investigator. Instead, she was faced with a dreadful flirt who had not offered a single idea on how to solve this mystery, and who seemed more interested in eating baked goods and winking at pretty women than he did in solving a murder.

It was dispiriting.

He materialized before her, bearing two pints of cider, and proceeded to settle himself opposite her. He looked irritatingly pleased with the state of the world and his place in it.

"So?" Georgie prompted.

He looked at her inquiringly.

"So?" he repeated pleasantly.

"Have you had any brilliant insights? That's why you're *here*, isn't it? A sophisticated man of the city, here to show us country simpletons how to solve a murder?"

Sebastian took a sip of cider. "I would never presume to tell a woman her own mind, but I can't help feeling that you don't like me very much."

"Everyone else likes you plenty," Georgie said, taking a grumpy sip of her own drink. "They can make up for whatever adoration I am insufficient in displaying."

"I find it rather refreshing, truth be told," he said. "Some women are simply *too* easy to charm, you know—it takes all the sport out of it."

"They're not foxes."

"Women and foxes, Georgie, are more alike than you might think."

"Don't you have *work* to be doing here? How are you going to help us solve a murder if you're chasing after every female with a distracting pelt? What would Mr. Fitzgibbons have to say about that?"

He looked suddenly shifty, which naturally caused Georgie's attention to sharpen on him. "He would not be . . . entirely surprised," he hedged.

"Meaning what?"

"Meaning that I may have recently found myself... entangled in a personal matter... with a lady who happens to also be... matrimonially entangled... with someone at Scotland Yard."

Georgie wasn't fooled by these linguistic gymnastics for a second. "You had an affair with a policeman's wife?" she hissed. "What is *wrong* with you?"

"A question my family has often had cause to ask themselves," he said reflectively. "And I shall simply say to you what I said to my sister when she learned of this predicament: the lady in question was extremely pretty."

Georgie blinked at him—and then, suddenly, a dark suspicion set upon her. "This is why you're here, isn't it?"

He arched a single eyebrow at her in a rakishly charming sort of way. Georgie was not remotely charmed. "My dear Georgie, I am here to help you solve the latest in a plague of homicides that has befallen your idyllic countryside home."

"But this is why *you*, specifically, are here," she insisted, feeling more certain of the truth by the second. "You caused a mess and immediately fled town?"

He sighed. "It wasn't an enormous scandal—the police lieutenant in question wanted it kept quiet—but Fitzgibbons was annoyed about the whole thing. He's on thin ice with Scotland Yard at the best of times, since they've butted heads in the past, and he was threatening to let me go, so I showed him your letter and volunteered to spend a few weeks in the countryside until matters died down. He thought if the lieutenant was under the impression that I'd been reprimanded somehow, he might not kick up too much of a fuss when I reappear."

Georgie snorted. "Are you really that good of an assistant?" Her tone was extremely skeptical; nothing that she'd witnessed so far evidenced a particularly keen investigative mind.

"Secretary."

"I beg your pardon?"

"I'm his *secretary*, not his assistant," Sebastian said, raising his glass to take another sip. "I—you know—handle his correspondence. Answer the telephone. Maintain his calendar." He waved a hand vaguely. "That sort of thing."

Georgie's jaw dropped, though she wrenched it closed a moment later. She set her pint glass down with a deliberate *thunk*. "Let me be certain I understand this," she said evenly. "I wrote to Mr. Fitzgibbons explaining that we'd had a string of murders in a village that had not seen a murder in the previous three decades, and that I was concerned that the death of our council chairman might not be of natural causes, and instead of taking these concerns seriously and coming himself, he sent us a womanizing secretary who can't keep his thoughts on the matter at hand for more than five minutes at a stretch before the next tantalizing lady catches his eye?"

"I don't think that's entirely—"

"Well, I do." Georgie stood up. "Thank you for the drink, Mr. Fletcher-Ford—but I believe our work here is done."

"I say, Geor—Miss Radcliffe," he amended hastily, at least wise enough to read whatever flashed across her face at that moment. "I thought we were to be partners!"

Georgie leaned forward and rested her hands on the surface of the table, meeting his eyes directly. "The only sort of partner I mean to be to you," she said, "is the sort who assists a shiny-shoed man from out of town in finding the next train back to London." She nodded toward the bar. "I believe Harry often has a copy of the timetable at hand."

She straightened, whistled for Egg—who had been snoozing beneath the table during this entire conversation, unperturbed by her mistress's metaphorical ruffled feathers—and said simply, "Goodbye, Mr. Fletcher-Ford. It has been a . . ." Here, manners failed her, and after a moment's consideration, she concluded with, "An event."

And then she turned and swept from the pub, hoping with every fiber of her being that she would never lay eyes on that useless man again.

This was her last, comforting thought before something collided with the back of her head with heavy force, and Georgie tumbled to the ground.

CHAPTER SIX

*B*eagles, for all their virtues, were not much use in a crisis.

"Egg, be quiet," Georgie muttered, her palms and knees stinging from where they'd borne the brunt of her landing on the cobblestoned path leading away from the Shorn Sheep. This had no effect other than causing Egg to bark even more loudly, and Georgie sighed. Suddenly, from behind her, there was the sound of running footsteps, and she somehow knew who it would be without even glancing up.

"Oh, no," she groaned, and the footsteps skidded to a halt beside her. From this vantage point, she could see a pair of extremely well-shined shoes.

"Are you delirious? Or concussed?" came Fletcher-Ford's voice, slightly breathless, and he was suddenly crouching beside her, his trousers maddeningly uncreased, a hand extended. Georgie took it, wincing at the rub of his skin against her scraped palm, and he helped her to her feet with a hand beneath her elbow.

"I'm not concussed," she said sharply, glancing up at him as she rose. He was looking at her with an expression of undisguised concern. "What are you doing out here?"

"I happened to glance out the window in time to see you topple," he said, letting go of her elbow and leaning down to offer a reassuring pat on the head to Egg, who immediately ceased barking.

"Traitor," Georgie muttered, casting a baleful look at her dog. Egg licked her hand by way of reply.

"Should you sit down?" Fletcher-Ford asked now, still looking concerned, and Georgie shook her head.

"I'm fine," she said, unable to suppress a wince at the jolt of pain the shaking caused to shoot through her head. She began to turn, then stumbled. Instantly, Fletcher-Ford's arm was at her back, steadying her.

She cut him a look. "This is . . . intimate."

"It's how I lure all my women," he said cheerfully, not loosening his grip. "Wait for them to get clubbed about the head and then rush in to cradle them as they recover their senses."

"So you admit that the only women who would welcome your advances are the ones who have recently sustained head injuries," she said, and he frowned, as if trying to work out where exactly he'd wandered into a trap.

She took advantage of his distraction to struggle out of his grip and put a healthy bit of distance between them. She braced her hands on her hips, the full impact of the events of the past two minutes finally landing with her.

"I was attacked!" she said, interrupting some monologue on Fletcher-Ford's part about the number of non-concussed women he'd lured to his bed over the years. "Someone hit me in the back of the head!" She glanced around wildly but saw no one other than a cluster of—she groaned internally—Murder Tourists, who were watching this series of events with some interest; clearly her attacker had already fled. "I *knew* there was something strange going on here. A perfectly healthy member of the local government doesn't drop dead without explanation, and now that I've started asking questions, someone is trying to silence me!" Even though her head was throbbing painfully, she couldn't prevent a thrill from coursing through her at this realization. She was right to be suspicious! She had been right to write to Fitzgibbons! And now...

She sighed.

Now she only had Mr. Fletcher-Ford to assist her.

Fletcher-Ford, for his part, was looking vaguely apologetic, which naturally caused her to direct a suspicious eye toward him—he did not seem the sort of man to be overly familiar with that emotion.

"Why do you look like that?" she demanded, and immediately his expression smoothed into something blander; it was a neat trick, and watching him perform it caused something to niggle at the edges of her mind, some half-formed thought that she didn't have the time to consider too carefully at the moment.

"It's only," he said, his tone still somewhat apologetic, even if his face no longer was, "that you weren't attacked."

"Excuse me?"

"No one attacked you," he repeated.

She raised her fingers to pinch the bridge of her nose. "I know we don't know each other well—"

"Yet," he interjected with a winning smile, and didn't quail in the slightest under the look she leveled at him, which was exceptionally annoying since there was no one in the entire village—including her own family—on whom that look wasn't at least somewhat effective.

"But," she continued, deciding that ignoring him entirely might prove to be the best (only?) way to deal with this man without entirely losing her sanity, "I promise you I'm not the swooning type."

"A shame, that," he said regretfully, shaking his head sadly. "I'm told I do an impressively manly spring-and-catch maneuver when ladies swoon in my presence." He looked at her hopefully. "Are you certain you don't want to try swooning, just to experience it?"

"My point is," she said determinedly, "I did not suddenly faint without provocation."

"Of course," he agreed, solemn as a vicar. "I should have spoken more clearly—bit of a problem of mine—"

"You don't say," she muttered.

"You weren't attacked by a *person*," he continued blithely. "You were attacked by a roof shingle." He nodded his head to the right; Georgie followed his gaze and saw that there was indeed a rogue roof tile lying in the dirt, cleaved neatly in two as though it had fallen from a considerable height.

"Oh," she said blankly.

"I don't doubt the severity of your injury," he hastened to reassure her in a soothing tone that made her want to collect said roof tile and bash *him* over the head with it. "But unfortunately, I don't think there's someone in your fair village trying to do you in."

This was irritating. It was not that Georgie wanted a would-be assassin to be lying in wait for her, but it *would* have been gratifying.

She huffed out a frustrated breath. "Fine. In that case, I'm grateful for your help—though it really wasn't necessary—but—"

"I was hoping I might change your mind," he said, cutting her off so smoothly that he somehow managed to make it seem as though he were doing her a favor—preventing her from saying something foolish or unreasonable—by doing so. "I know you're not convinced I can assist you, but I believe that I can." He was looking directly at her now, his expression considerably more focused and less affably vacant than Georgie had seen it at any point in the few hours of their acquaintance thus far.

"Mr. Fletcher-Ford," she said, trying to keep her tone pleasant; the past year's worth of dealings with the local police force had taught her the importance of remaining patient whenever a man tried to explain something to her, but she was extremely resentful of the fact that she'd had to develop this skill at all. "I'm certain that your work with Mr. Fitzgibbons has been most, um, enthusiastic—"

"You think I'm a mindless idiot who will get distracted by the next skirt that passes," he said. It wasn't a question.

"I don't think I would have phrased it like that."

"I believe you did, not five minutes ago," he said, with a smile so appealing it should possibly have been illegal. "I'll offer you this: Give me a week to help you solve this mystery, and at the end of that time, if we haven't sorted things, I'll pop back to London and sell Fitzgibbons a real song and dance about the dastardly crimes gripping a cheese-filled village, and how fame and fortune will undoubtedly follow whoever gets to the bottom of it. I can be quite convincing when I want to—I could have him on the next train, I'd wager."

"I don't think—"

"One week," he said. He was once again looking at her very intently as he spoke, despite the fact that they were standing on a public street with a curious beagle sitting at their feet. "I know you don't think much of me, but I've been employed by Fitzgibbons for nearly five years now, and I practically—well—" He broke off, shaking his head and looking frustrated, for reasons Georgie didn't understand. "I've more experience than you might expect," he finished after a moment.

"What aren't you telling me?" she asked; if there was one thing she'd learned of late, it was how to tell when someone was trying to keep a secret from her.

He extended his hand. "Give me a week, and see if you can work it out—you're the detective, aren't you?"

And Georgie—unable, and a bit unwilling, to argue with that—reached out, took his hand, and shook it.

Unfortunately, Georgie's accident meant that their tour of the village was clearly at a close, and the event she had been dreading could be delayed no longer:

It was time to introduce Sebastian Fletcher-Ford to her family.

This would be happening even sooner than she'd planned, because while Dr. Severin—who had been hastily summoned by a telephone call from Harry the barman—examined Georgie's head and then cleaned and bandaged her scraped knee, Fletcher-Ford had taken the liberty of phoning Papa, who was now on his way to collect them in the Radcliffe family motorcar.

"I'm perfectly capable of walking," she said for at least the third time.

"Of course you are," Fletcher-Ford agreed, hands in his pockets as he leaned against the wall outside the Shorn Sheep, looking around. At least the Murder Tourists had vanished while Georgie and Fletcher-Ford were inside the pub.

"It was just a knock on the head and a fall," she continued.

"Of course," he said again, nodding amiably. This was extremely vexing, because Georgie wanted desperately to quarrel with him, and he was making it impossible to do so when he insisted on agreeing with everything she said. If there was one thing she hated more than men disagreeing with her, it was men agreeing with her when she was trying to pick a fight. "But, my dear Georgie, better safe than sorry! That's what I always say." He paused, considering, his handsome face looking a bit troubled. "Well, that's what my nanny always used to say, actually, and I usually ignored her, but I like to think I've gained some wisdom with age, eh?"

"If this is you with wisdom, then the thought of what you were like when you were younger is absolutely chilling," Georgie retorted, crossing her arms.

"Do you like Gothic novels, Georgie?"

"Do I—what?" she asked, so puzzled by this non sequitur that she could barely formulate a full sentence.

"Just trying to work out whether I should take 'chilling' as a compliment, coming from you," he explained with wide-eyed earnestness. "In any case, since your father appears to have his own motorcar, and sounded positively delighted when I phoned him to come collect us—ah, that must be him!"

It was, of course; the sound of the Radcliffes' aging Morris Minor could generally be heard well in advance of its appearance, and it rounded a curve in the lane a moment later, coming to a halt before the Shorn Sheep. The driver's-side door opened, and Papa emerged, looking somewhat frazzled.

Fletcher-Ford's face brightened. "You must be Radcliffe! I'm Fletcher-Ford, we spoke on the telephone."

"If you would please try not to shout an introduction on the street to a man you're allegedly already acquainted with, that would be brilliant," Georgie hissed, then turned to face her concerned-looking father.

"Georgie, love, are you all right?" Papa asked, his brow creasing. He must have left the house in a hurry, she thought, since he appeared to be wearing one loafer and one house slipper. "What's this about a head injury?"

"I'm fine, Papa, please don't worry," she said, smiling at her father as she approached the motorcar and opened the door for Egg, who—sensing the opportunity to be spared the long(ish) walk home—sprang into the vehicle with a degree of spryness that was astonishing for a dog her age.

Papa, however, was not listening, as he was now wringing Fletcher-Ford's hand and offering him his profuse thanks.

"He merely helped me to my feet, Papa, it's not as though he rescued me from drowning!" she called churlishly, and Fletcher-Ford flashed her that maddening smile once again.

"That can be tomorrow's entertainment," he said, his smile widening as her scowl deepened. "Think how thrilling—all those wet garments!"

Georgie's jaw dropped, and yet somehow her father—too busy babbling his thanks—did not appear to have taken in a single word Fletcher-Ford had just said.

"Papa!" she called again, loud enough this time that her father at last broke off and looked back at her with some concern. "My head is aching. I'd like to go home and rest."

This, predictably, did the trick—her father was very worried by any physical ailment either of his daughters ever mentioned, which was why Georgie harbored such concerns about Abigail's newfound affection for Dr. Severin. If Papa had his way, the doctor would be summoned the moment his younger daughter so much as sneezed. In no time at all, Georgie and Fletcher-Ford—"You must call me Sebastian, sir, if I'm to stay in your home!"—were settled in the Morris (Fletcher-Ford having, with a great show of chivalry, offered Georgie the front seat and made a production of folding his long legs practically to his chest to fit in the cramped back seat, Egg panting happily beside him), and then they were rattling back down the high street toward Radcliffe Hall, having made a brief detour to the train station to collect Fletcher-Ford's luggage.

"Papa," Georgie said, "you should know that Mr. Fletcher-Ford—"

"I thought you were going to call me Sebastian," the man

in question put in from the back seat, leaning forward to be heard, his chin scant inches away from Georgie's shoulder. This close, she could smell whatever soap he used when shaving—sandalwood, she thought. It was not unpleasant.

"*Sebastian*," she said through gritted teeth, "is going to be an old family friend of ours, if anyone asks."

Papa frowned. "Why are we lying?"

"Not lying," Georgie said soothingly. "Merely . . . stretching the truth. We don't want the police to know what we're up to, you see."

"I thought you said Constable Lexington is part of this scheme?"

"He is," she said hastily. "But we don't want Chief Constable Humphreys or Detective Inspector Harriday to catch word of it—you know they've never particularly approved of my sleuthing."

"Hmph!" Papa said, sounding gratifyingly disgruntled. "They should be thanking you for doing their jobs for them, without pay."

"Exactly what I thought, sir," Sebastian agreed from the back seat.

"My *point* is," Georgie said, "we don't want them to know we're investigating, so Sebastian is going to be an old family friend staying with us for a week or so. Enjoying a countryside idyll, if you will."

"And in such lovely company," he said, winking at her. Georgie scowled.

Soon, they were pulling up before Radcliffe Hall, in all its ramshackle glory; a family of ducks was crossing the driveway as they arrived, which eventually necessitated Georgie hopping out of the Morris to usher the final duckling to safety before they could continue, so by the time they came to a halt outside the front door, Abigail and Mrs. Fawcett had emerged and were watching them with undisguised curiosity. Abigail, Georgie was relieved to see, had at least changed out of the dressing gown she'd been wearing earlier, and was now wearing a blue pin-striped shirtdress, her blond hair pinned back.

Much as Georgie was dreading everything about this meeting, there was something undeniably amusing about watching Abigail's jaw literally drop as Sebastian unfolded himself from the Morris and proceeded to tug his enormous, heavy suitcases from the boot with great ease.

"Abigail... Mrs. Fawcett... this is Sebastian Fletcher-Ford," Georgie said, suppressing a weary sigh as Sebastian deposited his luggage on the front steps and reached up to offer a kiss on the hand to her sister and housekeeper, both of whom turned pink. Georgie did not think she had even known Mrs. Fawcett was capable of blushing, prior to this moment.

"Delighted," Sebastian said, smiling at them. "A household full of lovely ladies—my favorite sort!"

Abigail giggled.

Georgie glowered.

"I'll show you to your room," she said, brushing past him to lift his relatively light hand-case, leaving him to trail behind her lugging the suitcases. She led him through the front doors, across the entry hall, and up a flight of stairs to the nicest of the guest bedrooms. Mrs. Fawcett must have been in to clean that afternoon, she thought, detecting the faintest scent of lemon oil and beeswax. A chipped willow vase of fresh wildflowers sat on the nightstand, and the bedding looked freshly washed. The room itself was of a decent size, filled—like all of the guest rooms at Radcliffe Hall—with mismatched bits of furniture that had been inherited over the years: Bookshelves of differing heights flanked the secretary against one wall, and there was an enormous dresser that had once been in Georgie's parents' room shoved against an opposite wall. The wallpaper was a slightly faded green-and-white print, and a couple of mismatched rugs covered the floor. To Georgie's eye, it looked cozy and inviting.

Behind her, Sebastian set down his suitcases, uttered a cheerful "Ah!," and then crossed to the large window that offered a view of the kitchen garden below and the fields beyond.

"I say, is that a chicken, Georgie?" he asked, hands on his hips as he took in the scene.

"Probably," Georgie said. "We've several—eggs don't grow on trees, you know." It could have been Wilhelmina, or Gladys, or Ethel, though probably not Mary Magdalene, who preferred to stick close to the henhouse after a near miss with a fox the month before.

"What a delightful place this is," he said, turning to beam at her. "I see there's a pond, even."

"Yes. Let me guess: You brought your swimming costume, in addition to the tennis racquet?" she said wearily.

His grin widened. "I didn't, actually—but, my dear Georgie, a swimming costume is not *really* necessary, is it?"

Was he . . . flirting with her?

Surely, surely not. She was not at all the sort of woman whom men like this flirted with.

Just to be certain to put a damper on it, however, she said blandly, as she turned to leave, "You might wish to rethink that—the water in the pond is horrendously cold, so I don't think it would do your naked form any favors."

His laughter followed her out the door.

CHAPTER SEVEN

"*I* have to say, Georgie, this is truly the most interesting thing you've ever done!" Abigail declared, flinging herself into a chair.

"Not the three separate murders I've solved in the past year?" Georgie asked dryly.

Abigail shook her head. "Sleuthing is one thing. But bringing home a posh blond man from London? *That* is fascinating."

It was just before dinnertime, and Georgie, Abigail, and Papa were in the drawing room, where they gathered each evening for drinks and perhaps to listen to the wireless before heading through for dinner. Very little of the glory days of Radcliffe Hall remained, but Georgie's mother had continued this tradition upon her marriage, even allowing the children, no matter how small, to join their parents, and Georgie had therefore been determined to continue it as well, after her mother's death. When Abigail and Georgie were young, this had involved mugs of extremely milky tea for them, while Papa had tea as well (only he'd poured whisky into it). As the girls had grown, however, they'd begun to dabble in a bit of wine or sherry, then champagne, and these days Abigail had become obsessed with cocktails, which she never had the opportunity to acquire anywhere else in Buncombe-upon-Woolly, seeing as the village did not offer much in the way of fashionable entertaining. She had acquired a copy of *The Savoy Cocktail Book* and was apparently determined to eventually work her way through the seven hundred recipes, although the Radcliffes did not entertain frequently enough for her to make much of a dent in it.

Tonight, the menu was aviations with a garnish of interrogation.

"This is only a professional relationship," Georgie said, accepting the glass her sister handed her. "We are working on an investigation together. He'll be back in London by this time next week."

"That's how it started with Lord Peter Wimsey and Harriet Vane, but I'm not convinced wedding bells aren't in their future," Abigail said, sinking down onto the faded velvet love seat opposite Georgie. Almost everything in Radcliffe Hall was somewhat faded, full of relics from the family's wealthier and more glamorous days, and the drawing room where they currently found themselves ensconced was a perfect example of this, featuring a set of mismatched sofas and chairs, a battered coffee table, a scarred and chipped sideboard that Abigail had turned into a bar, a bookshelf buckling under the weight of two complete (and extremely outdated) encyclopedia sets and decades' worth of issues of *National Geographic*, and wallpaper in a William Morris print that had likely looked spectacular fifty years earlier when it was hung, but which was showing definite signs of its age.

"Who?" Georgie asked blankly.

"From Dorothy Sayers's novels," Abigail said impatiently. "Don't you *read?*"

"Strangely, I find the *actual* murders in my day-to-day life sufficient and don't need to seek them out in novels," Georgie shot back.

"Clearly not sufficient, since you're determined to see a murder where there wasn't one, with poor Mr. Penbaker." Georgie had to swallow back a sharp retort at the "poor Mr. Penbaker," considering that not a week before his death, Abigail had been complaining vociferously about the fact that he'd refused to allow her to sell cocktails to the Murder Tourists on Murderous Meanders, a series of guided tours he'd arranged along the village's high street. The Murderous Meanders took place every Friday, Saturday, and Sunday, meaning Georgie's plans to commence a subtle investigation that weekend would be a bit more difficult with would-be amateur detectives popping out from around every corner.

"Besides," Abigail added, not seeming to notice Georgie's disgruntlement, "Dr. Severin examined Mr. Penbaker—surely if he'd been stabbed, he'd have noticed."

"I don't think he was stabbed," Georgie said patiently. "If he was murdered, he was poisoned. There are numerous poisons that can induce cardiac arrest."

"Your fondness for poisons is disturbing," Abigail said, sniffing and taking a dainty sip of her drink.

"I'm not *fond* of them," Georgie said, nettled. "In fact, I'd love it if people in this village could see their way to being poisoned a bit less frequently."

"No, you wouldn't," Abigail said, with a trace of smug knowing that Georgie found infuriating coming from her baby sister. "Because then you'd have nothing to do."

Georgie opened her mouth to protest, but at that precise moment there were footsteps on the stairs, and a few seconds later, Sebastian poked his head into the drawing room.

"Hello," he said cheerfully, beaming at the assorted Radcliffes.

"Hello!" Abigail said, brightening. "Would you like a cocktail?" She was already making for the bar; it was a great thrill for her whenever they had visitors, as she evidently found Georgie and their father to be somewhat dissatisfactory as far as cocktail hour company went.

Sebastian winked at her; Georgie contemplated homicide. "Strong drink and the company of two fetching maidens—who could resist?"

Abigail dimpled at him. "We're having aviations, if you'd like one?" She didn't go so far as to bat her eyelashes, but Georgie was certain she'd considered it, and felt like reminding her sister that earlier that same day, she'd feigned a dire illness to lure a certain village doctor to Radcliffe Hall, and could she perhaps make up her mind as to which inappropriate man to flirt with?

"I'd love one," Sebastian said, entering the room and taking a seat on the settee next to Georgie. He had changed his clothing, she noticed—he was now wearing a cream-colored jumper and a pair of gray trousers. Catching her glance, he said, "I didn't think this seemed like the sort of household to dress formally for dinner—unless I was incorrect?"

Georgie looked down at her outfit—the same one she'd been wearing all day, her blouse a bit limp and wrinkled by this hour.

"Not incorrect, unfortunately," Abigail said, turning to present him with his drink. "We're not very formal in Buncombe-upon-Woolly."

"All part of your charm," Sebastian said brightly, raising his glass to her. "Cheers."

"Georgie tells me you're a fellow Cambridge man," Papa said now, eyeing Sebastian approvingly. "Which college?"

Papa and Sebastian proceeded to fall into a lengthy conversation in which they compared colleges (King's versus St. John's) and reminisced about May Balls and afternoons spent punting on the Cam. Georgie and Abigail exchanged weary looks and dedicated themselves to their cocktails.

"Did you never think to attend, then, Georgie, old bean?" Sebastian asked sometime later, drawing Georgie out of her thoughts with a start.

"What?" she asked blankly, staring at him.

"Or Miss Abigail, of course," he added with a polite nod at her sister. "Attend one of the women's colleges, I mean," he clarified, seeing that she was still regarding him with confusion. "Girton, perhaps. Or Newnham."

"No," Georgie said shortly. "I couldn't possibly leave Papa and Abigail."

"And I was never all that good at schoolwork," Abigail said, not looking remotely bothered by this. "It was all right at our boarding school, but a Cambridge education would be wasted on me."

"However," Georgie said quickly, spotting an opportunity, "Abigail may still leave the village—she's been invited to spend the summer with our aunt in London." Perhaps the presence of a handsome man from the capital would make the prospect seem more appealing to her sister.

Abigail's face darkened like a sudden storm cloud. "Nothing's been decided yet," she said shortly. "You're not the only person who has responsibilities here, you know. I'm on the fete planning committee, and I wouldn't like to abandon them—the other ladies don't have quite the flair for the dramatic that I do, and I really think the quality of our fetes would suffer if I were to leave."

Georgie set down her glass. "Aunt Georgiana has already said that you're welcome to stay with her," she said with a frown. "There's no reason you should be dillydallying about letting her know if you're coming."

"If you're so eager for one of us to spend the summer with her," Abigail said, a definite edge creeping into her voice, "then why don't *you* go to visit instead?"

"Because I'm needed here," Georgie said, which she thought should have been obvious. Did Abigail not realize who kept the house running? Who ensured that Mrs. Fawcett was paid on time? That local boys from the village were hired each spring and summer to help with the landscaping around the ever-more-overgrown Radcliffe Hall? The surrounding farmland had been sold off decades earlier, so at least she didn't have to worry about tenant farmers, although the income would have been welcome. Did Abigail not notice the number of villagers who sought her out, asking her advice on matters ranging from the keeping of bees to the timing of their milk deliveries to the changes to the bus schedule to Cheltenham? And what of the three—three!—murders that Georgie had solved in the past year?

Abigail seemed unmoved by this explanation. "Of course you are," she said coolly, and then turned to their father and determinedly commenced a surprisingly detailed discussion of the mechanics of bell-ringing in *The Nine Tailors*, the latest novel by Dorothy Sayers, which both had evidently read for Miss Halifax's murder mystery book club at the library. (Georgie harbored a dark suspicion that, under other circumstances, both Papa and Abigail would be Murder Tourists.)

Sebastian turned to Georgie. "Didn't mean to strike a nerve," he said, sipping his drink with apparent satisfaction.

Georgie sighed. "It was my fault—it's a bit of a sore subject between us. I shouldn't have brought it up."

"It can be like that sometimes," he said contemplatively, popping the maraschino cherry from his drink into his mouth. "With siblings, I mean."

Just then, Mrs. Fawcett poked her head in to announce dinner, and in the rush of draining the dregs of their cocktails and moving to the door, Georgie let her conversation with Sebastian drop. But she couldn't help thinking, as they walked to the dining room, that when he spoke of siblings, there had been a slightly bitter edge to his voice.

But what on earth, she wondered, could a man like this have to be bitter about?

The next morning dawned as a perfect example of an English summer day—in other words, it was wet and chilly.

Georgie cast a gloomy look out the window as she dressed in a serviceable brown wool jumper and, after a moment's thought, a pair of tweed trousers that she usually wore only when working in the garden, or on one of her long countryside rambles to collect plant specimens; something about Sebastian's London polish made her want to appear as grubby as possible, out of some innate contrarian streak that she was usually more successful at repressing. She knew that she was not a great beauty like Abigail, and this fact had never bothered her one whit. For someone who spent a considerable amount of her time outdoors and in less-than-clean surroundings, clothing had always seemed like something of an afterthought, though she was conscious of her family's position within the village and tried to present an at least somewhat respectable figure.

However, she had never felt so acutely conscious of her own aesthetic appeal—or lack thereof—as she did with Sebastian. Her mind kept returning to the moment the day before when he had called her pretty—whatever could he have meant by it? Was he mocking her? For all his flaws, he didn't seem unkind, so somehow, she didn't think so. But that meant that he must have merely been being polite, she decided.

Because surely he hadn't *meant* it.

Shaking her head at these absurd thoughts, she finished dressing and prepared to head downstairs. Egg, who had a keen ear for the sound of raindrops on a roof and precisely nothing else, cracked an eye open, thumped her tail politely by way of saying farewell, and immediately went back to sleep on her cushion. Clearly Georgie would not have any canine company on today's adventures.

Down in the kitchen, Mrs. Fawcett was stirring a pot of porridge and humming what Georgie thought was a Noël Coward song; Georgie fetched a bowl from the cabinet and helped herself to a large portion of porridge, shamelessly spooning a generous helping of honey on top. Georgie kept hives in a corner of the kitchen garden and sold honey at the Saturday market in the village, as well as in a few of the shops on the high street.

"You'll rot all your teeth," Mrs. Fawcett scolded as usual, and as usual, Georgie replied with a cheerful, "And it will have been worth it."

She carried her bowl upstairs into the dining room—which always seemed particularly absurd in terms of its scale at breakfast time—to find Sebastian attacking a bowl of porridge with great gusto while regaling Papa with the tale of that year's Oxford-Cambridge boat race.

"... important that the Oxford crew was heavier than the Cambridge crew, on average," Sebastian was saying as Georgie entered the room, brandishing his spoon for dramatic effect, "and by the time they passed Craven Cottage, I thought Oxford was beginning to look tired, and I turned to old Tuppy and said—far sooner than I should have, I grant you—'I think Cambridge is going to win this,' and, by Jove, I was right!"

"An unusual experience for you, no doubt," Georgie said as she took her seat, and both men turned, startled, evidently not having noticed her entrance amidst Sebastian's thrilling tale of oar-based drama.

"Morning, Georgie," Sebastian said cheerfully, scooping up another heaping spoonful of porridge. "I say, have you tried your lovely housekeeper's porridge? It's remarkable; I told her, the best porridge I ever tasted was at the most delightful inn in Scotland, directly next door to the mill that produced the oats, and I was under the impression that there was simply something about the Scottish character that lent itself to oat-based goods, but your Mrs. Fawcett should consider donning a kilt and joining that fair nation, because this might be even better."

Georgie, as so often seemed to be the case when Sebastian was speaking, found herself somewhat at a loss for words, and latched onto one detail the way a drowning man might cling to a life raft. "I do not believe women wear kilts."

He frowned. "You're correct, dash it—though I must say that you would look remarkably fetching in one."

She frowned back at him and ate a spoonful of porridge.

"Just staying in character as a cherished friend of the family, bestowing a compliment upon one of its daughters," he informed her innocently, and then returned his full attention to his porridge.

Meanwhile, her father appeared to be hanging on Sebastian's every word. "I've not been to the Boat Race in . . ." He trailed off, his brow furrowing. "Well, I can't remember the last time. I ought to go again one of these years."

It would have been, Georgie knew, at least twenty years ago that he'd last gone—the race had been suspended during the war, and then her mother had died, and her father had not traveled any farther than Bath since then. Initially, it had seemed reasonable—he was grief-stricken, utterly devastated by his wife's death, with two young daughters to care for. And then, as the years had passed and Georgie and Abigail grew older, Georgie suspected that it had simply become something of a habit. Papa was not entirely isolated, for they did have visitors—friends from his Cambridge years would arrive for a fortnight spent discussing minor archaeological discoveries in remote English counties while eating shortbread before the fire; Aunt Georgiana would visit occasionally, usually as one of her marriages was on the rocks and she was looking to escape London. Mama's parents never visited; instead, Georgie and Abigail were periodically sent to Bath to stay with them, since they felt that the civilizing influence of town—even if the town in question was merely Bath—would be good for both girls, given their somewhat helter-skelter upbringing at Radcliffe Hall with a scatterbrained father and no mother.

But Papa himself, while happy enough to entertain visitors, did not venture afield, and so it was somewhat astonishing to hear him now discussing the Boat Race as if it were something he might consider attending in the future. It seemed almost unkind of Sebastian to bring back this glimpse of the father she recalled from her childhood, the man who had once taken her to London on the train for the day, to visit the Natural History Museum and feed the ducks in St. James's Park and select a box of violet creams at Fortnum's.

Occupied by these somewhat melancholy thoughts, Georgie devoured her breakfast in a hurry, and then interrupted a lengthy tangent from Sebastian about the merits of Cambridge blue as opposed to Oxford's darker hue to say abruptly, "Mr. Fletcher-Ford, if you are finished with your Scottish-quality porridge, I was hoping we might be on our way?"

Papa and Sebastian blinked up at her.

"Georgie," Sebastian said with a winning smile, "if we're to convince the fine people of this adorable hamlet of our deep familial connection, don't you think you'd better see your way back to calling me Sebastian, as you were yesterday?"

"Sebastian," she replied, her tone so syrupy it was practically dripping, "I will be departing through the kitchen door in approximately two minutes, and I will not be waiting a second longer, so if you intend to accompany me, I'd suggest you get moving."

"I do enjoy a woman telling me what to do," he said with a roguish wink.

He seemed not to notice her discomposure as he rose from the table, gave Papa an affectionate pat on the shoulder, and delivered his porridge bowl to Mrs. Fawcett in the kitchen, paying her all manner of compliments as he did so. Georgie trailed behind him mutely, trying to regain her equilibrium as she pulled on a mackintosh and a pair of muddy boots, and it was only once they were out the door and sloshing through puddles in the kitchen garden that she mustered her sangfroid once more.

Sebastian had other concerns, however. "My shoes may never recover from this," he said, looking down at his loafers mournfully. They were a deep brown leather with stylish little tassels, and had no doubt cost a sum that would cause Georgie to have apoplexy.

"You cannot possibly have thought those were a sensible shoe choice today," she said waspishly, opening her umbrella. Sebastian followed suit—he did, apparently, at least have sufficient common sense to have thought to carry one.

He neatly dodged a particularly large puddle at the garden gate, then opened the gate and stepped back, allowing her to pass through before him.

"Better than the alternative options," he assured her, once again looking dejectedly down at the damp leather. They set off down the long, now somewhat muddy lane leading from Radcliffe Hall to the village high street.

"Do you not come to the countryside often?" she asked after a minute or two of silence, the raindrops tapping a gentle beat on their umbrellas.

"Not much these days," he said, his tone slightly evasive; she glanced at him curiously, but he was still gazing around them at the surrounding fields, overflowing with buttercups and cornflowers, and his face bore its usual expression of absent-minded good humor. Despite the dreary weather, he positively radiated good health and vigor, his skin glowing, his expensive clothes tailored to show off his lean, athletic figure to best advantage. Even his golden hair seemed to be curling attractively in the damp. He looked like he should be racing about an athletic field somewhere, or rowing a boat, or carrying a willing maiden home. And yet, she could tell that he did not entirely welcome this line of conversation, despite every appearance he gave of ease and good cheer. He hid it well, but he was also very carefully *not* looking at her at the moment, and her curiosity was piqued.

"Did you grow up in London, then?" she asked, something within her now determined to weasel a bit of information out of him. How, she wondered, did one come to be a secretary to a famous detective? Presumably his path into the world of murder investigation had not involved as many direct connections to crimes (or, at least, to their victims) as hers had.

"No, in a little village in Cambridgeshire," he said. "Only moved to London after I left university."

So far, so unremarkable—similar to the biographies of many a poncy and overprivileged man of his ilk. But...

"So you do not visit your home often?" she pressed.

"At Christmas, usually," he said. "That's sufficient time with my family to last me a full twelve months, I find." His tone was all bland geniality, as usual, but Georgie looked at him sharply as he spoke. Spotting her curious gaze, he shrugged. "It's not an interesting story, old bean. We're just not terribly compatible."

"Do *not* call me 'old bean,'" she said shortly.

"All right," he agreed, waiting another beat before adding slyly, "old sport."

"For the love of—"

"Relax, darling Georgie," he said soothingly. "I'm only joking."

"I'm not your darling," she retorted.

"Not yet," he said, twirling his umbrella bit jauntily.

Georgie rolled her eyes heavenward as they continued

their rainy walk into the village—and it was only later that she considered that maybe, just maybe, he'd provoked her deliberately, so as not to talk about his relationship with his family any longer.

It was cunningly done, if so—which was odd, because prior to that moment, "cunning" was not a word she would have ever thought to apply to Sebastian Fletcher-Ford.

CHAPTER EIGHT

*A*rthur was awaiting them outside the *Woolly Register* offices, looking damp and irritable.

"If we're going to investigate a potential murder," he said as soon as Georgie and Sebastian were within earshot, "I'd appreciate it if the weather would cooperate."

"I don't suppose you recall the fact that when Lady Tunbridge was murdered at Radcliffe Hall at Christmas, I spent two hours in a snowstorm waiting for her lady's maid to emerge from the greenhouse where she was hiding?" Georgie reminded him.

Sebastian shook his head admiringly. "That was the one where the widow of a baronet was attacked by the daughter she'd had out of wedlock and abandoned at an orphanage years earlier? The one where you uttered the famous line, upon finding the corpse in her bed, 'I wish I hadn't bothered buying her a Christmas present'?"

Georgie stared at him. "How do you know that?"

Sebastian shoved a hand in his pocket, offering a modest smile. "I did my research."

"Meaning?" Georgie asked suspiciously.

"Well," Sebastian said, "while you were having your bumps and scrapes patched up by that doctor of yours yesterday, I happened to notice a couple of ladies sitting alone and I thought one of them looked dashedly familiar—"

"I imagine it's hard to keep track of all their faces," Georgie said.

"—so I took myself over to their table and introduced myself," Sebastian continued, ignoring her entirely, "and that is how I learned that one of them is a Miss de Vere—a high-society sort, her uncle's a marquess and the family seat is in Wiltshire—"

"Is there a point to this beyond proving that, mystifyingly, there's still an audience for *Debrett's*?" Georgie asked.

"—and it transpires that this is her third visit to the village this year," Sebastian said, with the air of a man about to drop some sort of bomb that made Georgie very nervous. "Because she is an *avid* follower of your exploits, Georgie."

"Oh dear God," Georgie said, looking at him in frank horror. "You do not mean to tell me you befriended a *Murder Tourist!*"

"I think she and her friend prefer the title 'Detective Devotees,' actually," Sebastian said. "They showed me their notebook—they've been tracking all of your articles that have made it to *The Times*, Crawley, and they're positively fascinated by the intrepid Miss Radcliffe. They believe that *The Deathly Dispatch* is far too enamored of Detective Inspector Harriday and does not give you enough credit, for the record." He shrugged. "In any case, they regaled me with all the tales of your detecting prowess in great detail—"

"Is this a nightmare?" Georgie muttered wildly.

"—which is why I now consider myself something of an expert on the crime-solving exploits of Georgiana Radcliffe," Sebastian concluded.

"The last thing we need is to encourage the Murder Tourists," Georgie informed him.

"I don't think they need any encouragement," he suggested. "Positively *obsessed* with murder, those two. Although they *were* quite fetching, so at least if they're dogging our steps, it will be pleasant scenery."

Georgie bit back the approximately half dozen scathing replies on her tongue and instead turned to Arthur.

"Are you busy with work today, or do you have time to do a bit of research for the investigation?"

"I've some time," Arthur said cautiously. "What do you mean by 'research,' though?"

Georgie bit her lip, scrunching up her nose a bit as she thought. "It occurred to me as I was lying in bed last night—I think we should try to compile a list of people who might have held a grudge against Mr. Penbaker. I was thinking that perhaps if you were to ask some questions around the village—pretending that you're writing some sort of feature on Penbaker's life for the *Register*—then you might be able to come up with a list of potential suspects for us to consider. No one would find it odd for you to be asking questions like that, seeing as you're a reporter."

Sebastian beamed at her. "Capital idea, Georgie."

"It's a good thought," Arthur agreed. "What do you plan to do today, then?"

"Focus on the most important thing," Georgie said grimly.

"And what's that?" he asked uncertainly.

"Working out whether Mr. Penbaker was, in fact, murdered."

"And how exactly do you plan to do that?"

"By speaking to the last two people to see him on the day of his death."

───

Dr. Severin's surgery occupied the front half of the small, tidy cottage where he lived, which was just around a corner and down a narrow lane from the village high street. Georgie had not been into the building in years—both Severin and his predecessor made house calls, and Georgie was a fairly healthy sort of person. The front of the cottage was occupied by a thriving garden, featuring any number of herbs and native plants—Georgie spotted elderflower, evening primrose, and feverfew. She knew that, in addition to more modern medicines, Dr. Severin also prescribed various tinctures to his patients—Papa had been advised to use oil of honeysuckle to treat a sunburn just last month—but she hadn't realized that he provided the necessary herbs himself. Georgie could not help but approve; Dr. Fitzpatrick, his predecessor, had been a kind man but one who turned up his nose a bit at so-called home remedies, even ones that Georgie knew for a fact were effective. When she'd learned that Dr. Fitzpatrick's replacement was a recent graduate down from Edinburgh, she'd expected a similar attitude to prevail, and had been pleasantly surprised.

Now, if only he were approximately thirty years older and very plain, and therefore not remotely interesting to Abigail.

The inconveniently young, broad-shouldered, and handsome doctor opened the door at Georgie's knock, an expression of polite surprise flashing across his face when he spotted Georgie and Sebastian on his doorstep. "Miss Radcliffe. Is something wrong—is your sister unwell again?"

Georgie did not think she imagined the note of eagerness that entered his voice at the question.

"Abigail's fine," she said a bit shortly. She cleared her throat. "Er, you remember Mr. Fletcher-Ford, don't you? From the inn yesterday?"

"I do." Severin nodded at Sebastian. "I hope your head is feeling all right today, Miss Radcliffe?"

"It is *not*," Georgie said, pleased that an excuse had so readily materialized. "It is aching something terrible, and I was hoping you would be willing to take a look?"

"Certainly," Severin said politely, standing back from the door so that Georgie might enter, and then offering Sebastian a curious glance. "Mr. Fletcher-Ford, you're welcome to wait out here—"

"I'm afraid I've been tasked with keeping dear Georgie here company today," Sebastian said, with the sort of easy smile that seemed to make people want to agree with him, no matter what he was saying. "I promised her father—old family friend, you know." His gaze was wide and guileless. Severin glanced at Georgie, frowning.

"It's fine for him to come in, too," Georgie said, and Severin's frown eased, though his thoughtful expression remained. He didn't say anything, however, beyond a simple "All right."

Once Georgie was seated in a chair in Severin's small examining room, she pondered how best to approach her questions. "You must keep quite busy, here in Buncombe-upon-Woolly," she said casually, examining her fingernails as if she were simply making idle chitchat.

Severin, who had been rummaging in a drawer, glanced over his shoulder at her. "Busy enough," he said, turning, a penlight in hand. He reached a finger beneath her chin to tilt her head back slightly. "A doctor's work is never done, after all."

He bent toward her, shining the light from the outer edge of her right eye toward the center. He repeated this on her left eye, then straightened.

"I mean," she attempted again, "what with all the ... murders." She bowed her head as if at church, allowing a beat of silence to pass before chancing a glance upward.

"Hmm." Severin leaned back with his hip against the large, antique-looking chest of drawers that housed many of his medical supplies and looked at her warily. "It's been ... interesting, yes. Can you recite the months of the year backward, please?"

"Ooh," Sebastian murmured, shaking his head. "Is that some sort of test for a head injury? Don't know that I could pass it even on my best day."

"Why does that not surprise me," Georgie muttered, then complied. Before Dr. Severin had the chance to open his mouth, she pressed, "And, naturally, you were the first to arrive when Mr. Penbaker died recently." She shook her head mournfully. "So tragic." She chanced a small sniffle, as if overcome by emotion.

"Yes," Severin said. "Although I wasn't under the impression you two were terribly close."

"What made you think that?" Georgie asked.

"Well," Severin said dryly, "there was your lengthy argument with him about the poison garden at the murder exhibition at the village hall."

"How did you hear about that?" she asked, nonplussed.

Severin snorted. "I think the entire village heard about it—Mrs. Chester said you were practically shouting."

Georgie sniffed disdainfully. "He mislabeled hemlock and hogweed. They don't even *look alike*. And," she added, working herself into a proper temper as the opportunity to opine about one of her favorite subjects presented itself, "just last week, I noticed that monkshood and foxglove had somehow been mislabeled, too. How can we ever expect the children of this village to gain any sort of basic botanical education if village-sanctioned exhibitions are relaying false information?"

"You know, Miss Radcliffe, you are not giving me the slightest reason to worry that you might be concussed," Severin said, the corners of his mouth twitching. "I think I should just send you to the chemist for some aspirin."

Sebastian cleared his throat; Georgie suppressed a sigh, fearing what was to come next. "The truth is, Severin, old chap, that Georgie here has been fretting something *awful* over Penbaker's death, ever since that knock on the head yesterday."

"Has she?" Severin asked.

"It made her reflect on . . . mortality, I suppose," Sebastian said with a sad shake of his head. "How quickly death can come for us all. We were talking about your erstwhile council chairman's tragic death last night—how you never know what day might be your last, don't you know?—and she began to wonder if perhaps there wasn't more to it."

There was something oddly transfixing about him as he spoke; his handsome face; wide-eyed, guileless demeanor; and the smooth, soothing tone of his voice made it difficult to turn away from him. She risked a glance at Severin and saw that his expression had softened.

Sebastian gave her a brief, small nod, and she tried again. "When Mr. Penbaker fell ill," Georgie said, leaning forward in her seat as Severin's gaze flicked back toward her, "was there anything about his condition that made you think it could be something more serious? Something like—"

"Poison?" Severin finished for her, then scrubbed his hands over his face in a gesture that conveyed extreme weariness. "Christ, I thought I was setting up a practice in a quiet village and that nothing at all interesting would happen here. Never seen so many dead bodies in my life." He shook his head ruefully. "Mrs. Penbaker rang me the afternoon of her husband's death because she returned home from a meeting to find him unwell—he was complaining of dizziness and chest pain, and by the time I arrived he'd suffered cardiac arrest. I was unable to revive him, as is often the case with heart attacks—they happen very quickly, often with little warning. It's a tragedy, but I found nothing unusual in it."

"Hmm." This was nothing more than what Georgie had already heard through the grapevine of village gossip, but she had hoped that hearing the tale directly from Severin would help her uncover some new, overlooked piece of information. "Had Mr. Penbaker complained of feeling unwell prior to that day?"

Severin paused, his brow furrowing slightly. "He had other complaints, but nothing that seemed unusual for a man of his age—he had terrible aches in his joints, for example, and he drank a particular tea that I blended for him to help with that. But otherwise, he seemed in fairly good health."

"How did Mrs. Penbaker seem when you arrived?" Sebastian asked; he'd spent the entire time Severin was speaking gazing idly around the room, not seeming to pay attention to the matters being discussed, but he'd now glanced up and was looking steadily at Severin.

"As you'd expect," Severin replied. "She was distraught. It was all the more startling, since she strikes me as a woman who is very collected." He shook his head with an unhappy twist of his mouth. "It is always difficult when a spouse is present during these sorts of events, no matter how unhappy their marriage."

Georgie blinked at this last, almost thoughtless addition. "Did you not think theirs was a happy marriage?"

Severin glanced at her for a moment, seeming to weigh his words, then said, rather carefully, "I have not lived here long, Miss Radcliffe, so you'd likely be better able to answer that question than I would. But based on my few encounters with them . . . no, I would not have said that the Penbakers had a particularly loving marriage."

Georgie glanced quickly at Sebastian, and just as quickly away again. Severin did not miss this.

"I don't know what you think you're investigating," Severin

said, "but if you're in search of a murder victim, I think you're wandering down the wrong path."

"Thank you," Georgie said gravely. "I do appreciate it when men tell me that I'm wrong."

To his credit, Severin flashed a smile of genuine good humor at that. "Fair enough, Miss Radcliffe. Good luck, then, I suppose."

In short order, he showed them to the door and bid them farewell. As soon as the door closed behind them, Georgie turned to Sebastian. "Are you thinking what I'm thinking?"

"Probably not," he said. "Unless you, too, are thinking that it has been positively *ages* since we ate that porridge—"

"It has been an hour at most."

"—and therefore we're overdue for a midmorning scone?" His eyes were wide and hopeful.

Georgie did not roll her eyes, which she thought a promising sign of personal growth. "*I* was thinking," she said impatiently, "that we need to work out a way to speak to Mrs. Penbaker next, without raising her suspicions."

"But first, may we acquire a scone?" he asked, offering her his most blinding smile.

"Only if you promise never to smile at me like that again," she said coldly, and he laughed—a genuine, surprised laugh—as he followed her down the lane toward the high street. And as they walked, she wasted at least ten seconds informing herself, quite sternly, that she did not like the sound of that laugh at all.

CHAPTER NINE

Georgie had come to an unfortunate conclusion: she was never to have any peace from Murder Tourists.

Disliking the idea of listening to Sebastian's complaints of hunger pangs for the rest of the morning, she led him to the Scrumptious Scone in the hopes that he would eat a quick scone (or four) and then they could be on their way. By the time they arrived at the tearoom, the rain had slowed to a drizzle, though the sky overhead remained unrelentingly dark. Georgie carefully skirted a rather large puddle outside the front door and stepped inside, the bell overhead jingling to mark her entrance; she felt her hair begin to frizz even further, if that were possible, as soon as she walked into the inviting warmth.

"Mr. Fletcher-Ford!" came a tinkling voice from one corner, and Georgie glanced over to see two Murder Tourists holding court at the choicest table, a pot of tea steaming before them. They looked—well, they looked like precisely the sort of women Sebastian might have sidled up to in a pub, Georgie thought grumpily; they were both extremely pretty, wearing the sort of pressed white linen dresses that were wildly impractical for countryside life, but which visitors seemed to delight in wearing on their holidays. They looked to be about Georgie's age; one had light brown hair that curled attractively around her chin, green eyes, and a sprinkling of freckles across the bridge of her nose, and the other had darker skin and a heap of shiny dark hair that fell in stylish waves just past her shoulders.

"Miss de Vere, Miss Singh," Sebastian said, smiling winningly at them as he led Georgie to the table next to theirs; both women beamed back at him. "Allow me to introduce Miss Radcliffe—though I daresay her reputation precedes her."

Georgie spared a frown for Sebastian at this introduction, which prompted an incoherent babble of delight and praise from the ladies the second Georgie's name was uttered.

"—read everything about you that we could manage—"

"—were here in January, after the Mistletoe Murder—"

"—and *imagine* our delight when we happened to plan another visit, and poor Mr. Marble died, too!"

Georgie, sensing that little in the way of reply was currently required of her, gave a discreet wave to Mrs. Chester, who appeared with a teapot and cups a moment later. A murmured word from Sebastian had her bustling away to the kitchen. The matter of food settled, Georgie turned her attention back to the rhapsodizing Murder Tourists, who were now watching her rather expectantly.

She cleared her throat. "Well, I am . . . glad . . . that our criminal activities have been so entertaining to you." She thought she was keeping her tone quite friendly, but the scolding sort of frown Sebastian leveled at her indicated that she might not have managed it as well as she thought.

"It's just that we're awfully fond of reading," Miss Singh explained, leaning forward in her seat. "Do you enjoy the novels of Mrs. Christie?"

"I have not read them," Georgie admitted, taking a sip of tea.

"What about Dorothy Sayers?" Miss de Vere asked. "I think I actually prefer hers—Harriet Vane is my type of woman. I do hope she's not going to let that idiot Wimsey convince her to marry him eventually."

"But Stella," Miss Singh said, turning to her friend and looking distressed, "think how *romantic* it would be."

"It's not romantic when an intelligent woman settles for a man who isn't as smart as her," Miss de Vere said definitively. "Though I will grant you that Wimsey does have a certain charm about him."

"And yet, Miss de Vere, do I not detect an engagement ring on your own hand?" Sebastian asked. He adopted an air of mournful disappointment. "Much as it pains me to even contemplate such a thing."

Miss de Vere smiled at him. "You're rather over-the-top with your flattery, Fletcher-Ford, but I won't deny you look *very* handsome when you pout."

"Would you believe that three separate women have told me the same thing?" he asked winningly.

"I wouldn't," Georgie said, and the rest of her table companions glanced at her, startled. "I would not believe that it was only three," she clarified, and Miss de Vere let out a hoot of laughter.

"I do like you, Miss Radcliffe."

"Well, Mr. Fletcher-Ford?" Miss Singh added, looking between Georgie and Sebastian with some interest. "Is Miss Radcliffe correct?"

"She is," he conceded, after a theatrical pause. "It was actually five."

Miss Singh laughed, delighted, while Miss de Vere gave Georgie a thoughtful look. "How is it that you have come to be here with Miss Radcliffe?" she asked, looking back at Sebastian.

"I'm an old family friend," he said easily. "Couldn't resist the opportunity to rusticate in the countryside for a bit."

Georgie ground her teeth together at the word "rusticate," but managed to avoid interrupting.

"And since I've been here," he continued, "Georgie here has been getting me up to date on all the violent happenings. Never realized the countryside was so dangerous," he added, with a regretful shake of his head. "I thought it was all cheese and lambs and village fetes, but now I'm a bit worried a murderer is going to pop out around every corner."

"Surely no one would try to harm *you*," Miss Singh said, gazing at him with something perilously close to adoration. "You're so . . . *strong*."

Sebastian beamed at her. "I've been known to carry the odd rowing team to victory with the strength of my arms, I'll grant you. Georgie, are you all right? That snort sounded quite unhealthy."

"Simple hay fever," she said blandly, and buried her face in her teacup.

"It *is* curious, don't you think?" Miss de Vere said, reaching for the teapot to refresh her own cup. "It's been an awfully long trail of bloody corpses for a village this size."

"They weren't really bloody though, were they?" asked Miss Singh thoughtfully. "An awful lot of poisonings." She reached into her handbag and produced a leatherbound notebook; when she opened it to the first page, Georgie caught sight of the words "DETECTIVE DEVOTEES: OFFICIAL NOTES" in block capitals, and suddenly wished it were a socially acceptable time of day to drink. Miss Singh nodded as she perused her notes. "Yes, three poisonings, and just the one stabbing at"—she darted a quick, starstruck glance at Georgie—"Radcliffe Hall at Christmas. Awfully odd, really. Agatha Christie would *never* let that many crimes in a row take place with the same method of killing. It really would seem like lazy writing, wouldn't it?"

"Perhaps," Georgie said, extremely dryly, "reality doesn't have as strong a concern for a satisfying narrative arc?"

"Too right, Miss Radcliffe," Miss Singh said, snapping her notebook shut.

"And more's the pity," Miss de Vere said. "If this were a proper novel, there would be a romance developing alongside all the mysteries. Miss Radcliffe, you haven't got a secret paramour, have you?"

"What an intriguing question," Sebastian murmured, taking a sip of his tea.

Georgie busied herself stirring her already-stirred tea. "I don't think we need romance in a mystery, Miss de Vere."

Miss de Vere frowned. "That's very dull of you, Miss Radcliffe." She sounded, briefly, as though she were disappointed that her heroine was not living up to her expectations, but quickly rallied. "I suppose you've too much else to do, though! Crime never ceases!"

"Well," Georgie said, once again feeling peculiarly protective on behalf of her village, "it *does*, actually. Most of the time there's no crime at all in Buncombe-upon-Woolly."

"That hasn't been our experience," Miss de Vere said.

"Truly," Miss Singh agreed. "Corpses everywhere! We met a group yesterday who had read the most *gruesome* details in *The Deathly Dispatch* of the state of Lady Tunbridge's corpse after she was stabbed." She shook her head, looking faintly horrified. "This is why I don't like *The Deathly Dispatch*—it provides a bit too much detail. I like my murders nice and cozy, don't you?"

"Absolutely," Sebastian agreed, dropping another lump of sugar into his tea. "What else do you ladies plan to do on your visit?"

Miss de Vere shrugged, reaching for the pot of strawberry jam on the table before her. "We might visit the murder exhibition at the village hall again—we've been three times already, but I do enjoy the poison garden—and the display featuring the Mistletoe Murder weapon. The bloody knife is *very* gruesome."

"You do realize that's not the *actual* knife that killed Lady Tunbridge?" Georgie asked. "It's one of Mrs. Penbaker's kitchen knives—I believe Mr. Penbaker asked the butcher for a bit of blood to make it look properly gruesome."

Miss de Vere and Miss Singh were identical portraits of disappointment. "You mean the blood comes from *an animal?*"

Miss Singh asked, her eyes wide and horrified. "I don't mind if it's human blood, but the thought of some poor creature being butchered..." She shook her head.

Miss de Vere glanced at the clock on the wall opposite their table and started. "Asha," she said, "the Murderous Meander starts in five minutes!" Both ladies drained their teacups, Miss de Vere reaching for her handbag and producing a shilling that she placed on the table. They rose, but then hesitated for a second, eyeing Georgie.

"Yes?" she asked cautiously.

"It's only..." Miss Singh trailed off, looking nervous, and then said in a rush, "would you please sign our notebook, Miss Radcliffe? The autograph of a *celebrity* sleuth would mean so much to us." She extended the Detective Devotees notebook and handed Georgie a pen, and Georgie, feeling that it would be unnecessarily churlish to refuse, quickly scrawled her name.

"Not a word," she said to Sebastian as the Murder Tourists departed amidst a few more breathless proclamations of their admiration. "Not a single word."

After they were at last blessedly free of both the Murder Tourists and the tearoom—though only after Sebastian had consumed enough scones to fuel an army—and were making their way slowly down the high street, Georgie reached out a hand to seize him by the elbow and yank him to a halt.

"I don't want to get my hopes up," Sebastian said, looking down at her, "but does this signal a thawing in relations? Are you hoping I might offer you my arm?"

"Perhaps I'll find another heavy object dropped on my head, and then your dream will come true," she said. "But until then, no. But do you know, Miss Singh's discussion of *The Deathly Dispatch* made me wonder—where do you think they get the information they print? I refuse to read it, but it sounds like they must have a source among the police—they're much more tight-lipped when giving Arthur information to report on. And they speak awfully favorably about Detective Inspector Harriday."

"Yet another mystery to add to our list. Remarkable quantity of them per capita here, don't you think?"

"I do think," she agreed coldly. "Which is, if you will recall, *the reason you are here*." She shook her head. "This is growing more maddening by the moment—Murder Tourists everywhere! Dr. Severin not being remotely helpful! Rogue newsletter writers!"

"Would you like to know what I do when I am feeling the weight of the world on my shoulders?"

"Not if it involves nudity."

"Ah." He fell silent.

Her mind was turning in confused circles, but then a thought occurred to her. "The Murder Tourists will all be on the Murderous Meander just now," she said, "meaning the murder exhibition at the village hall should be pretty quiet."

"Of course," he said wisely. "Eager to revisit the relics of your previous successes, to bolster your spirits for the difficult task that lies ahead?"

"No," she said shortly. "Mrs. Penbaker runs the exhibition, so this might be a chance to speak to her alone."

"Ah," he said, unfazed. "I suppose that makes sense, too. Shall we invite her to lunch?"

Georgie stared at him incredulously. "You just ate *three scones*, how can you possibly be thinking about lunch?"

"Not for *me*," he protested, looking wounded, then appeared to reconsider. "Well, I'm sure I wouldn't say no to a bite, if it were on offer—"

"Argh!" Georgie threw her hands up to clutch at her hair, feeling as though she were losing her mind. Surely this case wasn't worth it—why not just assume Penbaker had died of natural causes and send Sebastian on his merry way? She could already picture the days of peace that would await her in his absence. She could spend an entire day in her garden, she thought dreamily. Plants couldn't talk. She had never fully appreciated this particular virtue of theirs until now.

"But," Sebastian continued, apparently blind to her distress, "old Fitzy takes an awful lot of lunch meetings, you know." He paused significantly, as though expecting her to immediately change her tune in the face of this knowledge. "I'm very good at booking tables as a result." He looked at her hopefully.

"I think you'll find we do things a bit differently here," she said, crossing her arms. "Now, follow me, and for the love of God, do *not* flirt with Mrs. Penbaker."

"I wish I could promise you that, Georgie," he said, sounding honestly regretful. "But when the spirit of flirtation moves me, I find myself powerless in its grip." He shook his head sadly. "It is both a blessing and a curse, really."

"On second thought," she said, setting off down the street without bothering to confirm that he was following, "perhaps it is best if you don't say anything at all. Mrs. Penbaker is a bit more reserved than her husband was—I don't want you to scare her off."

"But Georgie, old bean," he said; glancing to the side, she saw that he was matching her stride, smiling at her winningly while dodging puddles that would ruin his ridiculous, impractical shoes. "Wives absolutely *adore* me."

"Yes," she agreed sweetly. "Rather too much, I expect. I believe it's recently got you into trouble, in fact?"

Rather than looking chastened, he merely appeared even more amused. "Touché, my dear Georgie. But this time, it will prove to be useful. Just you wait."

The village hall was located in the very center of town, directly opposite the green and behind a low stone wall. A tidy garden featuring roses, peonies, and lupins lined the short path leading from the street to the oak doors. Georgie noted with some disapproval that there was a patch of Himalayan balsam, but she had already learned that lectures on invasive plant species were not often well-received.

Something of her thoughts must have shown on her face as they approached, however, because Sebastian asked, "What is it?"

She blinked; she hadn't realized that her face was so transparent. "That's Himalayan balsam," she said, pointing to the pretty pink flowers. "They're not native to England, and spread easily and stifle native flora."

"You're very fond of plants," he said, and she glanced at him, a bit startled. "It's only—the cases you solved. A couple of them involved poisonous herbs—you seem to know a lot about them."

"Yes," she said, and then added, without pausing to consider, "I want to open a botanic garden at Radcliffe Hall someday, showcasing the native flora of Gloucestershire."

"Yes, I noticed the gardens earlier. Your doing?"

She nodded as she walked up the neat gravel path to the front door. "My mother loved to garden, and even had greenhouses built behind the house. After she died, I took over the gardening, since we can't . . . well, we can't afford a gardener anymore." She didn't see any point in pretending the financial situation at Radcliffe Hall was anything other than a bit desperate; surely he'd already noticed the chipped paint and worn furniture. "Anyway, I hope to expand the gardens eventually, but . . ."

"But what?" he prompted, reaching out a hand to her elbow to slow her approach to the door. She glanced over at him, surprised. He must have interpreted her look as a scold—which, for once, it wasn't—and quickly dropped her elbow.

"But . . . well, I suppose I don't really *know* anything about running a botanic garden," she said, shifting from one foot to another, twirling her umbrella in her hands. "I mean to say—I understand the plants, obviously, but I don't know all the ins and outs of a large-scale operation like that. I don't expect to manage something like Kew Gardens out in rural Gloucestershire, but even so . . . it would be helpful if I had a bit of experience, working as a gardener somewhere—Kew stopped hiring women as apprentice gardeners after the war, but there are other gardens . . . even horticultural colleges for women. . . ."

She trailed off, a bit uncertain. "I suppose it's not a very common goal for a woman, but—"

"I cannot imagine that stopping you," he said, and it did not sound like an insult; rather, there was something close to admiration in his tone, and Georgie decided to ignore this, because quite frankly she had no notion of what to do with the admiration of a man like Sebastian Fletcher-Ford.

"I'd once thought to go live with my aunt in London for a year or so," she continued instead, "if I could apprentice at Regent's Park, perhaps, or the Royal Horticultural Society, but..." She hesitated, but before he could prompt her to finish, she added, "I can't leave my family. They need me."

He opened his mouth to reply, but she turned and opened the door to the village hall, stepping through the doorway. The hall was primarily comprised of a single large room—they held an annual Christmas dance here, as well as the yearly cheese festival, which usually drew a sizable crowd each August. At the moment, however, the hall had been entirely taken over by... well, by murder. There was a giant map of Buncombe-up-on-Woolly displayed prominently near the entrance, with a dramatic red X marking each spot where a murder had occurred in the past year. (Georgie scowled at the X on Radcliffe Hall.) Beyond it, there was an entire display of newspaper clippings—from both *The Woolly Register* and (much to Arthur's displeasure) *The Deathly Dispatch*, and even a couple of stories that *The Times* had picked up—detailing the past year's gruesome events. The bloody knife that the Murder Tourists had mentioned had pride of place on a slightly faded cushion. The entire thing was garish and appalling.

"Well, this is delightful," Sebastian said.

"It isn't," she retorted as he strolled around the room, exclaiming excitedly each time he spotted something new. Georgie's gaze landed on the framed photograph of Detective Inspector Harriday and her frown deepened. Constable Lexington, she noticed, did not merit a mention, despite certainly having contributed just as much—if not more—to each investigation. A sudden hoot of laughter drew her attention, and she knew, with a sudden premonition of doom, what Sebastian had spotted.

"Georgie, is that *you?*"

She crossed the room to stand beside him near the back of the exhibition, where he was ogling a small framed photograph of Georgie—taken a few years earlier, because she had flatly refused to sit for a new photograph for the sake of this nonsense—next to an informational placard titled The Lady Detective.

". . . 'the village's own Poirot'—well, not sure that's quite accurate," he said apologetically, as if wary of causing offense. "You don't sound terribly Belgian, old bean."

"Dear God," she muttered.

". . . 'racing boldly against the clock as the snow fell heavily outside to confront a killer within her very own home'—I say, Georgie, this Christmas case sounds quite dramatic."

"It really wasn't. It involved a lot of standing around in the snow and tiresome telephone calls to the police—who couldn't get through the snow to reach us, very helpful—and Abigail making endless mince pies because she bakes when she's anxious."

"I do love mince pies," he said dreamily, but before he could drift too far into a baked-good-induced reverie, he was distracted by the framed copy of a letter in a neighboring display case. "And here is the letter from the orphanage, alerting the murderous maid to Lady Tunbridge's identity as the mother who abandoned her!" He sounded duly impressed. "Quite a distinctive smudge on the letter 'O' on this typewriter—wouldn't want to use it to send a ransom note!" He chortled.

"Fortunately, I don't think orphanage employees are in the habit of sending frequent ransom notes," Georgie said, as patiently as she could manage; even as she spoke, there came the sound of footsteps behind them, and Georgie and Sebastian turned in unison to see Mrs. Penbaker approaching.

"Miss Radcliffe," she said with a slightly forced smile, looking from Georgie to Sebastian and back again. "This is a surprise. I wasn't under the impression you were very fond of the exhibition."

Mrs. Penbaker was considerably younger than her late husband, in her mid-forties, with a head of cropped blond hair that showed only a few strands of gray. She was wearing a neat green dress with a pleated skirt and sensible loafers; a strand of pearls was at her throat.

Georgie's previous dealings with Mrs. Penbaker had always been scrupulously polite but not terribly warm, and she could not think that her husband's recent death would have made her any more welcoming, particularly to questions regarding it.

Fortunately, however, she had not accounted for Sebastian.

"Mrs. Penbaker," she said with a nod. "This is Mr. Fletcher-Ford—he's a family friend, visiting from London." Sebastian offered a complicated and elegant bow over Mrs. Penbaker's hand, as though she were a Regency debutante. Mrs. Penbaker raised her eyebrows at this display, but a hint of a smile played at the corners of her mouth, which Georgie took as a promising sign.

"I'm delighted to meet you," Sebastian said. "And I'm so sorry for your loss."

Mrs. Penbaker inclined her head with a slightly pained smile. "Thank you."

"It must be nice to see your husband's legacy live on, though," Sebastian said, all earnest solemnity.

Mrs. Penbaker looked a bit startled. "In what way?"

Sebastian widened his arms in a broad, sweeping gesture that encompassed their surroundings. "This *fascinating* exhibition. It's quite thorough."

Mrs. Penbaker smiled. "Thank you. Bertie and I worked quite hard on it—we even have a poison garden out back that Miss Halifax and a few of her book club members planted for us, showcasing plants that featured in crime novels."

"Delightful!" Sebastian said brightly, as if he could think of no greater pleasure than surrounding himself with herbs that might kill him. "The entire exhibition is an interesting idea. I understand that your husband was determined to find a silver lining in the village's recent misfortunes—terribly admirable." He leaned against the display case featuring the bloody knife, stuck a hand in his pocket, and cast an appreciative glance around the room. He looked, Georgie thought, a bit like he was posing for a catalogue: "A jumper-wearing man at ease in the country."

"Yes," Mrs. Penbaker said, regarding Sebastian as though he

were some sort of exotic tropical creature one might find at the zoo. "Well, Bertie had become very fond of murder mysteries himself—an interest he developed in the last year or so. And so he was less surprised than I was when increased numbers of tourists began arriving. Eventually, given their number, Bertie thought it sensible to at least offer some sort of official, village-sanctioned information on the recent misfortunes."

"So very wise," Sebastian said with an earnest nod. "You'd hardly want them getting all their information from *The Deathly Dispatch*, after all!" He chuckled easily.

"Miss Radcliffe has told you about *The Deathly Dispatch*, has she?" Mrs. Penbaker asked.

"Yes—well," Georgie said, thinking quickly, "that is, Arthur Crawley has received a tip that the *Dispatch* is going to do some sort of *dreadful* article implying that your husband was murdered. I was explaining to Sebastian here how they publish sensationalist garbage."

Mrs. Penbaker frowned. "Why on earth would they think that? Bertie had a heart attack."

"*We* know that," Georgie assured her. "But you know what the *Dispatch* is like." She shook her head darkly. "Just last week it published an article contrasting how many lambs were killed by foxes here this past spring compared to Bramble-in-the-Vale, as if we're some sort of hotbed for the murder of humans and animals alike."

"This county does love its hyphens, doesn't it?" Sebastian observed.

"Do *not* compare us to Bramble-in-the-Vale," Mrs. Penbaker insisted. "They have *three* hyphens. We only have two!"

"Of course, of course," Sebastian agreed, nodding. "I didn't mean to cause any offense—particularly not to a lady as lovely as yourself." This last was uttered in an intimate tone. "I don't suppose there's anything *you* could tell us about your husband's death—something we could pass along to Crawley, so he can write an article that clearly refutes anything that hack at the *Dispatch* publishes?" He offered Mrs. Penbaker a reassuring sort of smile. "It would pain me to see an upstanding woman like yourself caused distress by tabloid journalism." He shook his head.

Mrs. Penbaker regarded him coolly. "Do you know, Mr. Fletcher-Ford, that I used to know a man *just* like you?"

Sebastian smiled at her. "Do you remember him fondly?"

"No," Mrs. Penbaker said. "He was a dreadful flirt and broke my heart when he married my best friend after leading me on."

Sebastian leaned forward, his gaze fixed on her. "Then, my dear Mrs. Penbaker, he was nothing at all like me."

He winked.

Mrs. Penbaker, seemingly against her better judgment, relented and offered him a small smile.

Georgie exhaled a soft sigh of relief.

"What can I tell you about my husband's death?" Mrs. Penbaker asked briskly, crossing her arms over her chest.

Georgie rummaged for her notebook and a pencil. "I believe he was at home alone when he became ill?"

"Yes." Mrs. Penbaker nodded. "I was running some errands, and then was at the fete planning committee meeting."

"And when you returned home," Georgie prompted, "you found your husband unwell?"

Mrs. Penbaker nodded again. "He complained of being dizzy and short of breath, and his chest was paining him. I rang for Dr. Severin, but by the time the doctor arrived . . ." She shook her head.

Georgie began to hastily jot down notes. "And what time would you say this was?" she asked, glancing up.

Mrs. Penbaker cleared her throat. "I couldn't say for certain. My meeting usually ends at two, and I came straight home afterward."

"So by two-fifteen or so, then?" Georgie asked.

"I suppose so," Mrs. Penbaker agreed.

"And were you surprised by your husband's death?"

"It was quite sudden, as I've just explained. So it was shocking, yes."

There was nothing in her voice but cool, measured politeness. She was very self-contained, Georgie thought—she was not the sort of woman to give any sign of strong emotion.

"And Dr. Severin found nothing unusual about your husband's symptoms?"

"If he did, he told me nothing of it," Mrs. Penbaker said, still very cool.

Georgie glanced at Sebastian; this was going, truthfully, about as well as she had expected it might, but if he thought that his dubious charms could aid the progress of this conversation, now would be a rather helpful time for him to employ them.

Mercifully, he took the hint and leaned forward. "We are so sorry to bother you with what must seem like very odd questions, at such a difficult time for you," he said, his voice warm and soothing, and Georgie could practically see Mrs. Penbaker melting slightly before him.

"But," he continued, "we know how much your husband loved this village—Georgie here has spoken of him so highly, and in such glowing terms," he added, with a fond glance at Georgie, "that I can only mourn the fact that I did not get to make his acquaintance myself. And I cannot help but wonder if your husband had any known enemies who might have had cause to do him harm." He finished this pretty little speech, then leaned back against the display case, looking entirely at ease.

Mrs. Penbaker hesitated for a long moment; Georgie had the impression that she was thinking quite hard, considering her next words. At last, she looked directly at Sebastian and said, "My husband was quite obsessed with increasing tourism to Buncombe-upon-Woolly, you know."

Georgie snorted; everyone in the village knew this—it would have been rather impossible to miss. Sebastian split a curious glance between her and Mrs. Penbaker before asking politely, "Is there something I'm missing?"

"Mr. Penbaker was very... imaginative," Georgie said, with considerable diplomacy, "in his schemes for attracting new visitors."

A small smile played at the corners of Mrs. Penbaker's mouth. "What Miss Radcliffe is too polite to say in front of me is that my husband had ideas that bordered on lunacy—he tried, at one point, to introduce a flock of sheep to the village green, on a permanent basis."

Sebastian blinked. "For what purpose?"

"Our name," Georgie explained. "Buncombe-upon-Woolly. He thought we ought to really lean into the character of the name and become known for our friendly flock of village sheep."

"I take it this didn't work?" Sebastian asked.

Mrs. Penbaker shook her head. "It was absolute chaos—sheep everywhere. You couldn't drive a motorcar through the village for weeks. Eventually, he saw that it was folly, and the sheep were returned to their usual fields."

"Except for one," Georgie added.

"Poor Ernest," Mrs. Penbaker agreed.

"Our permanent village sheep," Georgie explained, seeing that Sebastian looked mystified. "He loved the village green so much that he could not be persuaded to return home. I'll introduce you to him, next time we walk past."

"I look forward to the honor," he said gravely.

"There was also the year he attempted to create a festival at harvesttime centered around racing pumpkins down the river," Mrs. Penbaker continued.

"And the year he tried to draw tourists for Bonfire Night by advertising the largest bonfire in the Cotswolds, and he ended up setting the roof of the school on fire," Georgie added.

"And when he thought we should have an annual weekend celebrating particularly large wheels of cheese, and he ended up dropping one and breaking a tourist's foot."

"If the tourist were allowed to eat the cheese afterward, I expect they might not have minded," Sebastian said thoughtfully. "What's a broken bone when compared with the joys of cheese?"

"And," Mrs. Penbaker added, after a brief, eloquent silence, "he was absolutely obsessed with the notion of besting Bramble-in-the-Vale. The council chairman there—Mr. Lettercross—was an old friend of his, but they hadn't spoken in fifteen years after a falling-out over the last bit of Bath Blue at a Christmas market—"

"I did not realize cheese could cause such lasting enmity," Sebastian said, looking duly impressed.

"Welcome to the Cotswolds," Georgie said.

"—and once Lettercross became the chairman of Bramble-in-the-Vale's village council, just the year after Bertie was elected here, it grew even worse."

"Bramble-in-the-Vale has always been a bit flashier than us," Georgie explained. "Their cheese is more famous, and their sheep have thicker fleece."

"It seemed as though no matter what Bertie did, Lettercross was always a step ahead," Mrs. Penbaker said, shaking her head. "Until the murders, of course. There haven't been any murders at all in Bramble-in-the-Vale."

"No Murder Tourists either, I expect," Sebastian said cheerfully.

Mrs. Penbaker frowned thoughtfully. "That's where you're wrong, actually. A friend of mine runs an inn in Bramble-in-the-Vale, and apparently they're positively overrun—loads of tourists who want a glimpse of the scenes of the crimes, but who are a bit nervous about staying in Buncombe-upon-Woolly itself, lest they become the next victim. So, even when Buncombe-upon-Woolly managed to at last accomplish something noteworthy, Bramble-in-the-Vale still benefited."

Georgie exchanged a glance with Sebastian, her mind racing.

A village leader with no love lost for Mr. Penbaker. And the money and renown that Murder Tourists could bring... without the actual murders?

It all sounded rather ideal for Bramble-in-the-Vale.

CHAPTER TEN

*B*y the time they met Arthur and Constable Lexington at the Shorn Sheep that evening, Georgie was beginning to feel weary. Investigating crimes in small villages was not for the faint-hearted—there was a lot of tea to drink, and scones to consume, and sheep to visit. (The last agenda item, strictly speaking, had nothing to do with their investigation, but Sebastian had been determined to meet Ernest, and so a lengthy detour to the village green had been necessary after bidding Mrs. Penbaker adieu.)

Sebastian, meanwhile, seemed the very picture of vigorous good health and cheer; despite the damp weather, his hair maintained a jaunty curl, his skin glowed alluringly, and his shoes remained astonishingly unmuddied (though this fact had been rendered less astonishing when Georgie had witnessed him furtively produce a handkerchief from his jacket pocket and bend to wipe at a muddy splatter that had had the audacity to besmirch the expensive leather).

Arthur and Lexington arrived together, with Arthur looking visibly disgruntled.

"Hello," she said cautiously, sipping at her half pint of cider. Next to her, Sebastian was lounging insouciantly in his chair, scanning the room—no doubt keeping an eye out for any potential romantic conquests once the evening's business was concluded.

"George. Fletcher-Ford," Arthur said, nodding at them as he shrugged off his damp jacket and slung it across the back of a chair. "Pint of bitter?" he tossed over his shoulder at Lexington, who nodded by way of reply. Georgie filed away this fascinating piece of information in her mind.

In a minute, Arthur was back, clutching a ginger beer for himself and sliding Lexington's beer across the table to him; Lexington accepted the pint glass with a nod at Arthur.

"Did you learn anything interesting?" Georgie asked, once Arthur had settled into his seat.

He shook his head, looking vaguely disgusted. "Lots of chatter about Penbaker being a bold visionary for all of his schemes to draw tourists—nice bit of revisionist history, there," he added with a snort. "But, in short, nothing that gave me the slightest suspicion that anyone I spoke to might be a murderer," Arthur concluded. "What about you?"

"We," Georgie said conversationally, "have decided to go on an expedition to Bramble-in-the-Vale tomorrow."

The effect of these words was instantaneous; Lexington, who'd been about to take a sip of his drink, froze with his glass raised halfway to his lips and offered an eloquent grimace; Arthur, who *had* taken a sip of his ginger beer, choked on it and proceeded to cough quite dramatically, not subsiding until Lexington reached over and thumped him helpfully on the back. Once his lungs were clear, Arthur said, horrified, "*Why?*"

Sebastian, who had watched all of this with keen interest, now turned an inquiring gaze to Georgie. "Is this village home to a prison?" he asked. "Are its inhabitants known to be petty thieves? Do they steal horses? Murder puppies?"

"Worse," Georgie said darkly. "They're *charming*." She shook her head and took a sip of her cider.

Sebastian blinked, then looked from Georgie to Arthur to Lexington, who all gazed back at him solemnly. "More charming than . . . here?"

"Have you forgotten all of our corpses?" Lexington asked dryly. "Bramble-in-the-Vale is lacking in homicide victims."

"And our shops aren't as adorable," Arthur added. "And far fewer of their names involve puns."

"We don't even have a bookshop," Georgie put in, offering the final piece of information that should settle this debate. "No small village can be truly charming if it's lacking in a bookshop."

"You've a library," Sebastian pointed out. "With a book club, even!"

"A *murder*-themed book club," Georgie reminded him.

"Why the devil do you want to go to Bramble-in-the-Vale, though?" Arthur said, looking horrified anew at the very notion.

"We want to speak to the council chairman," Georgie explained. "It has been brought to our attention that they seem to be benefiting rather nicely from our little crime spree—loads of the Murder Tourists are staying there instead and popping over here to look for dead bodies before returning at the end of the day."

"A good thought," Arthur said pensively, reaching for his ginger beer.

"What do you intend to do?" Lexington asked, a bit skeptically. "Just march into the council office and demand an audience?"

Georgie and Sebastian exchanged a sheepish glance.

"Er," said Sebastian.

"More or less," said Georgie.

"I feel the need to remind you that we're meant to be investigating *discreetly*," Lexington said, giving them a stern look.

"What if," Arthur said slowly, "I came along, and made as if I were writing an article about the village."

"Why would *The Woolly Register* be writing an article about Bramble-in-the-Vale?" Georgie asked, distaste practically dripping from her voice.

"We could bring the Murder Tourists," Sebastian said, straightening in his seat.

"Excuse me?"

"The Murder Tourists," Sebastian repeated. "Miss de Vere and Miss Singh—we met them in the tearoom today, don't you recall?"

"I do," Georgie said. "Why would we bring them with us, though?"

"Well," Sebastian said reasonably, "if *they* appeared to be touring the village, and Crawley here was reporting on—I don't know—the phenomenon of all the Murder Tourists visiting, you'd just need to make sure this council chairman became aware of it, and he'd practically be running toward us."

"Hmm," Georgie said.

"It's not a bad idea," Arthur said thoughtfully.

Lexington shook his head. "If this somehow ends in all of you getting arrested," he said darkly, "just know that I will not be getting you out of prison."

"That's the spirit!" Arthur said, clapping him on the back.

And Georgie did not think that she imagined his hand lingering slightly longer than necessary.

"This," said Miss Singh, for at least the third time since alighting from the train, "is *so* charming!" She looked around, wide-eyed, seemingly captivated by the sight of the improbably adorable high street, strung with colorful bunting and populated by a gaggle of giggling children, several attractive villagers clutching baked goods, and some sort of pop-up string quartet that appeared to be serenading the passersby, for God knew what reason.

"Ridiculous," Georgie muttered, staring around her with a jaded, suspicious eye. The weather was vastly nicer than it had been yesterday; she had awoken early to the sight of sunlight streaming through her turret window, and had taken Egg on a morning walk that the beagle had enjoyed with a veritable spring in her step. The sky was clear—virtually cloudless, and with that particular shade of blue that signaled dry air, no hint of rain or even humidity that could ruin a perfectly good hair day. Georgie had spent more than her usual amount of time dressing that morning, at last selecting a green sailor dress that had caused Sebastian, when he first spotted her at breakfast, to proclaim, "Why, Georgie, you look entirely ravishing," which had made her scowl by way of reply.

They had collected Miss de Vere and Miss Singh from the Sleepy Hedgehog, where they were staying, and then met Arthur at the tiny village station and boarded the ten o'clock train; Bramble-in-the-Vale was only one stop down the line, and they'd disembarked ten minutes later, blinking in the morning sunshine and soaking in the sight of a village that looked *precisely* like Buncombe-upon-Woolly, if Buncombe-upon-Woolly had been an illustration in a children's picture book, rather than a real place.

"I say, are those *rival* cheese shops next door to each another?" Sebastian asked, looking delightedly at the Great Stilton and the Grand Gloucester.

"Yes," Georgie said, sighing. "They're owned by an elderly pair of twin brothers."

"How *charming*," Miss Singh said, clapping her hands delightedly.

"I know," Georgie said darkly. "It's unnatural."

Beyond the competing cheese shops, there was also a soap shop (featuring a wide selection made with Cotswold-grown lavender), a bookshop, an art gallery, and an ice cream shop, as well as the usual array of butcher–baker–grocer–et cetera that characterized any village high street.

"You're frowning," Sebastian said, glancing down at her.

"I don't mind—it is my favorite of all your expressions—but I don't know if you're precisely giving off genial goodwill in a way that will encourage confidences from the locals."

Georgie, who had immediately begun to smooth her expression the second Sebastian had proclaimed her frowns to be his favorite, attempted a cheerful smile.

"A bit grimace-adjacent," he advised, and she tried again. "Better."

Thus armored, they struck off down the high street toward the center of the village. It was a Saturday and the entire village buzzed with cheerful energy. Miss Singh and Miss de Vere stood out in their London finery—Miss Singh was wearing a polka-dot skirt suit, and Miss de Vere a pink silk dress with a decorative lace collar and diamante buttons—and Sebastian looked to be some sort of annoyingly handsome storybook prince come to life, in his white linen suit, but they did not stand out quite as much as they did in Buncombe-upon-Woolly, because Georgie quickly realized that Bramble-in-the-Vale was absolutely *overrun* with tourists. She was impressed in spite of herself; this undoubtedly was what Mr. Penbaker had been aiming for with his various schemes, but never quite managed to accomplish. And, begrudgingly, she acknowledged that Bramble-in-the-Vale radiated a similar quaint village appeal, just in a slightly more attractive way. It was as though Buncombe-upon-Woolly were a rough sketch, and Bramble-in-the-Vale the finished painting.

Arthur, who was viewing all of this with the mistrust that came naturally to all Buncombe-upon-Woolly natives when visiting their more fetching rival, cleared his throat. "Do we have any notion of where Councillor Lettercross might be on a Saturday morning?"

"Yes," Georgie said with a grimace. "Mrs. Penbaker told us that he hosts a sort of open house at the council office, so that villagers might stop by and say hello, share any of their problems—that sort of thing."

"How—" Miss Singh began.

"Charming," said Georgie, Arthur, and Miss de Vere.

"Well," Miss Singh said, looking a bit sheepish. "Rather."

The council office was a pretty stone building covered in ivy, with cheerful bunting strung over its door, which was flung open to let in the fresh air. Georgie's footsteps slowed as she approached, and she glanced at Miss de Vere and Miss Singh. "Are you certain you understand what you're doing?" she asked in an undertone. Sebastian had been the one to approach the ladies the evening before, loitering at the Shorn Sheep until they had once again put in an appearance, and Georgie was feeling rather nervous about commencing a plan that she had not been entirely in control of from inception to conclusion.

"Miss Radcliffe," said Miss de Vere, a steely note creeping into her voice, "you need not worry in the slightest. We are Detective Devotees, and we are going to help you solve this case."

"Not a case," Georgie said hastily, shooting an alarmed look at Sebastian. "Merely a bit of . . . curiosity."

"Hmmm." Miss de Vere sounded skeptical. "Well, I am a master of discretion, so you needn't worry that I'll give anything away."

"She is," Miss Singh put in with an appreciative nod. "It's quite useful." She and Miss de Vere exchanged a glance.

"All right, then," Georgie said, still a bit reluctant but not seeing anything else for it than to let the women and Arthur go about their work. She turned to Sebastian. "Ready to do a bit of sneaking about?"

"Always," he said readily, before adding, "It feels quite relaxing to be doing so without having to remove a single article of clothing or risking an irate husband trying to kick me in the—well," he said, looking winsomely bashful. "*You* know."

Georgie was momentarily lost for words, and with a grin, he reached over with a finger, which he stuck under her chin to close her gaping mouth.

"You know, darling Georgie, you're *frightfully* easy to rile," he said cheerfully, and then offered her his arm. "Shall we?"

As they walked away, Miss de Vere, Miss Singh, and Arthur approached the entrance to the council office, the women exclaiming loudly on the enchanting setting and beautiful weather. Arthur had his notebook out and appeared to be taking copious notes. They vanished inside, and Sebastian and Georgie ducked round the corner of the building and waited, poking an occasional cautious head around the side to watch the entrance.

Less than five minutes later, the Murder Tourists and their reporter companion emerged again, this time in the company of a man dressed in—Georgie grimaced—a pin-striped suit, flashing a blindingly white smile. She recognized him as Lettercross; she'd seen the man in passing on more than one occasion. He was speaking in a booming voice, and his words easily carried to Georgie's ears.

"—say that you are staying in Buncombe-upon-Woolly itself? I don't wish to alarm you, but I must say it seems a rather *dangerous* place these days. If, perchance, you were interested in visiting somewhere similarly charming but a bit safer..."

His voice faded as they continued out of earshot, moving at a somewhat meandering pace; Lettercross appeared to be pointing out any number of town landmarks to Miss Singh and Miss de Vere, who were playing their roles to perfection, all nodding eagerness. Arthur was scribbling dutifully away, and Georgie spotted Lettercross giving him a considering glance, which suggested that Arthur's plan—of giving a strong impression that the article he was writing was likely to be picked up by the London papers—had been a success.

They waited another minute or so, to be safe, and then Sebastian offered her an easy smile and extended his arm, which Georgie took, trying hard not to notice its firm, reassuring strength beneath her hand. She and Sebastian approached the entrance to the council office, moving at a leisurely stroll that suggested that they were nothing more than a couple out for a pleasant Saturday meander around the village.

"Hello," said a smiling woman sitting behind a tidy, elegant Queen Anne–style desk. She was very pretty, with rosy cheeks, bright blue eyes, and chestnut hair that was cut stylishly at her shoulders and pinned back with pearl hairpins. A typewriter sat on her desk, as well as a neat stack of papers and a diary that, at a glance, looked to be full of appointments. "Can I help you?"

"I am Miss Radcliffe," Georgie said, "here to see Mr. Lettercross."

The woman straightened a bit in her seat at the sound of Georgie's name, but then wrinkled her brow. "I'm so sorry, he's just stepped out—was he expecting you?"

"No," Georgie said, "but Mr. Fletcher-Ford and I have come on the train from Buncombe-upon-Woolly, on official village business, so it's rather important."

"I see," the woman said, her smile fading. "Well, if you'd like to wait for him to return..." She gestured at a pair of armchairs in a striped silk pattern that flanked the fireplace opposite her desk.

"We would, thank you, Miss..." Sebastian trailed off with an inquisitive smile.

"Lettercross," the woman said, dimpling at him.

"Ah," he said. "Then am I to assume that Mr. Lettercross is—"

"My father, yes," she confirmed. "I'm his secretary."

"How delightful," he said, grinning at her, and she smiled back, her cheeks coloring further beneath the power of that smile. He leaned his hip against the edge of her desk. "Do you enjoy your work?"

Georgie, who at this point thought the best course of action was to draw as little attention to herself as possible and allow Sebastian to get on with it, shrank back toward the armchairs, watching this forceful display of charm the way she might have observed animal behavior at a zoo.

"I do," Miss Lettercross said, smiling coyly up at Sebastian. "You meet such... interesting people."

"I'm so glad to hear it," he said, his smile—if possible—widening. "I myself am just visiting from London, and I've begun to hear the most alarming tales of, well"—he dropped his voice dramatically—"*murder* in Buncombe-upon-Woolly." He shook his head regretfully.

"Oh, they're not just tales," Miss Lettercross said, leaning forward now, a bit breathless. "There have been *four murders in the past year*. It's very shocking." She shook her head. "I have been following them all, and—well—" She flicked a glance at Georgie, who promptly made a great show of looking around the room, as if she were not listening to a word being uttered. "—Miss Radcliffe has helped the police solve some of them, you know."

Georgie stilled briefly; she supposed it was unsurprising that word of her exploits would have traveled the scant miles between the two villages, particularly given the existence of *The Deathly Dispatch*.

"But," Miss Lettercross continued, "it's only a matter of time until . . ." She trailed off in theatrical fashion; Georgie thought that Abigail would have approved of this performance.

"Until?" Sebastian prompted.

"Until a killer strikes again," Miss Lettercross said, her tone ominous. Sebastian allowed a second or two of appropriately impressed silence and then wrinkled his brow slightly.

"Why do you say that?" he asked, all innocent curiosity. "I thought that the culprits had been apprehended in all of the cases."

"Well," Miss Lettercross said, faltering, "they have, yes— but once a village becomes a Murder Village, it is impossible to dispel the criminal atmosphere that descends upon it. It's like a plague!"

"A plague of . . . murder?" Sebastian asked.

"Yes." Miss Lettercross gave a quick, sharp nod.

"This all sounds very alarming," he said solemnly. "I was reading the latest issue of *The Deathly Dispatch*, and the account of Mr. Marble's final moments was harrowing."

Harrowing, and completely fabricated, considering no one had been present, Georgie thought irately, but she did not interrupt, sensing that Sebastian was really getting into the spirit of the thing.

"Yes, well," Miss Lettercross said with a little shake of her head, "you needn't worry about anything like that happening *here*." She gave Sebastian a flirtatious smile—one he returned easily.

"Such a relief," he agreed. "The articles in the *Dispatch* caused a chill to run down my spine, I don't mind telling you."

"Well, perhaps you ought to consider Bramble-in-the-Vale when you are planning your next holiday, Mr. Fletcher-Ford," Miss Lettercross said. The faintest smugness crept into her voice, and she darted a quick glance across the room at Georgie. It took everything within Georgie not to allow her natural protective instinct on the part of Buncombe-upon-Woolly to rise up and loosen her tongue.

"Perhaps," Sebastian agreed, sticking his hands in his pockets and commencing a stroll around the room. "I don't suppose you have the latest issue of *The Deathly Dispatch* to hand, have you? The one I was reading was last week's edition."

Miss Lettercross's smile faded slightly. "No, I haven't."

"A pity." Sebastian shook his head. "I've only recently arrived in this part of the country, you see, and am trying to learn as much as possible about . . . well . . ." He lowered his voice. "I just found the reporting in the *Dispatch* to be reassuringly thorough. The article comparing the effects of various sleeping pills and powders!" His expression turned appreciative. "Admirable research! Just the sort of journalism I like to support."

"Well," Miss Lettercross said, watching him carefully, "I believe there will be a new issue on Monday morning." A canny gleam lit her eye. "If you should feel the need to return to Bramble-in-the-Vale to procure a copy..."

"What a delightful prospect." His smile widened even further.

"Why," Georgie asked, causing both of the others to start, as if they'd forgotten her presence entirely, "would he need to return to Bramble-in-the-Vale?"

Miss Lettercross turned to her, her flirtatious smile vanishing. "I'm sorry?"

"To get a copy of the *Dispatch*," Georgie said. "The newsagent in Buncombe-upon-Woolly always has copies. Why should he return here?"

"Oh." Miss Lettercross looked, briefly, a bit flustered. "Well, I believe we get our copies earlier—"

"And why is that?" Georgie asked, suddenly very curious.

"I, er—I heard someone speaking of it. A tourist who had been in Buncombe-upon-Woolly, who retreated here in search of a bit more..." Here, a delicate pause. "... upscale, refined entertainment."

Georgie was tempted to snort. It was hardly as if Bramble-in-the-Vale were Paris, after all.

Sebastian, meanwhile, seemed to think that a bit of smoothing of ruffled feathers might be in order, for he directed the full force of his smile once more upon Miss Lettercross. "Have you lived here all your life?"

"Yes," she said, tearing her eyes from Georgie after another long moment had passed. Her expression—which had turned a bit wary under Georgie's line of questioning—softened once more now that she was looking at him.

"And you've worked for your father for . . . how long?" he asked, his tone still casual as he turned to look out the window at the high street beyond.

"Four years—just since I finished school," Miss Lettercross said.

Sebastian glanced over his shoulder at her and smiled. "He must feel very fortunate to have you."

Miss Lettercross preened a bit. "I like to think so."

Georgie watched this exchange with a sour taste in her mouth. It struck her that, when explained in simple terms like this, her own biography and Miss Lettercross's sounded virtually identical.

"Do you still live at home, then?" Sebastian asked, his attention still focused on Miss Lettercross.

She nodded. "My father says he'll be devastated when I marry and set up my own household—*not*," she added hastily, her gaze upon Sebastian turning worried, "that there are any candidates for matrimony." The unspoken *yet* was so loud and clear that it was nearly deafening. Georgie felt a frown tugging at the corners of her mouth and hastily attempted to smooth it.

Sebastian's smile widened, and Georgie watched as Miss Lettercross flushed further under his regard. Georgie decided that the moment was ripe to commence the next step in their plot, and so gave a bit of a wobble, emitted a faint "oh!" and—as the eyes of the other two turned toward her—proceeded to collapse into an armchair.

"My dear Miss Radcliffe," Sebastian said, all solicitous concern. "Are you all right?"

"I don't know," Georgie said, making her voice a bit faint. "I suddenly felt unwell."

Sebastian crossed the room to her in a trice, crouching down by her chair, raising a hand to her brow.

"I'm not feverish," she muttered to him under her breath.

"Be quiet and act like an invalid," he muttered back, in a voice entirely different from that of the polite, worried companion he'd been acting a moment before.

She tossed her head fretfully against the back of the chair. "I suddenly felt rather dizzy . . ."

Miss Lettercross, by this point, had risen from her desk and was hovering behind Sebastian, watching the proceedings. "Would you like some tea, Miss Radcliffe?" she asked, and Georgie gave a weak nod. The English were such a reliable people—the moment a spot of trouble arose, they could be counted on to offer to prepare tea.

"If you don't mind," she said, attempting to make her voice a bit feeble.

"Not at all," Miss Lettercross said with a nod, and then she vanished through a small door in the far corner of the room.

"How much time do you think we have before she returns?" Georgie asked, straightening in her chair as soon as the door closed behind Miss Lettercross.

"A few minutes, at least," Sebastian said, already moving toward the open doorway directly behind Miss Lettercross's desk, which presumably housed Mr. Lettercross's office. He glanced over his shoulder. "Stay there—for deniability. I'll take a poke around his office, and you can let me know if you hear her returning." With that, he disappeared into the room beyond, leaving Georgie alone in the antechamber.

Feeling she might as well make herself useful, she wandered toward Miss Lettercross's desk, with the vague thought that she might have been responding to some piece of correspondence on her father's behalf that would somehow be damning. She wasn't certain what she expected to find—or what proof she thought Sebastian might stumble across in Mr. Lettercross's office—but the desk's contents were decidedly dull, simply stationery and pens and stamps and tiresome letters to and from various constituents. She peered closer at one of them, frowning—one of the villagers appeared to be complaining that this spring's crop of kittens were insufficiently rotund and adorable. She shook her head, then stilled, listening carefully. She'd thought, for a second, that she'd heard the sound of footsteps.

"Georgie," Sebastian hissed, poking his head back into the room. "You need to come see this."

"What is it?" Georgie asked, glancing over at him in surprise from the stack of papers she had resumed flicking through, which now appeared to be several pages of notes written in Miss Lettercross's hand; there was an air of barely concealed excitement hovering around him. She recognized it, after a moment, as the same sort of energy that she herself had experienced during her previous investigations, once she'd realized that she'd stumbled upon an important clue.

He shook his head. "His desk drawer isn't locked, and—well, just come look." He waved an impatient hand, and Georgie followed him. Mr. Lettercross's office was a bit of a mess; Georgie found her hands nearly twitching with the desire to organize the haphazard piles of papers and teetering stacks of books.

"Look," Sebastian hissed, reaching for a large brown paper envelope that he thrust toward Georgie. "Look at this!" Georgie reached into the envelope and pulled out a large stack of newspaper clippings. She frowned down at them as it took a moment for their contents to sink in.

"These are all of Arthur's stories in the *Register* about the murders," she said.

"And *The Times*, too—see?" Sebastian pulled a clipping from deep in the stack to show her. "He's saved everything that made the news about the murders."

"That's . . . odd," Georgie said, still staring down at the crumpled bits of newspaper in her hands.

"It's *suspicious*," Sebastian corrected her, his tone grim but his gaze bright and alert. She felt as though she were seeing an entirely different version of him to the one she'd known until now. She didn't have time at the moment to pause to analyze how she felt about this.

"I suppose it is," she said, then paused, her heart suddenly leaping into her throat. This time, she was certain she heard footsteps. Glancing at Sebastian, alarmed, she thrust the envelope back onto one of the piles on the desk, and then slipped from the office and back into the antechamber, Sebastian on her heels.

"Oh, wait—" She whirled. "Can you intercept her? I wanted to look at one last thing on her desk."

With nothing more than a nod, he was off, taking long strides toward the door that Miss Lettercross had vanished through. Georgie darted back to the desk and seized the stack of papers, flicking through it with increased haste, scanning the words before her as quickly as possible, her eyes widening.

"—some help with that?" she heard Sebastian say, his words growing louder, and she just had time to arrange the papers back in some semblance of the neat stack they'd been in when she'd arrived, and then fling herself back into her armchair.

"I could have managed it myself," Miss Lettercross said to Sebastian, who was bearing an enormous tea tray laden with a teapot and cups, along with a tin of biscuits.

"Nonsense," he said cheerfully, depositing the tray with great care on the desk, which was the only available flat surface, and directing the full, radiant force of his smile on Miss Lettercross. "You've already gone to the trouble of preparing all this for us; the least I can do is the heavy lifting."

"It was no trouble," Miss Lettercross said, dimpling at him. "I wouldn't want you to return to London thinking our village inhospitable, after all."

"I could never," Sebastian assured her, his own smile widening even further, and Georgie was annoyed to discover that she felt like a bit of a third wheel at the moment. She cleared her throat, and Sebastian crossed the room toward her, laying a cool hand on her brow, once more the solicitous companion to an ailing young lady.

Miss Lettercross busied herself with the teapot, and Georgie watched a frown furrow her brow for a moment as she glanced at her desk, but a second later the frown was gone, leaving Georgie to wonder if she'd imagined it. Miss Lettercross poured two cups of tea, then reached for the sugar bowl, calling, "One lump or two?"

"Two," Sebastian said, revoltingly, as Georgie said, "One, please." She was tempted to ask for none, just to make a point, but, since she didn't actually enjoy unsweetened tea, thought that might be cutting off her nose to spite her face.

Miss Lettercross handed the two cups of tea to them. She and Sebastian sat for some minutes, sipping, making idle chitchat, and casting significant looks at each other. Georgie realized that they hadn't worked out a way to make their escape without appearing suspicious.

"How long do you expect Mr. Lettercross to be out?" Sebastian asked Miss Lettercross after about a quarter of an hour; she was seated behind her desk, sharpening one of her pencils, and glanced up at him.

"He didn't say—did you need to be going?" She sounded extremely disappointed.

"It's just that if Miss Radcliffe isn't feeling well, I wonder if perhaps I ought to take her home, and we can return another day," Sebastian explained, his voice soothing and very reasonable. Georgie thought, wildly, that he was likely quite good at calming animals.

She took another sip of tea and stifled a yawn against the back of her hand. "That might be for the best...."

"I don't want you to overtax yourself," Sebastian said, turning to her with wide, concerned eyes. He yawned, too. "It's been an exhausting few days, dear Georgie."

"I'm not your dear anything," Georgie muttered, the words

coming strangely slowly. She felt rather as though, in attempting to speak, she was swimming against a current, feeling sluggish and unwieldy.

"So you say," he agreed amiably, stifling another yawn, and dimly, as if at the very corner of her brain, Georgie began to register a feeling of vague alarm.

She glanced over at Miss Lettercross, who was watching them closely. Her mind flicked back to the contents of that stack of papers—or what she'd managed to absorb of them in the scant time she'd had to look through them—and her eyes narrowed as they met Miss Lettercross's gaze.

"Miss Lettercross," she began, and Miss Lettercross was now rising from her seat and walking toward her, her expression concerned.

Sebastian, who had reached for the tin of biscuits, was now helplessly stifling another enormous yawn, frowning faintly. "Georgie," he said, "do you know, I think there's something odd afoot here?"

But by this point, Georgie felt as though she were at the bottom of a deep well, calling up to him—and then, shortly thereafter, she was aware of nothing at all.

CHAPTER ELEVEN

When Georgie opened her eyes, she was disturbed to find that she was being cradled. The thread count of the cotton against her cheek left no doubt as to who was doing the cradling, despite the currently fuzzy state of her mind.

"Ugh," she said, shutting her eyes firmly in the hopes that this would prove to be some sort of bad dream.

"I'm going to choose not to take that personally," came Sebastian's voice from above her, sounding amused. "I would also like to note that this is becoming a bit of a habit. Have you a particular penchant for slumping dramatically to the ground, Georgie? Do you find it adds a bit of titillation to a courtship?"

This was sufficient to wake Georgie up in a hurry, though it was only much later that it would occur to her that this had perhaps been precisely his aim. She pushed at him until he helped her to an upright seated position.

"There *is* no courtship," she reminded him icily, once she

had blown a curl out of her face. She could only imagine what state her hair was in just now, but it likely didn't matter—wherever they were was so dimly lit that Sebastian appeared merely a shadowy outline before her.

"So you like to remind me," he agreed mournfully, and Georgie shook her head, feeling the strangest desire to smile. She glanced around, trying to make out their surroundings in the darkness. After a moment, she realized . . .

"Are we in a cellar?" she asked, frowning.

"It does appear so," he confirmed. "Beyond that, I know no more than you do—I only came to about ten minutes before you did. I don't mind telling you that you gave me a bit of a fright, though; do you know you breathe remarkably slowly when you're unconscious?"

"I'm so sorry," she said, rather acidly. "I'll try to remedy that the next time I find myself unexpectedly rendered so. How did we get into a cellar?"

"I expect our lovely Miss Lettercross drugged us," he said a bit grimly. "As I'm not in the habit of suddenly falling unconscious and then waking up next to a printing press." He gave an uncharacteristically irritated snort. "I should have stopped drinking that tea the second I noticed it tasted a bit bitter."

Georgie blinked. "A press?" She squinted in the darkness.

"Just behind me," Sebastian said. "Your eyes will adjust in a minute or two."

"Why on earth is there a printing press in . . . well, in whoever's cellar this is?"

"I expect it's the cellar of the very same council office that we were in prior to having our tea," he said. "Since I doubt Miss

Lettercross could be out dragging our unconscious bodies around in broad daylight without attracting a few strange looks."

"I can't believe she got us both down here," Georgie said. "Even if it's only a flight of stairs—she's not that large."

"Well, perhaps she'll put in an appearance and answer that question for us," he said, sounding a bit weary. There was an edge to his voice that Georgie had never heard before; she supposed drugging, kidnapping, and imprisonment would try even the sunniest of dispositions.

"Surely she will, if only to give us some bread and cheese to nibble on so that we won't starve."

"Speak for yourself. I am accustomed to a certain caliber of meal, Georgie. I'm not at all suited to prisoner fare. If you see me eat a crust of stale bread, it is a sign that death is imminent."

"What a cheerful prospect," she said sweetly. He laughed.

"So," he said, leaning back to rest his weight on his hands and gazing around at their surroundings. "I don't wish to leap to conclusions, but do you think it's possible—given the old drugging-and-kidnapping treatment—that Miss Lettercross might have something to hide?"

Georgie sobered; it was a testament to how fuzzy her head remained that the implications of their current situation hadn't yet sunk in. She felt a faint niggling at the edge of her mind—something important, something she was forgetting. If only her thoughts did not feel so terribly sluggish—a lingering effect, no doubt, of whatever their tea had been laced with.

"We've no proof the Lettercrosses have anything to do with Penbaker's death," she said.

"She recognized your name, that's certain. It makes sense, if her father was keeping all the news clippings about the murders." He frowned; Georgie's eyes must have been adjusting to the dim light, because she could now vaguely make out the features of his face again, despite the shadows.

"Georgie," he said, his voice thoughtful, "have you ever considered that the murders in Buncombe-upon-Woolly could be . . . linked somehow?"

Georgie frowned. "What do you mean?"

"Well," he said slowly, clearly still working it out in his head, "you've noted yourself how odd it is, there having been this sudden rash of murders."

"Yes," Georgie agreed. "But more because I'm concerned about—I don't know. Copycat killers, I suppose?"

"Always a possibility," he conceded. "But what if there was something more linking the crimes?"

"But I *solved* the crimes," Georgie reminded him. "Well, three of them, at least. And there was nothing at all to connect them."

"I suppose," Sebastian said, still sounding thoughtful. "Just, seeing all the news clippings that Lettercross had saved . . . it made me wonder."

"If he somehow orchestrated a series of crimes in Buncombe-upon-Woolly to . . . what? Make Bramble-in-the-Vale look good?" She could hear how skeptical her tone was.

Sebastian shrugged. "We're here in the first place because we realized they had something to gain from the continuation of Buncombe-upon-Woolly's crime spree."

"None of this answers the question of why on earth Miss Lettercross would want to kidnap us."

"I don't think *I* was the target," Sebastian said.

"So... what? She recognized me when I walked in and gave my name, and thought that this was too perfect an opportunity to miss? To kidnap..." She trailed off, her mind working. "But what does she gain from kidnapping *me*?"

"Perhaps she plans to hold us captive indefinitely, and somehow make it look like the culprit is someone from Buncombe-upon-Woolly." He offered this horrifying prospect very casually, and Georgie gaped at him. "What?" he asked, a bit defensive. "I'm thinking like a criminal, Georgie!" He shifted forward so that he could sit cross-legged, bracing his elbows on his thighs. He looked far more comfortable than he had any right to look, considering he'd been dragged into a cellar while unconscious. Although he *did* bear a few signs of the labors that had been involved in that effort—even in the dim light, she could see that his hair was a bit mussed, and at some point before Georgie had awoken, he'd removed his suit jacket and rolled up his shirtsleeves. His hands were now clasped loosely together as he regarded her intently, his brows lowered in either thought or worry.

"I suppose she could plan to store us down here and starve us to death," she said thoughtfully. Her eyes landed on something bulky shoved against one wall, past Sebastian's shoulder: Now that her eyes had adjusted to the dark, she could see that he was correct—it was some sort of printing press.

She frowned, the niggle returning to her mind, more powerful this time—and then, suddenly, in a flash, it came to her.

"Sebastian." He jerked his head toward her at the sound of his name. "I think Miss Lettercross writes *The Deathly Dispatch*."

"How the deuce did you work that out?"

"The notes I saw on her desk, just before she returned with the tea—they were all about the murders, all sorts of grim little details, and lots of . . . speculation, too. The sort of thing Arthur—or any legitimate journalist—would never publish for fear of libel." She paused, suddenly recalling a comment Sebastian had made while talking to Miss Lettercross. "Didn't you say the *Dispatch* had written an entire article about sleeping powders?"

He inhaled sharply. "Yes—it was comparing how quick-acting they were and how long their effects lasted. It would make sense, then, that she would have some sort of fast-acting sleeping powder to hand, if she's Agent Arsenic."

Georgie scrambled to her feet and then immediately wished she hadn't—her head spun a bit, and she'd not realized while seated quite how woozy whatever had been in her tea was still making her feel. Sebastian's hand was suddenly at her back, steadying her, as he, too, rose to his feet, and she turned to find him standing closer to her than she'd expected. At this proximity, his advantage in height was particularly pronounced, and she had to tilt her head back slightly to look up at him. It was a brief, fleeting moment—and then she looked away.

And back at that *printing press*.

"Of course," she murmured, stalking toward it. "She'd want to hide it somewhere that no one else would see. . . ."

"Well," Sebastian said, his tone a bit apologetic, "if we are correct in assuming this cellar *is* beneath the village council office, then it's not precisely private."

Georgie waved an impatient hand. "But it's hidden—so no

one would see her using it. I wonder how she's been distributing them to all the shops; it's not as if she could just waltz in herself with a stack of them...." Her eyes landed on a wooden crate whose lid had not been refastened, and she moved closer, crouching down to slide the lid back enough to view its contents.

"See?" she hissed, reaching inside to pull out a single sheet of paper, full of cramped print, none of which she could make out in the darkness. She glanced around. "Is there any chance there's a torch—or even just a candlestick—down here?"

They spent several minutes making as thorough a search as they could manage of the surrounding shelves, which were piled with all sorts of clutter, before Sebastian muttered a triumphant "Aha!" and brandished what appeared to be a Christmas-themed candelabra, the base wrapped in paper ivy and papier-mâché holly berries. He produced a matchbook from his pocket—"Never know when an attractive woman will need a light from a handsome gentleman!"—and a moment later, newly able to see, they leaned forward to begin reading *The Deathly Dispatch*.

"... grisly hotbed of crime," Georgie muttered, her eyes scanning the page. "... can only speculate about what dark forces are at work here ... perhaps it is the police themselves, trying to create work..." She looked up at Sebastian, who was, she realized, trying not to laugh. "For heaven's sake. These are *conspiracy theories.*"

Sebastian nodded, schooling his expression into something approaching gravity. "They are. Though, in the interest of fairness, I suppose that one could accuse *you*, dear Georgie, of harboring similar ones."

Georgie gaped at him. "That's not remotely the same! I was just—"

"Asking questions?" he asked innocently, pointing to the bottom line of the newsletter. Georgie squinted down at it in the dim light, and read, "'We do not profess to accuse anyone of a crime—we are simply *asking questions*, as concerned citizens. And we wonder how long it will be before the residents of Buncombe-upon-Woolly realize that their lives might be easier in a neighboring, less violent village.'"

"I wonder if they've real estate holdings they're trying to hawk," Sebastian said thoughtfully.

"I wouldn't put it past them," Georgie said darkly. "This is lunacy. This entire village is full of lunatics."

"Feels a bit pot-kettle," he said. "I don't notice any resident sheep on *their* village green, after all." For some reason this made Georgie laugh—*truly* laugh, the sort of loose, unconstrained sound that she hadn't thought him capable of drawing from her. She saw surprise register on his face for a moment, replaced just as quickly by slow-dawning delight. He began to smile, and this made her laugh harder for another second or two before she got herself under control. Even when her laughter ceased, however, his smile lingered.

"Fair point," she managed, once her laughter had subsided. "Shall we try to escape, then?"

"I expect we ought to," he agreed, and this time they *both* laughed.

Within a few minutes, however, they were feeling decidedly less amused.

"It shouldn't be so hard to break out of a cellar," she said, standing with her hands on her hips and scowling at the door at the top of the stairs they'd been trying to force their way out of without any success for a few minutes now. "It's not as though it was designed to hold captives!"

"We're hardly operating under optimal circumstances," Sebastian pointed out. "You went out without a hairpin, which I believe ought to be illegal for any lady claiming to be an amateur sleuth—"

"All right, then, if you'd like to produce *your* hairpin any second now, I'd be delighted," Georgie said, nettled.

"And there's a dead bolt, in addition to the lock on the doorknob. Hardly ideal for an easy lockpick."

"I expect Arthur and Miss de Vere and Miss Singh will raise the alarm once they notice we've vanished," Georgie said, before a horrifying thought struck her. "Unless—oh God, you don't think Mr. Lettercross has murdered them, has he?"

"Definitely not," Sebastian reassured her, and he reached out, for just a moment, and squeezed her hand, the strength and warmth of his hand strangely soothing. "They're Murder Tourists—the golden goose! He's no doubt hoping they'll up sticks and settle in the village; he's not going to *murder* them."

"But when they *do* raise the alarm," Georgie said, "do we really think that Miss Lettercross will say, 'Oh gosh, we didn't realize Miss Radcliffe was with the *Murder Tourists*, let's let her out immediately!'" She shook her head. "We could be trapped down here for ages."

She sank down on the bottom step and, after a moment's hesitation, patted the spot next to her. He took the invitation; the steps were narrow enough that their bodies were pressed against each other, the heat of his skin evident through both her clothing and his. Nonetheless, she didn't shift away, and neither did he.

"I expect Fitzgibbons has been in dozens of situations like this and made his way out," she said, feeling a bit glum. If she couldn't escape from a cellar, she honestly didn't think she was cut out for the life of a detective.

There was a slightly longer pause than she expected, and she slid a sideways glance at him; he was frowning.

"He has," he said at last, and Georgie looked at him expectantly. She knew that he must be aware of her head turned toward him, her gaze on his face, but he continued to look straight ahead and at last heaved a sigh—the sound was weary, and resigned, and completely out of character for him. Or, at least, for who she *thought* he was; she was beginning to think her impression of him might not be at all accurate.

"Fitzgibbons is . . . well, he's been doing this a long time," he said, still not looking at her. "When I began to work for him, his prior secretary warned me that Fitzgibbons was, if not precisely work-shy, then certainly uninterested in any investigations that were overly taxing."

"But," Georgie protested, "all those famous cases! He solved the Case of the Acton Arsenic Ring! And the Strand Shoplifting Spree!"

"Yes," Sebastian agreed. "He did—fifteen years ago, or more. He's too much of a spendthrift to retire—you should see what he spends on pipe tobacco alone—"

"Alarming testimony, indeed, coming from a man with a jumper for every day of the year," Georgie interrupted, but there was no heat to the words, and a quick glance showed that Sebastian's mouth had curved slightly at her interruption.

"—but he's no interest in taking on any complicated cases."

"Complicated," Georgie repeated.

"Interesting," Sebastian clarified, with an unhappy twist of his mouth. "And since I'm his secretary, I see all of his correspondence—I know what sorts of cases he's invited to consult on. I see the desperate people asking him for help. And he's not interested in any of it—he only cares about who can pay him the most, for the least effort. So he spends a lot of time following the wives of rich men, trying to catch them out in affairs."

"Is that how he met you?"

That *did* provoke a proper smile from him. "No. Only a matter of time, though, darling Georgie."

This time, however, she noticed the brittle note to his voice as he spoke, and she suddenly had a sneaking suspicion that there was more to the story of his romantic entanglements than she'd yet learned. Which was likely, since she'd not wasted any time at all in leaping to the least flattering conclusions about him, from the moment she'd first met him—was it only two days earlier?

"You know," she said quietly, before she had time to second-guess the words spilling from her mouth, "I'm beginning to suspect you're not half as much of a womanizing idiot as you seem determined to convince me you are."

He glanced at her quickly, looking away again just as fast. "What makes you think so?"

"You're smarter than you let on," she said, mulling the matter over in her own mind. "You prattle a lot about beautiful women and biscuits and pretend that the only skill you possess is scheduling lunches and sending prettily worded letters, but occasionally you let your guard down. I think there's more to Sebastian Fletcher-Ford than a playboy who seduces women and wears nice jumpers."

"You like my jumpers, do you?"

"I think you're single-handedly keeping half the sheep farmers in England employed."

"I like to do my part where I can," he said modestly, flicking at what she *would* have thought was an invisible speck of dust on his cuff but which, given their current circumstances, might have been entirely real.

"How *did* you come to work for Fitzgibbons?" she asked curiously, wondering what path had led him to this line of work.

Another pause. He was once again staring straight ahead, his jaw tight, his brow furrowed. She did not expect him to answer her, and yet, after another long moment, he said, "I'm a bit of a disappointment to my family, you know."

"Are you?" she asked. She hadn't paused to consider much about what sort of family he came from, other than that it must be posh (the double-barrel surname, the Cambridge education, his general aura).

"Yes. I'm the youngest of three, and my brother and sister are . . . impressive."

"Impressive how?"

"Impressive in their accomplishments. My brother is a mathematician. My sister's a poet, married to an artist. My father's a classicist at Cambridge. My mother was a suffragette, and still writes articles on women's rights. The Fletcher-Fords are a famously intellectual set. And then there's . . . me."

"Meaning . . . ?"

He let out a frustrated sigh. "Meaning that I was never half so serious as the rest of them. I liked sports, and flirting with pretty girls—having a good time. Nothing so out of the ordinary, really, but when everyone expects you to be just as brilliant as the rest of the family, and you seem a bit, well, *unserious*, you quickly realize that you're seen as a bit of a disappointment." She was definitely not imagining the bitter note in his voice now. "After a while, it was easier not to fight it. If I was a disappointment because I hadn't known my entire life path since I was a child, like my brother and sister, then I might as well try to be the best, biggest disappointment I could be."

"By, perhaps, having affairs with unsuitable women?" she asked shrewdly.

He shrugged. "That, and—well, my marks at Cambridge weren't anything to write home about. I spent more time with my friends than I did at my studies. I scraped through, but when I finished at university, my parents called me home to the family pile for this absurd dinner at which they sat me down and asked what, precisely, I intended to do with my life. The implication was that I couldn't hope to be as successful as my siblings. There were all sorts of suggestions—had I considered working at a museum? Or perhaps going on an archaeological dig?"

"An—I beg your pardon?" Georgie asked. She could not imagine the state of his clothing were he to spend his days digging away in a pit somewhere under the Mediterranean sun; everything about this image was entirely incongruous.

Sebastian shrugged. "As I said, my father's a classicist, so he could pull some strings—I expect he thought it was the only way I'd ever find gainful employment."

"What did you read at Cambridge?" she asked curiously.

"Languages."

She blinked; had she been given a dozen guesses, she didn't think she'd have landed on that answer. He did look at her now, and smiled, the dazzling, rakish grin that he seemed to have perfected over the years, although she thought that now, in the candlelight of the dusty cellar, as he sat here with her confessing his secrets into the silence, it looked a bit strained. Perhaps, she thought, it had always looked that way, and she'd simply not been paying enough attention to notice.

"All the better to make my romantic conquests," he said. "Got to be able to communicate in as many languages as possible. I learned French and Latin at school, then studied Greek and German at Cambridge. I can tell you that studying German at the time didn't make you enormously popular," he added dryly, and Georgie nodded, recalling the suspicious treatment that a German couple who'd lived in the village when she was a girl had received during the war, for all that they'd lived in England for forty years by that point.

"In any case," he added, a bit more quietly now, "it wasn't much *use* as far as degrees went, if I didn't want to teach or remain on at Cambridge for a doctorate. I took the Foreign Office exam, but it didn't work out—I scraped through the written portion, but the oral interview was a disaster. I think they thought I was a bit of an idiot. Turns out what works for making friends at university, or seducing pretty girls—always smiling, always up for a laugh—doesn't serve you as well when you want powerful men to take you seriously. That was the moment I realized that I might have gone a bit too far at turning myself into someone who would annoy my family. And so when my father mentioned that Fitzgibbons was looking for a secretary, and that he'd recommended me for the role—he's an old friend of Fitzy's—I went along with it. I needed something to do, after all, and it was easy enough—no danger that anyone would expect too much of me." There was an almost embarrassed note to his voice now, and Georgie, who had turned her head to look at him at some point while he was speaking, continued gazing at him now in the soft candlelight. The effect of him—of his face, his hair, his clothing, that *smile*—was lessened in their present circumstances, and yet she found him almost more compelling here, for reasons she couldn't articulate.

"Do you enjoy the work?" she asked after a long beat of silence.

He shrugged. "It's an awful lot of paperwork—Fitzgibbons still receives a mountain of correspondence, and is constantly being invited to various ceremonies that he's only too delighted to attend, since it gives him the chance to puff out his chest and preen and be the great detective. But I'm actually quite organized, and I find it rather satisfying, even if . . ." He hesitated, and Georgie held her breath, waiting for him to continue. "Even if," he said, after another couple of seconds, "I wish sometimes that he was still the Delacey Fitzgibbons I thought I was coming to work for. The great detective in truth. I'd like to help *that* man—like to make myself useful. It's hardly taxing work these days."

He sounded a bit glum as he spoke, and Georgie realized that two days ago she would not have thought him remotely interested in any work that might be described as "taxing."

"Have you ever thought of striking out on your own?" she asked curiously. "Setting up your own agency? Surely a history of employment with Fitzgibbons would speak well of your abilities—he could even refer cases to you that were too laborious for him."

"Ha. No." He laughed, but it was dark and a bit sharp and so totally unlike any noise that she had heard him make thus far in their acquaintance that she was momentarily taken aback, any further response she might have uttered dying on her lips. He glanced at her, and it was difficult to tell in the shadowy darkness, but she thought she saw his features soften slightly. "Sorry. It's just—Fitzgibbons would never refer a single case to me. He won't refer cases to *anyone*—he likes being highly sought after, even if he accepts almost none of the work that's sent to him."

Georgie frowned. "I don't think I like Fitzgibbons very much, based on all you've told me."

"I don't dislike him," he said mildly. "I just . . . wish that the man I knew was the one he'd once been." He paused for another moment, then glanced at her. "Because, I must say, of the detectives I've had to work with, Miss Radcliffe, *you* are by far my favorite."

She did not know why, after two days of his calling her "darling Georgie," largely to irritate her, she suspected, it should feel so much more intimate now to hear him address her so properly. Perhaps because she suspected that this was the first conversation she'd ever had with him that had involved no artifice on his part whatsoever.

"For what it's worth," she said, suddenly and impulsively, without considering her words for even a split second, "I think you'd make a splendid detective. Should you ever gather the courage to become one."

"Courage, is it?" he asked. "I'd like to remind you that I awoke in a darkened cellar with an unconscious lady whom I thought for a split second might be dead, and yet not a single whimper of fear escaped my lips."

"That's not the sort of courage I meant."

"And yet, it's the sort I've got."

And it occurred to her, then, that he might have just betrayed something of himself—something he did not quite intend to share with her. Because she did not think she'd been imagining the strain in his voice when he'd uttered the word "dead."

And she wondered, for all his "darling Georgie" and his flirtation and his smiles, if Sebastian Fletcher-Ford might care for her, just a little.

Just enough that the notion of her being dead might be the tiniest bit unbearable.

And, suddenly, recklessly, she wanted to know if this was true.

"Well," she said coolly, ignoring the fact that her heart, for incomprehensible reasons, had started beating more quickly in her chest, "I'm alive and well, so there's no need for fearful whimpering."

He turned to look at her now.

"I know," he said quietly. Then, quick as lightning, he reached out to take her hand in his. "It might take my body a bit longer to catch up, though." And she realized, once she worked past the utter confusion in her mind at the feeling of her palm pressed against his, that his hand was trembling.

Because he'd been afraid for her.

She felt herself leaning toward him, as if drawn by some magnetic force. His eyes were fixed on hers, the perfect angles of his face softened by candlelight, and with his free hand he reached up to cup her cheek in his palm.

"Georgie," he murmured, angling his face down toward her—

And then, suddenly, there was the sound of a key in the lock above them, and they jerked apart and scrambled to their feet, their hands still clasped, as a sudden shaft of light briefly blinded them, and a scolding voice said, "I just really don't think a kidnapping was called for!"

Georgie squinted upward, to find . . .

Miss de Vere and Miss Singh beaming down at them.

"Hello," Miss de Vere said with a pleased smile. "Did you require a rescue?"

CHAPTER TWELVE

"It was a simple misunderstanding!" said Miss Lettercross, wide-eyed and tearful.

"It was not," Georgie said stonily. "It was, in fact, a crime that I'm half tempted to have you arrested for." This was not entirely true, merely because pressing charges against the Lettercrosses would draw police attention to what Georgie and Sebastian and Arthur and the Murder Tourists had been doing in Bramble-in-the-Vale that day, and she'd rather not have to answer any questions along those lines.

"With what proof?" Miss Lettercross asked, suddenly canny, and Georgie eyed her with some suspicion. Those rosy cheeks and guileless blue eyes masked a certain slyness that Georgie didn't like in the slightest.

"I think my own testimony would provoke at least a few questions," she shot back, and Miss Lettercross sighed.

"Miss Radcliffe, I cannot express to you what a shocking series of events this has been," Mr. Lettercross put in at this juncture, with a stern look at his daughter. Perhaps sensing that having the daughter of a local government official accused of kidnapping was not the best look for Bramble-in-the-Vale, he had been practically falling over himself to apologize from the moment the cellar door had been opened, and Georgie had noticed, with some uncharitable satisfaction, that despite his white, toothy smile, he had a rather weak chin that was prone to a bit of a wobble under stress.

"I'm certainly intrigued to hear you attempt to explain why Mr. Fletcher-Ford and I were drugged and left in a cellar by a member of your family," Georgie said, smiling at him with some venom. They were gathered in Mr. Lettercross's office; Miss de Vere and Miss Singh occupied the two chairs that were clustered opposite the desk, whispering to each other excitedly, while Arthur was leaning against one wall, notebook and pen in hand, scribbling furiously away. Mr. Lettercross and his daughter were behind his desk, the latter perched on the arm of the chair her father occupied, while Sebastian was looking out the window at the throngs of Murder and Not-Murder Tourists who lined Bramble-in-the-Vale's winding streets and the grassy slopes of its quaint canals.

"It was an accident," Miss Lettercross insisted, sounding a bit annoyed. "It wasn't as though I was going to leave you in that cellar to rot!"

"How," Georgie asked, "does one 'accidentally' drug a pot of tea?"

"And stow a couple of unconscious bodies in a cellar?" Miss

de Vere added, with the confidence of a woman who has read many—perhaps too many—crime novels.

Miss Lettercross narrowed her eyes at Miss de Vere, clearly under the mistaken impression that the Murder Tourist was the sort of woman who was easily cowed.

"And why," Arthur added, his attention still on the notebook in his hand, "did you happen to have sleeping powder so conveniently at hand?"

Georgie smiled thinly. "I believe I can answer that one. You see, one might keep such a thing around if one were planning to write an article about it."

Arthur's pen stilled. "Write about it?"

"Yes," Georgie said, her attention still fixed on Miss Lettercross. "Isn't that right, Agent Arsenic?"

Miss Lettercross dropped a glass of water onto her lap, prompting some colorful language. Arthur glanced at Georgie, his expression startled, and she gave him a small shrug. "You learn interesting things while trapped in a cellar." He raised an eyebrow at her and returned his attention to his notebook, his pen now moving at lightning speed.

"I don't know what you're talking about," Miss Lettercross said, not remotely convincingly. "I suppose all those murders in your crime-ridden little village have left you seeing intrigue wherever you look—"

"I don't have to look very hard for it," Georgie pointed out dryly, "considering it only took me half an hour in your company to find myself unconscious in a cellar."

Miss Lettercross deflated.

"I'm sure this, er, *misunderstanding* is something that we're all eager to put behind us in . . . whatever way that might be possible," Mr. Lettercross said.

Georgie regarded him stonily. "*Was* it a misunderstanding? Was your daughter not, perhaps, trying to create another crime worthy of reporting on, since news has been scarce of late?"

Miss Lettercross rolled her eyes. "Please. As if I'd want to report on a crime in Bramble-in-the-Vale! Our village is a peaceful respite where the tourists may return after a day of walking your grim, crime-ridden streets—"

"*I* think Buncombe-upon-Woolly is adorable," Miss Singh said. "And I have never once felt unsafe!"

"Except for the time we walked into the village library right as their crime book club was meeting, and Miss Halifax was describing the effects of arsenic in too much detail," Miss de Vere said with a shudder. "I wasn't convinced she didn't have some in her pocket, just to experiment with."

Georgie cleared her throat, thinking that they were perhaps veering a bit far from the topic at hand. "If you weren't trying to create a mystery worth writing about, then would you mind explaining *why* you kidnapped us?"

"I panicked, once I realized you were investigating," Miss Lettercross said, sounding disgusted with herself. "I was suspicious as soon as I realized who you were—and all the questions about the *Dispatch* set me on edge—but when I went to get tea, I waited on the other side of the door a bit to listen, and I realized you were searching my father's office."

"I knew I heard footsteps," Georgie murmured to herself, before shaking her head and saying, "And you somehow thought drugging and kidnapping us would make us *less* suspicious?"

"Did you miss the bit where I said that *I panicked?*" Miss Lettercross asked, sounding very testy indeed. "I couldn't simply let you prance off home—not when it seemed likely you might have worked out who I was." She shrugged. "It was easy enough to offer the butcher's apprentice a pound to help me drag you down into the cellar to keep you out of sight, and I thought I'd simply ask my father what to do about you when he returned. I thought we could attempt to reason with you somehow, after the sleeping powder wore off. You woke up sooner than I anticipated," she added, casting a reproachful look at Georgie and Sebastian.

Miss de Vere tutted. "Agatha Christie was right! English villages are simply full of would-be criminals!"

"I'm not a criminal," Miss Lettercross said indignantly, shooting her a withering look. "I'm a journalist."

"I don't think the profession wants to claim you," Arthur said, shaking his head.

"You're simply jealous because I have a broader readership than you."

"You *don't*," he shot back, looking outraged. "Besides, no one believes your articles full of wild speculation and conspiracy theories."

"I am merely giving a voice to the eager public, ravenous for information," Miss Lettercross said smugly.

"Where *do* you get your information?" Georgie asked sharply. "Not the conspiracy theories, I mean—the actual details of the crime scenes. You seem to know things that no one who wasn't present at the time of the murders would know."

Miss Lettercross folded her hands. "I have my sources."

"Would you mind expanding on that?" Arthur asked. "Because, naturally, in the exposé of *The Deathly Dispatch* I plan to write, it would be unfortunate if I had to accuse its publisher of being a criminal...."

Miss Lettercross blanched. Next to her, Mr. Lettercross's chest swelled with indignation.

"Now, see here, young man," he blustered. "I will see you in court for libel if you attempt to accuse my daughter—"

"Of doing exactly what she's actually done?" Arthur finished for him. "Somehow, I like my chances."

"Oh, for—" Miss Lettercross began, and then broke off, shaking her head. "Detective Inspector Harriday is my source!"

"Detective Inspector Harriday," Georgie repeated.

"Yes," Miss Lettercross said impatiently. "We've been walking out together, and with a little, ahem, enticement, he told me all sorts of details about the cases."

"He's an old family friend," Mr. Lettercross explained. "Grew up here in the village." Arthur was scribbling furiously, and Mr. Lettercross cast an anxious look at him. "However, I would hate for any of this to damage his career—"

"I wonder how he'd feel if we phoned the police, and he learned that his paramour likes to engage in a bit of kidnapping in her spare time?" Georgie said thoughtfully, and both Lettercrosses looked even more alarmed.

"Or we could simply let my article do the talking," Arthur murmured, not looking up from his notebook.

"Very true," Georgie agreed, nodding.

"Miss Radcliffe," Mr. Lettercross said, a note of desperation creeping into his voice, "I understand that this has been extremely distressing—especially coming on the heels of such a violent crime wave—"

"Now, now," Sebastian interjected smoothly. He had been silent for several minutes, leaning against the windowsill with his arms crossed across his chest. In his white suit, he looked the very picture of a wealthy tourist at ease, if one ignored the dirt on one cheekbone, and the wrinkled, smudged state of his trousers. "In my experience, both Miss Radcliffe and Mr. Crawley are very reasonable people, and I'm sure they'd *hate* to spoil the reputation of an upstanding family in a friendly neighboring village." Both Lettercrosses looked at Sebastian now like shipwreck victims who had spotted a life raft. "In fact, I daresay Mr. Crawley could be convinced to, ahem, *ignore* this little out-of-character transgression, if he were granted an interview with the one and only Agent Arsenic . . . who would, without revealing her identity, admit to spreading conspiracy theories, and reveal police leaking of information that was not intended to be public."

Miss Lettercross looked flustered. "If you reveal Detective Inspector Harriday—"

Sebastian raised a hand to stop her. "I think that simply citing 'an unnamed source among the police' should be sufficient—wouldn't it, Crawley?" He glanced at Arthur, who was still scribbling away.

Arthur nodded, a bit reluctantly. "This should be a good enough scoop without naming names."

Sebastian nodded, satisfied. "And then, of course, the only other matter would be to answer any questions that Miss Radcliffe might have for you and your father. Just until she is reassured that you don't pose any further risk to the public—unless you'd prefer her to telephone the police, and see what questions *they* have for you instead?"

Both Lettercrosses shook their heads vehemently at this, and Sebastian took a sip of tea, looking pleased with himself.

"What questions could you possibly have for *me*?" Mr. Lettercross asked, having recovered sufficiently to look indignant. "I am not responsible for my daughter's illicit journalism career, or for whatever misguided choices she might have made—"

"Oh, I like that!" interjected Miss Lettercross, sounding very annoyed.

"I make it a point to never count on a man to stick with you when you find yourself in a tight spot," Miss de Vere advised, with the air of someone providing sage counsel to the king.

"Aren't you engaged?" Miss Lettercross asked, glancing at the emerald on Miss de Vere's left hand.

"And therefore speak from experience," Miss de Vere said smoothly, and Miss Lettercross slumped, apparently unable to think of a satisfying reply.

"I'm curious," Georgie said to Mr. Lettercross, "about your relationship with Mr. Penbaker."

"Bertie?" Mr. Lettercross looked surprised—genuinely so, Georgie thought. "Well, we used to be the closest of friends, but I won't deny that we grew apart in recent years."

"Because you were each obsessed with besting the other's village?" Georgie pressed.

Mr. Lettercross leaned forward, all wounded outrage. "Certainly not! Bramble-in-the-Vale is a long-standing destination for refined Londoners with taste—and an appreciation for the finest cheeses," he added, with a canny look at Sebastian and the Murder Tourists. "And on that note, I don't know if you've had the chance yet to try the offerings at the Great Stilton—"

"If you could try to stay on topic," Georgie interrupted.

"My point is, Buncombe-upon-Woolly isn't our rival—the very notion is insulting!"

"Hmm," Georgie said skeptically. "And I suppose you didn't rejoice when the murders started occurring in Buncombe-upon-Woolly, drawing visitors to *your* village, too?"

"Certainly not!" Mr. Lettercross said, attempting a look of wounded innocence. "I am a moral, upstanding citizen! I care for my fellow man! Unlike Bertie Penbaker," he added darkly.

Georgie's brows knit. "What do you mean?"

Mr. Lettercross looked uncomfortable. "I wouldn't really wish to say, with ladies present."

"Oh, you needn't worry about us," Miss de Vere said. "We're very good eavesdroppers, and you simply wouldn't believe the sorts of things men have said when they didn't realize we were listening." Next to her, Miss Singh was nodding eagerly.

"And I have personally walked into a bedroom to discover a corpse with a bloody knife still stuck in its chest. I promise, you do not need to worry about my delicate sensibilities," Georgie added.

"The Mistletoe Murder at Radcliffe Hall!" Miss Singh whispered to Miss de Vere, looking impressed.

"That was my name for it!" Miss Lettercross said, sounding pleased to hear her work being cited.

"For Christ's sake," Arthur muttered.

"Penbaker was not a faithful husband!" Lettercross burst out, and then cast an apologetic look at the Murder Tourists.

"How do you know?" Georgie asked, frowning.

"Well, as I mentioned, we used to be friends," Lettercross said a bit sullenly. "And I know that early in his marriage there was someone.... She moved away from the village and married someone else. But when I was in Buncombe-upon-Woolly last August for the cheese festival, I popped by the council offices to say hello to Bertie—pay my respects, you know, a friend and colleague—"

"He wanted to gloat," Miss Lettercross said with an eye roll, "about Bramble-in-the-Vale being named the Cotswolds' Most Beautiful Village for the third year in a row."

"That's quite enough from you, Meg," Lettercross said, with a reproving look at his daughter.

"Don't like it when *you're* the one being reported on by the journalist in the family, eh?" Sebastian observed idly. Lettercross glowered.

"My point is," Lettercross said, "I popped in unannounced, and saw that there was no one about—too much cheese to eat!—but Bertie's door was cracked, and I thought I might just peek inside, but he was in there with some floozy!"

"A floozy," Georgie repeated. "I don't suppose you'd care to elaborate?"

Lettercross shrugged. "I didn't get a good look at her face—dark hair? Wearing a dress?"

This could describe three-quarters of the women in Buncombe-upon-Woolly, and so was not precisely helpful.

"Why are the women always called floozies in these situations?" Miss de Vere asked. "Why isn't Mr. Penbaker a—a—"

"A man-floozy!" Miss Singh suggested, looking pleased with herself.

"I was hoping for something a bit pithier."

"Ah." Miss Singh deflated slightly. "You're the one who's good at that sort of thing, Stella."

"I shall think about it and get back to you," Miss de Vere informed the room, and lapsed into thoughtful silence.

"So you saw Mr. Penbaker in a compromising situation with an unnamed woman," Georgie said; for all that she agreed with Miss de Vere's objection regarding the phrasing, this was undeniably the best clue they'd stumbled across yet. Perhaps this trip to Bramble-in-the-Vale *hadn't* been an entirely wasted excursion.

"Yes," Lettercross said simply. "Whereas I promise you, *I* have never been unfaithful."

Miss Lettercross rolled her eyes again. "My mother died when I was a baby," she said to Georgie. "So please don't imagine that he's had to exercise any great willpower."

Lettercross flushed. "That's not the point. The point is—"

"Yes, yes," Georgie said, growing a bit weary of this entire conversation, her head aching from whatever sleeping powder Miss Lettercross had given her. "The point is, you're an upstanding citizen and while you're not above capitalizing on our misfortune, you certainly don't rejoice in it." She spoke the words a bit wryly, since she was fairly certain he would joyfully welcome another corpse materializing any day now. However, despite the initial suspicions that had brought them to

Bramble-in-the-Vale, she somehow couldn't believe that he'd had anything to do with Mr. Penbaker's death—he didn't strike her as any sort of great criminal mind.

"Now," she said, settling back in her seat, "I think it's time, Miss Lettercross, that you got to talking—Mr. Crawley, after all, has an exclusive to write."

CHAPTER THIRTEEN

"Let me be certain I understand this," Lexington said, rubbing his fingers against his temples. "You took a couple of tourists on a jaunty little excursion to Bramble-in-the-Vale, enlisted them to deceive a member of local government, managed to get yourselves kidnapped by said local government official's daughter, then blackmailed them into granting Crawley an exclusive interview rather than allowing the wheels of justice to operate?"

He sounded, Georgie thought, very, very tired.

"I think you're forgetting the bit where we learned that an esteemed colleague of yours is leaking private information to the local press," she pointed out.

"I don't think we should be so loose with the word 'press,'" Arthur muttered.

Lexington stared at both of them for several seconds, then

shook his head. "I think I need something stronger than tea," he said, staring darkly into his teacup.

They were gathered in the Scrumptious Scone, because Sebastian had declared the moment they'd disembarked from the train that being kidnapped had given him a powerful appetite. The tearoom was bustling as ever, but they'd procured a table tucked away in one corner that gave them some modicum of privacy. Miss Singh and Miss de Vere had regretfully waved away the invitation to join them, as they needed to collect a book from the library before it closed. ("We are reading *Death of a Ghost* for the Book Clue Crew this month—Miss Halifax said we're welcome to join the book club, even though we don't live in the village!" Miss Singh had informed them excitedly. "Mr. Penbaker himself told us the book was very good!")

They'd had the good luck to run into Lexington as they were walking down the high street, and he had agreed to join them, though at the moment he appeared to be very much regretting that decision.

Sebastian, meanwhile, had a platter of sandwiches before him, and was eating his way through the stack with even greater speed than usual. "I've been traumatized," he informed Georgie. "The only way to soothe myself is through sandwiches. They'll help me emotionally escape that cellar."

"Yes," she said. "Your harrowing experience has clearly marked you for life." She sighed, taking an unenthusiastic nibble of her own sandwich. Her mind was racing, turning over the morning's events and the subsequent revelations, and she was feeling a bit discouraged.

"Did you learn anything at all useful?" Lexington asked, noticing her expression.

She pinched the bridge of her nose, grimacing a bit at the headache that lingered in the wake of that cup of drugged tea. "Just one: Penbaker was having an affair."

"*Allegedly*," Arthur added, sounding a bit unconvinced. "Forgive me if I take everything Lettercross said with a grain of salt."

"This village has an *awful* lot of attractive women," Sebastian said, with the tone of a connoisseur. "Might be difficult to narrow it down."

Lexington had gone scarlet and busied himself slicing the crusts off his sandwich. Without missing a beat, Arthur reached across the table to steal one of his crusts; Lexington gave him a stern look.

"Waste not," Arthur said with a shrug.

Georgie, meanwhile, was frowning down at her plate, something niggling at the back of her mind. She glanced out the window in time to see a pack of Murder Tourists walk past on that day's Murderous Meander, one of them clutching a book. Georgie blinked, then clapped her hands together.

"Miss Halifax!" she said, startling her lunch companions into silence.

"Excuse me?" Arthur asked.

"Don't you recall what Miss Singh said as she was leaving for the library? Something about Mr. Penbaker recommending a book to her—the one they're reading for that godforsaken book club this month."

"And . . . ?" Arthur asked. "We know he liked to read crime novels."

"Yes," Georgie agreed, "and we know, according to Mrs. Penbaker, that it was a *relatively new interest*, as of . . . approximately a year ago. I wonder what could have possibly sparked it?"

"Perhaps the fact that his own village seemed to be turning into a Murder Village?" Lexington suggested.

"Perhaps," Georgie conceded. "But perhaps it was his new paramour."

"Ah," Sebastian said, nodding. "That's not a bad thought, Georgie. Librarians are famously licentious, you know."

"No," Georgie said. "I don't know."

"Well," Sebastian began, in a tone of fond reminiscence, "there was a librarian at Cambridge who was *extremely* flexible—"

"That's enough of that," Georgie said hastily, watching Lexington blush even harder. Arthur, she noticed, was eyeing the constable with interest.

"So," Arthur said, dragging his eyes away from Lexington, "you think that Penbaker commenced an affair with the village librarian, which inspired his interest in crime novels, and she poisoned him in some sort of crime of passion?"

"It would hardly be the first time a jealous lover committed a crime," Georgie pointed out. "Perhaps Mr. Penbaker ended the affair—or Miss Halifax realized that he was never going to leave his wife and grew enraged." She paused, contemplating. "And didn't Mrs. Penbaker mention that Miss Halifax had helped plant the poison garden? It wouldn't be difficult to slip a clipping of something into a bag—or perhaps she has her own poison garden at home!"

"I suppose it's possible," Arthur said, rubbing his chin. He stole another of Lexington's crusts and glanced at his wristwatch. "I'd better be off—I want to head to the *Register* and get working on this exclusive exposé of *The Deathly Dispatch* and its sources."

"I'd write quickly," Lexington advised, "before the Lettercrosses tip off Harriday and he tries to threaten you into silence."

"I expect the local police are going to look on Buncombe-upon-Woolly even more fondly after this," Georgie said. "Which means it's all the more imperative that we make progress on this investigation before they get wind of it. We need to speak to Miss Halifax."

"How do you propose to do that?" Lexington asked, polishing off a sandwich. "I hardly think this is an appropriate conversation for the library."

"No," Georgie agreed, leaning back in her seat. "I'll think about it tonight—I'm sure I can come up with a plausible excuse. One that does *not*," she added, seeing Sebastian opening his mouth to speak, "involve you lying around the library reading a book in a state of undress, waiting for our allegedly licentious librarian to stumble upon you and demonstrate her"—Georgie grimaced—"flexibility."

"Darling Georgie," Sebastian said, glancing up from his loving contemplation of baked goods, "I'm flattered. You didn't even insinuate that I don't know how to read!"

✑

Dinner at Radcliffe Hall that evening was somewhat subdued. Georgie, still processing the day's revelations, felt little desire to chat over the meal—Mrs. Fawcett's excellent pork chops and roasted vegetables—but, somewhat more surprisingly, Abigail didn't seem to be feeling very chatty, either. Papa and Sebastian talked amiably of Cambridge professors whose names were meaningless to Georgie, and did not seem to mind—or possibly even to notice—the relative lack of contributions from the female half of the table.

It was June, and so even after dinner, there were a couple of hours of daylight left. "I'm going to take Egg for a walk," she said, as Mrs. Fawcett cleared the plates. Papa merely nodded, and Abigail murmured something about reading a book in her room, but Sebastian glanced at her. "Fancy some company?" he asked.

In truth, Georgie wasn't at all sure that she did; it had been a long, odd, confusing day, and she couldn't shake the feeling that something about her perception of Sebastian Fletcher-Ford had shifted since that morning. It seemed incredibly churlish to say no, however, so she merely nodded and went to fetch Egg from the kitchen, where she was hovering around Mrs. Fawcett's ankles, hoping to be slipped a leftover slice of meat.

Georgie shivered slightly as she and Sebastian walked out the front door, glad she'd grabbed her favorite gray cable-knit jumper to slip over her dress. Sebastian had ditched his suit jacket when they'd returned home that afternoon and was now wearing a navy-blue jumper that looked so soft Georgie nearly reached out a hand to stroke it. The air had cooled as the sun sank lower in the sky, and around them the world was alive with the sounds of the countryside: birds warbling their evening songs, sheep bleating, the distant shout of parents in the village calling children in for bed. Egg, after a long day spent at home engaged in her profession (napping), walked with a spring in her step, but the fact that she stopped to sniff approximately every five feet meant their progress was slow.

"You did well today," Georgie said, after a few minutes' meandering in silence. Sebastian was walking beside her with his hands thrust in his pockets, head down as though deep in thought. At the sound of her voice, he looked sideways at her.

"And *you* did well to manage to keep from sounding surprised as you said that," he replied, with the air of a schoolteacher offering a pupil praise.

Georgie didn't smile, but she wanted to. She wondered if he could tell.

"I meant it," she said instead. "It was—well, being kidnapped and trapped in a dusty cellar would have been considerably worse if you hadn't been there."

"You'd have been just fine," he said quietly, and she glanced at him, surprised. "You're the most self-sufficient person I've ever met."

"Surely not more so than the great Delacey Fitzgibbons," she said, trying to inject a note of levity into a conversation that had somehow almost immediately come to feel a bit heavy, before remembering—too late—his revelations of the morning. She grimaced by way of apology. "Or not so great, I suppose."

"Not so great, indeed," he agreed, sounding a bit glum.

"But," she said, thinking back to their conversation in the cellar, "you *wanted* him to be great."

Another quick glance at her before looking away, just as

quickly. "I did, rather," he confirmed. "I knew I only got the job because of my father—likely only got into Cambridge because of my father, truth be told, so that experience was nothing new—but I thought that if I could help this brilliant detective solve tricky cases . . . well."

"Did you want to become a detective yourself?" she asked curiously.

"I think—" he began, then broke off abruptly, shaking his head. "It doesn't matter."

She wondered suddenly how many people took the time to ask him a question like this—not about Fitzgibbons specifically, but anything more serious about his own hopes. Whether perhaps serving as a secretary to a vain, self-important man and sleeping with half the society women in London was not entirely what he had envisioned for his life.

"It does," she said, despite the fact that two days earlier she would not have been able to fathom the notion of this man saying anything of value. "It matters to me."

She didn't look at him as she said this; it felt peculiarly intimate, especially after that moment in the cellar earlier—the moment she had spent the better part of the afternoon trying her hardest not to think about. Because, unless she had completely lost her mind, then she and Sebastian Fletcher-Ford had almost kissed. But if that *were* true, then she still, clearly, had completely lost her mind.

"I thought that it might be my . . . I don't know." He blew out a frustrated breath. "I don't want to say 'my calling,' because it's not as though I were going to save the world or anything, but . . . everyone else in my family has always known exactly what they're meant to be doing. And then there's . . . me. I thought it might be nice, if the job with Fitzgibbons worked out, to come to family dinners and have my own thing to discuss." He shook his head. "I should have known that no one would hire me for a job that would actually mean anything."

And Georgie, in that moment, *hated* Delacey Fitzgibbons, and his stupid monocle, and his bushy mustache, for making Sebastian feel this way.

But all she said was, "For what it's worth, I think Fitzgibbons is missing out. Because you're rather good at this."

"Do you think so?" There was a vulnerable note to his voice, one that made him sound oddly young.

"You're good at—I don't know—you're good at *people*, I suppose," she said, waving a hand. At some point, they'd slowed their steps, and now they drew to a halt entirely, turning to face each other. They were standing in the middle of the path that cut through the wildflower meadow that ran alongside the lane leading up to Radcliffe Hall; in the evening sun, he looked even more golden and perfect than usual, the light framing his face, the breadth of his shoulders casting Georgie in his shadow.

"And I'm not," she added, in a rush now, speaking without entirely considering what she was going to say next. "I've lived here my entire life—my family has lived here for hundreds of years—and yet it feels like people trust you more readily than they do me."

"Does that bother you?" he asked, looking down at her, his expression inscrutable—another adjective that, even twenty-four hours ago, she would never have thought to apply to Sebastian Fletcher-Ford.

"I don't know," she admitted, and it made her feel a bit off-balance to admit this, as though it were a shameful confession. She was good at knowing things, at working things out. To admit to not knowing... it made her feel not at all like herself.

She wondered—in a sort of idle, glancing way, without looking at the question head-on—if that might not be a *nice* thing, every once in a while.

"People are easy," he said, still watching her very carefully, as though searching for cues. "If you're friendly, if you like them, they'll like you in return. I've never had any trouble with that part of things."

"What gives you trouble, then?" she asked, and wondered, in some dim corner of her brain, when she had grown so desperately curious about the man before her—a man about whom, upon meeting, she'd thought she already knew all there was to know.

"The part where I try to say anything that people take seriously." He scrubbed a rueful hand down the side of his face, the gesture rough, impulsive, and considerably less elegant than most motions she'd seen him make thus far in their acquaintance.

"You don't make it easy for them," she pointed out.

"You'd have thought my family, at least, might have given me the benefit of the doubt." Something close to bitterness crept into his voice then, and Georgie, without thinking, reached out and took his hand.

He glanced down, his expression softening at the sight

of their interlinked fingers. Georgie, face heating, made as if to withdraw her hand, but he held on tighter, his skin warm against her palm.

"Georgie," he murmured, reaching out a hand to trace her cheek. Her skin burned in the wake of his touch.

"Don't do that," she said, unable to bring herself to pull away, and instantly his hand stilled, then vanished from her cheek, leaving a kiss of cool air in its wake. "No," she said hastily, even as she watched him open his mouth, presumably to apologize. "I mean—that is—I only meant, don't . . . I'm not one of your women in London."

A frown creased his ordinarily smooth forehead. "What do you mean?"

"I'm not someone to—to be trifled with!" she burst out. "Don't try to pretend that someone like *me* is who you'd usually flirt with. I know—I know that Buncombe-upon-Woolly must seem terribly provincial to you, and I expect you're bored, and I know there aren't any glamorous, dissatisfied wives here to flirt with, but—"

"But what?" he asked, his tone suddenly brittle.

"But don't . . . toy with me," she finished, humiliation warming her cheeks. "Just because I'm here, and it's convenient. I know I'm not the sort of woman you'd actually be interested in—"

"Do you," he said, a sharp edge evident in his voice.

"Don't flatter me," she snapped, suddenly weary of everything about this ridiculous day. Egg—who had been happily sniffing a patch of wildflowers a few feet away—looked at her, emitting an anxious whine from the back of her throat. "I know you flirt with everything that moves, but if you could leave me out of it, I'd appreciate it." The words came out sounding harsher than she'd intended, but she didn't wish them unsaid. It was better to state it bluntly, so he'd know where they stood. So he understood that she wasn't prepared to be yet another notch in his bedpost.

"Do you know," he said now, and there was nothing the slightest bit vague or amiable in his voice, "that you are possibly the most irritating woman I've ever met?"

"*That* I would believe," she said, hands on her hips.

"But you *wouldn't* believe that I'm not toying with you? That just because I've a bit of a—well, a history, shall we say—doesn't mean that I can't be genuinely interested in you?" He was still frowning, and he ran a hand through his golden hair, mussing it. He crossed his arms over his chest and looked a bit exasperated. He swallowed, as if suppressing something else he wished to say, and Georgie, against her will, found her eyes drawn to the movement of his Adam's apple.

"I don't—perhaps it's best if we just . . . don't," she said, biting her lip. She found herself suddenly unable to look him in the eyes. She was not a complete novice when it came to romance—there had been one of the village boys that she'd kissed behind the church when she was seventeen, curious to see what all the fuss was about; and, too, Arthur's cousin, who had spent an entire summer in the village the year she was twenty, with whom she'd engaged in rather more than kissing—but she could never recall anyone making her feel as annoyed, and embarrassed, and entirely discombobulated as Sebastian was making her feel in this particular moment.

She gave a sharp whistle, and Egg looked up quickly in wounded affront. "Egg, that's enough. Let's go home."

She turned on her heel. Sebastian fell into step beside her but mercifully didn't attempt to say anything else the entire walk back. They parted on the kitchen stairs, and Georgie retreated to the safety of her room for the rest of the evening—but found that even after night fell, sleep was a long time in finding her.

CHAPTER FOURTEEN

When Georgie arrived at the breakfast table the following morning, Sebastian was nowhere in sight. Papa and Abigail were already seated at the table, which gave Georgie pause; Papa usually beat her to breakfast, but Abigail almost never did, and it was only half eight.

"You're up early," she said to her sister, sitting down and smiling gratefully at Mrs. Fawcett, who slid a plate containing two poached eggs and a couple of slices of thick, streaky bacon in front of her.

Abigail, who had been staring into her teacup in a listless sort of fashion, glanced up at her. "I've started leaving my curtains open at night," she said, which seemed like a complete non sequitur, until Georgie's tired, overstimulated mind caught up a moment later.

"So . . . the sun woke you?" she asked. She reached for her

fork. Abigail's room faced east, and she'd sewn thick, dark curtains for her bedroom windows years earlier, blocking out much of the morning light during the long days of summer.

"Yes," Abigail said, taking a fortifying sip of tea. Now that Georgie looked at her more closely, she saw that her sister *did* look rather tired; there were faint purple circles beneath her eyes, marring her otherwise flawless complexion.

"Why don't you keep your curtains drawn?" Georgie asked, slicing into her egg and using a piece of bacon to mop up some of the runny yolk. "That seems a simple solution."

Abigail suddenly looked a bit evasive. "I heard . . . somewhere . . . that it is good for the body to let natural light awaken it."

Georgie was instantly on alert, with an elder sister's keen instincts. "'Somewhere,' is it?"

"Yes," Abigail said airily, not quite meeting her eyes. "I can't recall where." She reached for a slice of toast from the rack before her and began buttering it. A moment later, she frowned. "Papa, have you been using the butter?"

Georgie glanced at their father, whose face was, per usual, hidden behind a newspaper. The top of his head was visible, however, and Georgie could see the skin reddening beneath his thin layer of hair.

Abigail, too, seemed to spot this, and take it as confirmation. "You know Dr. Severin said you should be careful about how much butter you eat!"

Georgie opened her mouth, then shut it again, curious to see how Papa would handle this scolding from his younger daughter.

Papa lowered the newspaper and gave Abigail his best attempt at a stern stare (which, to be clear, was not very stern).

"Dr. Severin is young enough to be my son," he said. "And he seems prejudiced against the finer things in life. It must be that austere Scottish upbringing."

"He's from Hertfordshire," Abigail said smugly. "He merely studied in Edinburgh."

"Regardless," Papa insisted, "a little bit of butter on my toast won't kill me."

Abigail's and Georgie's gazes dropped to the butter dish—where a substantial quantity of butter appeared to have been hollowed out from Mrs. Fawcett's carefully crafted medallion—and then to their father's plate, where a half-eaten piece of toast provided clear evidence on what he considered to be a "little bit of butter."

Abigail reached out her hand and neatly plucked the remaining half of his toast from his plate without asking.

She took a bite. "Delicious," she said, smiling at Papa. Papa, for his part, swelled like a bullfrog for a moment before rapidly deflating beneath the force of her smile. Within a few more seconds, he was smiling fondly back at her.

And Georgie had not had to say a word.

Hmm.

She cleared her throat. "I think I'll take Egg on a walk this morning," she announced, then immediately winced in regret as there was a sudden, frantic scrabbling beneath the table (where Egg had been lurking in hopes of dropped crumbs), and a moment later her beagle was at her side, her soulful eyes staring pleadingly into Georgie's own. She should have known better than to utter the word "walk" aloud unless she was ready to immediately slip her shoes on and depart. "In a few minutes," she informed Egg, then offered her a bit of her namesake on a piece of bacon by way of mollifying her.

"I'll just go wake Sebastian," she said reluctantly; she had come to the conclusion that she owed him an apology, after leaving things on such an uncomfortable note the evening before, although it was not an enjoyable prospect.

"He went out already," Abigail said. "He was finishing breakfast just as Papa and I arrived."

"He did," Georgie repeated blankly. She had assumed that a man like Sebastian would like a good lie-in. Why did he insist on not behaving the way she expected him to? "Well, that's . . . good," she managed, ignoring the shameful bit of relief that came with the knowledge that she could avoid him for a while longer.

"You know, Georgie, I quite like Sebastian," Abigail said.

"Based on five seconds' acquaintance?" Georgie asked waspishly.

"No," Abigail said, not rising to the bait, "based on all our midnight chats."

"Midnight *chats?*" Georgie asked, incredulous.

Abigail nodded, taking another bite of toast. "He's fond of a late-night biscuit, it turns out, and you know I love a midnight cup of cocoa. We've run into each other in the kitchen the past couple of nights."

Georgie turned to her father. "Papa, do you hear this?" A sudden thought struck her, and she added cannily, "Don't you think it would be better for Abigail to be in London with Aunt

Georgiana, where she's not likely to run into unmarried men in the kitchen in the dead of night?"

Papa cocked his head thoughtfully. "Given your aunt's colorful love life, I don't know that she'd be any safer from that there than she is here."

This was undeniably true, and Georgie supposed she should have known better than to expect any help from Papa in her attempts to encourage Abigail to spread her wings.

"Besides," Abigail added serenely, "Sebastian was a perfect gentleman. We simply talked about baked goods—a mutual interest of ours." She tilted her head at Georgie. "And I do not think that *I* am the Radcliffe sister who is at risk of falling prey to his charms."

Georgie took that as her cue to leave. "Don't be ridiculous," she said, rising to her feet. "I'm old enough to withstand a bit of flirtation from a bored man with nothing better to do."

"I'm not being ridiculous," Abigail called after her as she made her exit, Egg trotting eagerly at her heels. "And Sebastian doesn't strike me as being the slightest bit bored."

Georgie did not deign to reply, and instead led Egg down the stairs into the kitchen. A nice long walk with the dog and then a morning spent in the garden were exactly what she needed. It would be good for her—remind her of the important work she had to do around here, which would fill her days after the Sebastian Fletcher-Fords of the world, and all the Murder Tourists, had long since fled back to the bright lights of the capital.

After her life had gone back to *normal*, in other words.

Which was, she insisted to herself, just the way she liked it.

A few hours later, Georgie was on her hands and knees in a pair of dungarees, digging happily in the dirt.

She and Egg had taken a long, muddy ramble through the surrounding hills, an endeavor that had involved clambering over fences, traipsing through sheep-dotted fields, and then walking back home along the narrow dirt path that ran along the shady banks of the Woolly River. She had brought her rucksack and a few jars with her, and had happily collected some plant specimens to take home and study; she would have thought, after a lifetime in this village, that there would be no more delights to uncover in terms of the flora that grew around them, and yet the thing that she loved so much about the natural world was the fact that it seemed to have limitless variation. Something new was always cropping up underfoot.

It was, in other words, the exact opposite of what it was like to live in a small village like Buncombe-upon-Woolly—at least, until people had started getting murdered.

And, added a sly voice inside her head, *until Sebastian Fletcher-Ford turned up.*

Georgie had ignored this, and upon returning home had donned her worn, stained dungarees that she wore exclusively when gardening, tied her hair back from her face with the silk scarf that her mother had once used for exactly this purpose, and then taken herself off to the kitchen garden, which she had been somewhat neglecting of late, given the other issues occupying her mind. She didn't know how much time had passed—Mrs. Fawcett had tried to summon her indoors for lunch at some point, but she'd waved her off; Georgie tended to slip into something of a trancelike state when she was in the garden, the earth beneath her hands. Now, however, a sudden shadow was cast over the ground before her, and she glanced up, her neck aching and, she suspected, slightly burned from the sun, to see Sebastian standing over her.

"Hello," she said, straightening enough to sit back on her heels and peeling off her gardening gloves.

"Hello," he said, crouching down next to her, wearing a pair of carefully pressed gray wool trousers, a collared shirt, and a jumper of the palest blue, like the early morning sky. She was suddenly acutely conscious of the frizzy mess of her hair, the muddied state of her dungarees, and the smudges of dirt that no doubt were on her cheeks. Something about the way he looked at her made her feel like crawling out of her own skin. It was dreadful, and somehow also *not* dreadful, all at once.

"You were gone an awfully long time," she said a bit cautiously.

"I've been back awhile—Mrs. Fawcett makes an excellent roast beef sandwich, did you know?"

Georgie *did* know; they were her particular favorite. As if on cue, her stomach growled, and Sebastian extended his hand, which contained something wrapped in a carefully knotted napkin. She unwrapped it.

"You brought me a sandwich." Unable to help herself, she took a bite, suddenly ravenous; the cold beef, sharp cheddar, and horseradish sauce tasted as nice to her as anything she'd eaten in recent memory.

"Mrs. Fawcett mentioned that you'd not come in for lunch, so I offered to bring you something. She said that you forget to eat when you're in the garden—not something I can personally relate to, obviously, and it sounded extremely alarming." He smiled easily at her.

Georgie lowered her sandwich, frowning. "Why are you being nice?"

"Georgie." He placed a hand on his breast. "I am *always* nice. How have you not noticed that yet?"

"But we quarreled last night!" she burst out, finding everything about this conversation thus far utterly mystifying.

"I don't know if I'd say 'quarrel,'" he objected. "I think we were . . . seeing things from differing perspectives."

"I was . . . unkind," she pressed.

"Well, actually, I've been thinking about that." He paused, looking at her. "Do you not like your sandwich?"

Georgie glanced down at the sandwich still in her hand. "What? No. It's delicious."

"Good." He waited expectantly, and Georgie sighed, taking another bite.

"You were thinking," she prompted, once she'd swallowed that mouthful.

"About what you said last night," he agreed.

Georgie inhaled deeply, reaching for her patience. "*And?*"

"And," he continued, "I don't think you were *really* trying to be unkind to me. I think you were trying to protect yourself, instead."

Georgie gaped. "What is *that* supposed to mean?"

He was silent, and she quickly took another bite of sandwich. "It means," he said promptly, "that I don't think you believe I mean it when I flirt with you."

"Of course I don't."

"Well," Sebastian said, "perhaps you ought to try."

"Try what?" She felt the way she had when she was eight and had to learn long division. Nothing anyone had said had made the faintest bit of sense.

"Try believing it," he said. He looked at her very steadily, and Georgie was acutely conscious of the fact that she was halfway through eating a sandwich, and quite possibly had horseradish sauce on her face. When he looked her in the eyes like that—when he wasn't trying to be seductive or flirtatious, or asking inane questions, or doing anything other than speaking to her in a quiet voice while looking her straight in the eyes . . .

Well, it made it difficult to think about anything else.

"Why did you go to the village this morning?" she asked, grasping desperately at the change of subject in the hopes that it would make her feel on steadier ground once again.

"I wanted to take a look around," he said with a shrug. "I've not explored it yet without you, and I thought it might be interesting. Forgot it was Sunday, though—not many people about at nine on a Sunday morning. *Though*," he added, a rapturous expression crossing his face, "the bakery was open, and Georgie, I swear, those Chelsea buns are life-changing."

"Your feelings have been noted."

"Not adequately," he said mournfully. "Not until I've erected the equivalent of Michelangelo's *David* will my sentiments be appropriately memorialized. And we wouldn't even need to worry about offending anyone's virtue! Baked goods don't have genitalia," he explained, apparently mistaking Georgie's expression for one of confusion, rather than reflecting a desperate attempt to both eat a sandwich and refrain from hysterical laughter at the same time.

"Anyway," he continued, "once I emerged from my Chelsea-bun-induced stupor, I noticed there were suddenly an awful lot of people about, so I—an intrepid sleuth—naturally followed them, and that's how I found myself in that fascinating little church of yours. I particularly enjoyed the stained-glass window featuring three sheep."

"*You* went to church?" Georgie asked, trying and failing to not sound astonished by this development.

He widened his eyes innocently. "I like to remind God of my existence from time to time."

"I doubt that's necessary. I'm certain you pop up in various people's confessions often enough that you're never far from the front of his mind."

"You do know how to flatter a man, Georgie."

"That wasn't flattery."

"The fact that you think so is part of what makes you so delightful," he said, looking more pleased than could possibly be healthy. Men like Sebastian, Georgie had decided, were far too accustomed to things going their way, which was why she liked to be as much of a pebble in his shoe as possible.

"I wasn't going to stay—I really just wanted to see who would show up, and if they did anything interesting—but then I realized that food was going to be provided, so I had to stay."

Georgie blinked. "The . . . coffee hour, afterward?" she ventured.

He shook his head. "No, the bit where you get wine and a biscuit. Best part of the entire experience—I was famished by that point. It had been at least an hour since that Chelsea bun."

"Oh my God." She burst out laughing. "You're a heathen."

"Guilty," he said cheerfully, gazing fondly at her as she continued to laugh helplessly. "My parents are dreadful atheists, I'm afraid, so I was raised without any religion at all—I couldn't even tell you what the Trinity is."

"The fact that you are aware of its existence is encouraging, at least."

"Women are fond of getting rather popish in moments of great passion. Start shouting about all sorts of things."

"I am fairly certain that this conversation is sufficient alone to see you sent to hell, without even considering all your other sins." She shook her head, finally able to get her laughter under control, and realized that something in his gaze had shifted as he watched her suppress her giggles. "What?" she asked, brushing awkwardly at the knees of her dungarees in a futile attempt to dislodge some of the clumps of dirt that were rapidly settling into the fabric.

"Nothing," he said, with a shake of his head and a look of faint confusion, evident in the slight wrinkling of his brow. "Anyway, what was I saying?"

"Something blasphemous about the body of Christ."

"Ah, right, the snacks. Well, once the service was over, I noticed Miss de Vere and Miss Singh, which I found surprising—wouldn't have taken them for churchgoers. Anyway, I went to have a little chat with them—never leave a pretty woman unacknowledged, that's my motto—"

"Believe me, I am aware."

"And they were yammering away about that book club at the library—you know, the one they had to go fetch the book for, yesterday afternoon? And it suddenly gave me an idea."

"So help me God, if your idea involved seducing someone in the church graveyard—"

"I am *shocked*, darling Georgie, at the places your mind goes. And while taking the Lord's name in vain, no less!" He tutted, shaking his head, but was unable to prevent the curve of his mouth that Georgie found herself matching against her will. For a moment, they crouched there under the bright June sun in the quiet kitchen garden, Egg snoozing in a patch of shade, smiling helplessly at each other, and Georgie felt a rush of such fierce, uncomplicated joy that it nearly set her off-balance.

"Your idea," she prompted.

"Right. Well, we need to speak to Miss Halifax, don't we?"

"Yes," she said slowly.

"*And* we don't want to leap in with the accusations, do we? We want her to trust us?"

"We do," she said, summoning her patience.

"*And* we know that her favorite thing on earth is books—"

"Well," Georgie said, out of some sense of fairness, "I don't know that we can assume that, just because she's a librarian. She might have other interests."

"Cats and cardigans, yes. And, apparently, illicit love affairs with local government figures."

"Sebastian, *what is your point?*"

"Ah, yes." He brightened. "*I* am going to pose as a Murder Tourist, eager to join her book club."

"You what?"

"Think about it, Georgie! We'll pop round her cottage—apologize for calling unexpectedly—flatter her a bit, talk about some detective novels, profess to be *desperate* to join this week's meeting—and, along the way, we'll see what information we can weasel out of her."

"I don't know why you think she's suddenly going to spill her secrets and confess an illicit affair, just because you pretend to want to join the—whatever it is they call themselves."

"The Book Clue Crew," he said promptly, and Georgie shuddered.

"And to answer your question," he added, "people . . . tell me things." He spread his hands in a gesture to imply that he didn't understand it, either. "I noticed it first when I was at university, but when I started working for Fitzgibbons, I realized it could be an advantage. Once, Fitzgibbons was late for an appointment with a client—a wife who suspected her husband was unfaithful—and I had to keep her entertained. By the time Fitzgibbons arrived I'd given her a cup of tea and she'd told me every dark secret about her marriage. Things that she didn't think were important, even, that I told Fitzgibbons later, that helped him track down the husband and catch him in the act. And ever since then, I've realized that . . . well, a lot of people are just . . . lonely. And if someone lends them a sympathetic ear, they're willing to tell that person just about anything."

Georgie watched him as he spoke, his eyes drifting away from hers to land on Egg's supine form. Belatedly, she became aware of the fact that her knees were beginning to protest this treatment, and she clambered gracelessly to her feet, trying not to resent the fact that Sebastian followed suit in a vastly more elegant fashion. Despite how bumbling and idiotic she'd—incorrectly—thought him when she first met him, she'd never failed to appreciate the sheer physical grace of him. He was a man who looked to have been built for motion—tall and fit, with the sort of lean muscle she associated with tennis players. He never moved without looking certain of where he was going; even the simple act of rising from a crouch seemed graceful, like a choreographed dance.

He gazed down at her, so handsome and golden in the sunshine that it made her catch her breath. Just as she'd never been terribly bothered about her own appearance, so, too, had she always viewed handsome men with some suspicion. They were all flash, little substance—not to be trusted. Had she not believed more or less precisely that of Sebastian? And yet now, when she let herself move past the fact of his handsomeness, and instead merely appreciated it . . .

Looking at him made something in her chest tighten.

"Don't look at me that way," he murmured, his eyes crinkling a bit at the corners as he continued to gaze down at her.

"What way?" she managed, hating that the words came out the slightest bit breathless.

"Like you want me to kiss you," he said, not breaking eye contact, and if she'd thought her chest felt tight a moment before, she properly struggled for breath now.

"I would think," she managed after a moment, "that *you*, of all people, would not be one to complain about that."

"I don't know," he said, leaning toward her, close enough that, with his height advantage, she had to tilt her head back slightly to meet his eyes. He wasn't smiling, but his eyes were. "I hate to mention it, but I have *rather* got the impression that my, ahem, romantic history is a bit distasteful to you, Georgie."

His tone was teasing, but Georgie realized that he was serious—he was asking her a question.

And with only a single moment's hesitation, she said, "I might change my opinion on that matter, if all that practice proves to have been worth it."

And, taking that for the invitation it was, he leaned down and kissed her.

Georgie had kissed people before—first out of scientific curiosity, to see what all the fuss was about, but then, too, because she wanted to kiss the person in question. And the kissing had been nice. Enjoyable. Not worth throwing one's life away for, as the heroines had done in some of the romances Abigail tore through at a frightening pace (and which Georgie occasionally snuck off the shelf to read in the privacy of her turret), but still a pleasant enough experience.

This, though, was not pleasant.

This—the feeling of his mouth on hers and his hand coming to cup her cheek, the press of his thumb against her jaw, tilting her face to precisely the angle he wanted; the feeling of his arm curving around her waist, pulling her toward him—

Well, "pleasant" was certainly not strong enough a word.

She stepped closer to him, fisting her hands in the fabric of that ridiculous, soft jumper, feeling the heat of his skin, the muscles of his abdomen tightening when she pressed her palm flat against him, and his arm snaked around her waist, pinning her to him. His tongue was at her lips, and then stealing inside her mouth, and a pulse beat low and heavy in her stomach.

No, this wasn't pleasant. Or polite. It was . . . consuming.

When he pulled away from her at last, she stared up at him, her heart pounding in her chest, her lips still tingling, and for a moment, she did not know what to say.

"What's the verdict, then?" he asked, sounding a bit smug. "Was the practice worth it?"

"I'm not answering that," she said, with whatever shred of dignity remained to her, and he tipped his head back and laughed—a loose, happy, uncontrolled sound, one that made her want to laugh helplessly in reply. In the bright June sunshine, the long column of his throat shone golden before her. She wanted to bite it. Her thoughts must have shown on her face, because he opened his eyes and caught her gaze, and something in his darkened, and he tugged her toward him once more, giving her another kiss—quick and fierce this time. When they broke apart, their breathing was a bit unsteady, and he winked at her.

And Georgie didn't even bother to attempt a frown.

CHAPTER FIFTEEN

They decided to call on Miss Halifax just before dinner, when it was nearly certain that she'd be at home. Georgie was not at all confident that this plan of theirs was going to work—despite Sebastian's blithe assurances that he was going to morph into a crime-novel-obsessed Murder Tourist before her very eyes—but she still thought it was better to approach Miss Halifax at home than attempt a sensitive conversation at the library or in line at the butcher's.

At the appointed hour, Georgie was standing at the base of the stairs, awaiting Sebastian and ignoring the clattering sounds emanating from the kitchen downstairs, where Mrs. Fawcett was preparing a Sunday roast while Abigail was hard at work on some sort of elaborate dessert. Georgie had spent the better part of an hour attempting not to look like the sort of person who had been kissed in the kitchen garden by a man whom she'd caught admiring his reflection in a spoon on multiple occasions. When he appeared, however, all such thoughts fled her mind.

"What on earth are you wearing?"

"My Murder Tourist disguise," he said cheerfully, sketching a bow. Said disguise involved nothing more than a pair of round, wire-rimmed glasses and a tweed jacket. With *elbow patches*.

"*This* is what you think Murder Tourists look like?" she demanded.

"Well, not really," he said, bounding down the last few steps and leading her toward the door. "But I wanted to convey that I take literature seriously, and so thought an outfit change might be in order."

"Do you truly think tweed denotes bookishness?"

"Georgie, it's an *aesthetic*," he said, as if trying to explain something very simple to a confused child. "I have to convince Miss Halifax that I am positively aquiver with bookish yearning." He opened the door, then stepped back to allow her to pass through first. "Now, shall we?"

"Only if you promise never to use the word 'aquiver' again," she said, and breezed past him into the evening sunshine.

Miss Halifax lived in a small cottage along one of the narrow cobblestoned lanes that branched off the village high street, and she answered the door a few moments after Georgie and Sebastian's knock.

"Miss Radcliffe," she said, looking startled. "This is . . . unexpected."

"Miss Halifax," Georgie said, and tilted her head at Sebastian. "This is Mr. Fletcher-Ford—he is an old friend of my family's, staying with us at Radcliffe Hall, and he is an enormous fan of Agatha Christie's mysteries. I mentioned your book club at the library to him today, and he was keenly interested and wondered if you might be able to accommodate him at this week's meeting."

Sebastian stepped forward, extending an eager hand, which Miss Halifax shook a bit warily.

"Could this not have waited until tomorrow?" she asked, sounding perplexed.

"I'm to blame for that, I'm afraid," Sebastian said, before Georgie even had the chance to open her mouth. "I was so delighted once Georgie here told me about your book club—the Book Clue Crew, is it?—that I absolutely insisted we come to see you right away, so that I could start reading the selection this very night."

"I see," Miss Halifax said, still sounding as though she had doubts as to their collective sanity. "Well . . . would you like to come in for a minute?"

"I can think of nothing I'd like more," Sebastian said with a wide smile, and in no time at all they were led through the cottage—which was small, but cozy and well-kept—and into the kitchen garden, where Miss Halifax had managed to squeeze a table and chairs. "I like to eat out here in the summer," she explained, "and since it's clear this evening . . ."

It was, indeed, a fine evening; the air felt cool and fresh after the rain that had briefly swept through late that afternoon, and there was a damp, earthy smell of early summertime that Georgie could not resist inhaling happily. Miss Halifax vanished back into the cottage momentarily, and Georgie fell into her favorite habit while in other people's gardens: examining the plant selection. Miss Halifax had a few lovely rosebushes that were in full bloom—she narrowed her eyes, considering. A Parsons' Pink and a polyantha, if she wasn't mistaken. There were also some foxgloves and delphiniums. She nodded approvingly; lots of nice, standard flora native to the Cotswolds—and, she couldn't help but notice, no lethal poisons in sight. This was the sort of garden she liked—not fussy; it looked as though nature itself were creeping up from between the paving stones and around the trellises, and Miss Halifax had merely exerted the lightest touch to influence its growth.

"What is your favorite plant?" Sebastian asked, apropos of nothing. He was gazing at his surroundings, reclining in his chair with a relaxed posture, looking perfectly at ease, as always. Even the ridiculous glasses and tweed jacket somehow didn't detract from the image.

His question, however, startled her. "My favorite plant?" she repeated.

He nodded. "You must have one—I see how you love them."

"I do," she said. "Only . . ." Only no one had ever thought to ask her.

"I love bluebells," she said, feeling a bit shy as she spoke. "They feel like a harbinger of everything I love about the countryside—they don't appear too early, like daffodils, when it's still wet and cold and we're not in full bloom yet. They wait until spring is on the cusp of overflowing, when the air starts to smell sweet and the days begin to truly grow long and the sun is warm and I don't want to wear woolens anymore—well, not all the time, at least," she said, with a rueful glance down at her serviceable jumper, which she'd donned after a hasty bath that afternoon. "They just symbolize to me all the best things about spring—about England—about . . . well, everything."

She fell silent and immediately began to second-guess everything she'd just told him. Did it make her sound silly? Something she always worried about, when people learned of her interest in plants, of her dream of opening a botanic garden, was that she'd be perceived as a silly girl who liked pretty flowers. And now, when Sebastian Fletcher-Ford, of all people, asked her what her favorite plant was, she'd not been able to think of anything unattractive but interesting, or sneakily dangerous, but instead had chosen the most basic symbol of English springtime imaginable. A *child* would have chosen bluebells, for heaven's sake. But she hadn't lied—they *were* her favorite.

While she was pondering all this, he merely regarded her thoughtfully, then nodded and said, "They suit you."

And then he said nothing else, as if this were the sort of observation that required no further explanation, as though he hadn't left Georgie feeling ever so slightly off-center.

Miss Halifax returned at this juncture, a bottle of whisky in one hand, three tumblers precariously balanced in the other. Georgie's brows rose; Sebastian looked delighted.

"Why, Miss Halifax, what *excellent* taste you have," he said, springing to his feet to relieve her of her burden and examining the label on the bottle with an expert eye. "A twelve-year Macallan, one of my favorites."

Miss Halifax smiled modestly. "I don't get the chance to break it out very often—don't want to shock any of the St. Drogo's social club ladies, after all."

Sebastian poured a couple of fingers of whisky into each

tumbler and raised his glass in a toast. "To murder! The fictional sort, of course! Ha! Ha! Ha!"

Miss Halifax regarded him for a long, perplexed moment before taking a sip of her own drink. Her hair was pinned back less severely than it was when she was at work, and the soft chestnut locks shone in the evening sun. Georgie realized that she was a bit younger than she'd thought—probably only in her late thirties.

Georgie took a cautious sip of whisky. Aside from the occasional hot toddy Mrs. Fawcett had forced on her during illnesses, she'd never had it before, and she discovered that, once she got past the initial burn in her throat, she rather liked the feeling of warmth that settled in her stomach.

"So," Miss Halifax said, setting her glass down on the table. "You wish to join the book club?"

Sebastian leaned forward, all eagerness; the gold frames of his glasses gleamed in the evening sun. (He had confided in Georgie on the walk into the village that he only used the glasses for reading, and even then, only when particularly small print gave him a headache.)

"If it wouldn't be an imposition," he said to Miss Halifax, wide-eyed and earnest. "I know I would be a last-minute addition, but when the book comes so highly recommended..."

Miss Halifax frowned. "Recommended by whom?"

"Well"—here, Sebastian lowered his voice to a reverent hush—"Miss de Vere and Miss Singh told me that the late Mr. Penbaker *himself* had read and recommended the book."

"Ah," Miss Halifax said, her tone neutral, and she took another sip of her whisky.

"I had not realized he was such an avid reader," Georgie said, attempting to convey mild surprise without overdoing it. Acting was not her strong suit. "Did he come to the library often?"

Miss Halifax leveled a shrewd glance at her. "He was involved in all aspects of village life, so yes."

"Mmm," Georgie agreed. "What did he like to read?"

"Mysteries," Miss Halifax said. "I introduced him to Mrs. Christie's work. I loaned him my copy of *The Murder at the Vicarage*, and he finished it two days later and wanted to spend an hour talking about it, the next time we met. When I decided to create the Book Clue Crew, he had plenty of suggestions for which books we should read—*not* that I needed them," she added, with the weariness of a librarian who was tired of other people telling her how to do her job.

"You'd have thought he'd get quite enough of murder mysteries in his own village without having to look for it in fiction."

"I suppose," Miss Halifax said, shrugging. "Although he was actually writing his own murder mystery, inspired by the village's crime spree. I've the draft lying around somewhere. But perhaps that's why he enjoyed reading them so much—they offered an escape from all the dreadful things happening here."

"Did he seem like he needed an escape?" Georgie asked. "Did there seem to be anything bothering him? Some weight upon his shoulders?"

Miss Halifax paused, her glass halfway to her lips. "I think you'd have better luck asking his wife that question, Miss Radcliffe. There's no reason I would know, after all."

Georgie allowed approximately three seconds of silence to elapse before she said, "Isn't there?"

Miss Halifax met her eyes levelly. "Miss Radcliffe, are you trying to accuse me of something?"

"I don't know," Georgie replied. "Was there something you wished to confess?"

Sebastian cleared his throat, and Miss Halifax's gaze flicked to him. "I don't think Miss Radcliffe means to cause any offense, Miss Halifax." He smiled at her, then took another leisurely sip of his whisky. "It is only . . ." He trailed off, appearing a bit regretful.

"Yes?" Miss Halifax asked, looking as though she were curious in spite of herself.

Sebastian sighed, shaking his head. "It's the other Murder Tourists, you see. They've got a bit . . . nosy."

"Nosy," Miss Halifax repeated.

Sebastian glanced around, as though worried one of said Murder Tourists might be lurking amidst the rosebushes, hoping to glean a juicy morsel of gossip, and leaned forward a bit in his chair, lowering his voice. "They've convinced themselves that you were having some sort of illicit affair with Mr. Penbaker." He let out a chuckle, as though inviting Miss Halifax to enjoy this absurdity with him.

Georgie looked at Miss Halifax, who had gone a bit pale, her glass clutched tightly in her grip. Georgie got the sense that she was thinking—very quickly.

"Where did they get such an idea?" Miss Halifax asked, after slightly too long a beat of silence had elapsed. She seemed to be attempting to look relaxed, but couldn't quite manage it.

Sebastian shrugged, taking another sip of his drink. "I expect they've been reading too many of Mrs. Christie's books—

convinced themselves that secrets are lurking around every corner in a quaint village like this, waiting to be uncovered. We are a passionate fan base, after all. I wouldn't be surprised if some of us got a bit carried away! They'll be fabricating murders next!" He let out another chortle. "But I expect if Mr. Penbaker showed up at one of your book club meetings, they might have got the wrong idea, and then rather run with it."

"It wasn't the wrong idea, though, was it?" Georgie asked, her voice quiet.

Miss Halifax looked at her, startled, as if she'd almost forgotten her presence. "Excuse me?"

"It wasn't the wrong idea, about you and Mr. Penbaker? All of this about him loving mysteries—it was just a way to cover that you were sneaking around together."

"It wasn't," Miss Halifax said sharply, looking offended at the very notion. "Bertie *loved* mysteries, and he had excellent taste."

"Is that how it started between the two of you, then?" Georgie asked.

Miss Halifax hesitated, then nodded. "Last summer, he was in the library one day and saw that I was creating a display of Mrs. Christie's books. He was curious, so I explained their popularity to him, and the fact that she occasionally uses a quaint village setting for her murders. That's how I ended up loaning him the first book, and from then on . . . well, once we started talking, one thing led to another . . ."

"Was he worried about the possibility of his wife finding out?" Georgie asked.

"I didn't get the impression his marriage was a terribly happy one."

"But still," Georgie pressed.

Miss Halifax sighed. "If you're asking me to get to the heart of Bertie Penbaker, I'm not certain I can be of much help—he was a difficult man to truly know, I think. I'd be surprised if his wife wouldn't say the same thing." She hesitated. "He was handsome and arrogant, and he thought a lot of his own cleverness—he never worried that we'd be caught; he was convinced he was too intelligent to slip up." She shook her head. "He was right, in the end; no one knew. Or so I thought," she added a bit dryly.

"Can you think of anyone who would have wanted him dead?" Georgie asked bluntly; given the nature of Miss Halifax's own secrets, she wasn't too worried about her spreading gossip around the village about Georgie's investigation.

Miss Halifax regarded her curiously. "Bertie died of a heart attack," she said. "So I don't think it really matters whether anyone would have wanted him dead, does it?"

Georgie gave her a thin smile. "Humor me. Was there anyone who resented him?"

"Aside from his scorned wife?" Miss Halifax asked wryly, but just as quickly shook her head. "I don't think she knew about us—and I don't think she would have done anything about it, even if she did."

"Why not?"

"I don't think she cared for him enough to kill him. I don't know why—he didn't speak much of her, and I don't know her very well. But I can't imagine that their marriage was the sort to provoke that strong of a reaction." Miss Halifax paused, then seemed to replay her words in her own head and went still. She then added, very delicately, "*If*, that is, he was murdered."

"If," Georgie agreed.

"I don't suppose you're going to tell me *why* you think he might have been murdered?"

"Call it a hunch."

"It seemed to me that he was quite popular in the village—mystifyingly so, honestly, when you consider all those inane schemes he was always cooking up, trying to improve tourism. The pumpkin race!" She rolled her eyes. "But he had a strong personality—I think he's the sort of man people look up to, even if they perhaps shouldn't." She shrugged. "I've honestly never heard anyone speak of him in a way that would make them seem a likely suspect for murder."

"Were you still seeing him at the time of his death?" Georgie asked.

Miss Halifax shook her head. "I wasn't," she said. "We argued, and I ended things."

"What did you argue about?" Georgie asked.

"The sort of thing you always argue about with a man like that—the fact that he was dreadfully selfish and viewed our relationship in terms of how *I* might benefit him, might make his life easier, but never, ever in terms of how he might . . . support me." Her voice went a bit quiet at the end. "It blew up something terrible a couple of weeks prior to his death—it was my birthday, and he'd promised to spend it with me, but instead he was out half the night, first at dinner with the Marbles and then doing heaven knows what. We quarreled about it, and he refused to admit that he'd done anything wrong, and

I broke things off. And then, a fortnight later, he was dead. I suppose you think that I had something to do with that? That's why you're here?" She didn't wait for a reply before continuing. "If you somehow think that I caused him to—what was it? Have a heart attack?" She shook her head and then smiled. "Miss Radcliffe, I'm not convinced the man truly *had* a heart. But if he did, I promise you, I'd nothing to do with stopping it."

Georgie met her gaze for a long moment and then looked away. Because somehow, despite the credible motive that Miss Halifax had provided, Georgie believed her.

Which meant that, once again, they were without a viable suspect.

Unless, despite Miss Halifax's doubts, Mrs. Penbaker was *not*, in fact, ignorant of this love affair—and was rather more bothered by it than Miss Halifax believed.

Because *that*, actually, seemed a rather excellent motive for murder.

CHAPTER SIXTEEN

"All right," Arthur said a couple of hours later from his perch on the arm of the sofa in the drawing room at Radcliffe Hall. "What do we know so far?"

Georgie and Sebastian had returned home after leaving Miss Halifax's, and had placed a quick telephone call to Arthur, who had materialized within ten minutes, lured in no small part by the promise of a Sunday roast, courtesy of Mrs. Fawcett. The meal was over now, however, and Papa had retreated to his study, while Abigail vanished upstairs, leaving Georgie, Sebastian, and Arthur to hole up in the drawing room to confer. Sebastian had charmed his way into being left with an entire tin of biscuits, and he was now munching them happily, hip propped against the bar, legs crossed at the ankles, the very picture of contentment.

Georgie, feeling a bit like a schoolgirl who had been called upon in class, straightened and raised a finger. "First, we know that Mr. Penbaker had, until recently, a mistress." A second finger. "Second, we know that he had a wife who may or may not have been aware of the existence of the mistress." Another finger. "And third, we know that there were no witnesses to his sudden heart problems, until his wife returned home—alone—and he died shortly thereafter."

"Fourth," Arthur continued, "we know that he was apparently a complete tosser. I can't believe we let this idiot run our village council for *years*."

"No one else on the council had the energy to argue with him, I expect," Georgie said darkly. Mr. Penbaker had been a bit of a shock to the village politics when he'd taken up the role of council chairman five years earlier, after the previous, long-serving chairman had stepped down to spend his golden years knitting sweaters for his seven spoiled whippets. Mr. Penbaker had enthralled the electorate with all his talk of increasing tourism to the village and making it a hot spot for well-heeled Londoners looking to spend a weekend engaging in wholesome countryside pursuits, though in practice his schemes had been considerably more unhinged than promised.

Georgie sighed, rubbing her temples. "The point is, after all we've learned, we're left with one obvious suspect."

"The wife?" Sebastian asked, polishing off another biscuit.

"Yes." Georgie shook her head. "Who seems a plausible candidate to have murdered her husband, but we need to somehow prove that he *was* murdered, which seems a bit of a tall order, since no one else in the village seems remotely concerned by his sudden death."

"Georgie," Arthur said, sounding a bit uneasy. "Do you think it's possible . . ." He trailed off.

"What?" Georgie asked sharply.

"Well, we don't *know* that Penbaker was murdered. You might be looking for a crime where there hasn't been one."

"I am aware of that," Georgie said evenly. "Which is why Sebastian is here, if you'll recall."

"But it's been *days*—"

"Four days."

"—and we've not uncovered anything to suggest—"

"Mysteries don't get solved in a day, Arthur!" Georgie snapped, crossing her arms over her chest and feeling oddly defensive. "They take work! You should know this—it's not as if your articles materialize overnight! If you're too busy with other stories to help us, that's fine, but *we* are going to continue investigating."

"I never said I didn't want to help." Irritation crept into Arthur's voice. "But I do have a *job* to do, and I was just asking—"

"You were just asking if we're all wasting our time here," Georgie snapped. "And I don't like the implication!"

"Georgie," Sebastian said quietly, "I don't think Crawley was trying to *imply* anything."

"He was," Georgie insisted, feeling her cheeks heating in the way they only did when she got properly upset. One of her least favorite traits in herself was the fact that she cried when she was angry; it felt weak and stupid, but it was almost impossible to control, and she could tell by the prickling at the corners of her eyes and the burning at the back of her throat that she was close to tears now. "But if there's the slightest chance that there's something that's been missed, then it's *our duty* to work out who's behind it—"

"It's not, though," Arthur said shortly.

Georgie stared at him. "What do you mean?"

"I mean it's not *our* duty. We're not policemen."

"But this is important," Georgie insisted. "It's our village—our home. We can't let it turn into a ... a crime-ridden cesspool of sin and vice!"

In unison, Arthur and Sebastian craned their heads around to take in their cozy surroundings, the worn furniture, the lingering smell of recently baked biscuits. There was a wireless tucked on a shelf, playing the BBC; a couple of windows were open, letting in the fresh air, late-evening sunlight spilling in and casting their surroundings in a golden glow. The smell of roses wafted in from the back garden. Faintly in the distance, Ernest could be heard baaing.

Still in unison, they turned back to look at Georgie, who waved her hand impatiently.

"All right, I'll grant you that it's not exactly Whitechapel," she admitted. "But still!" She glared at Arthur accusingly. "I thought *you* of all people would be just as eager to get to the bottom of this—you're certainly building quite a reputation for yourself based on all your articles!"

"I never said I wasn't," Arthur said. "Especially seeing as ..." He trailed off, looking suddenly a bit shifty in a way that Georgie recognized, given that she'd known him since he was five years old, and had known him to commit more than one minor crime over the course of their childhood.

"Seeing as what?" she asked suspiciously.

"Seeing as," he said, "I've had a job offer in London . . . but I don't want to take it, not until we've finished with this investigation."

Georgie felt as though she'd been struck in the chest, all the air knocked from her lungs. "A job offer in London," she repeated.

Arthur nodded. "With *The Times*. It's not a terribly glamorous position—they need a new reporter on the courts beat, and they've been impressed by the articles I've written on the murders."

"So you've already accepted?" Georgie asked.

Arthur shook his head. "Not yet. I've asked for a few days to think."

"And when were you planning on telling me about this?"

"I just have," he pointed out.

"Only because it came up!" Georgie said. "I don't suppose you would have even mentioned it otherwise? I'd have just popped round to yours one day and found your bags packed?"

"If you keep haranguing me about it, that prospect sounds more and more appealing," he shot back.

"Not to butt in," Sebastian said as Georgie and Arthur glowered at each other. "But I think everyone here cares about this case. So if we could perhaps focus on the matter at hand? Mrs. Penbaker?" he prompted.

"Right." Georgie sighed, running a hand through her hair, which was doubtless already in quite a state. "I don't think we can show up to ask her more questions—not when we've already done so once. She'll get suspicious."

"If you would like *me* to ply her with my masculine wiles,"

Sebastian said brightly, "I'd be more than happy to." He looked it, too. A little *too* happy, in Georgie's opinion.

"No," she said shortly, refusing to interrogate the tiny thread of jealousy working its way through her. "I think we need to be a bit sneakier."

Arthur frowned. "What do you have in mind?"

"I think," Georgie said, her mind racing, "that we need to do a wee bit of breaking and entering."

Arthur's jaw dropped. "You want to break into Mrs. Penbaker's house?"

"Well, think about it!" Georgie said crossly. "If there's any sort of evidence connecting her to her husband's death, that's where it's likely to be!"

"I expect it wouldn't be that difficult to break in," Sebastian said around a mouthful of biscuit. "This seems like the sort of village where no one locks their doors. That's always where crimes take place, you know," he added, with a wise nod. "The sort of place where someone says, 'We never thought it would happen here!'"

"*And* we know she's out of the house at predictable times, because she runs the exhibition at the village hall!" Georgie said excitedly.

"So, what? You're just going to stroll up to the front door and let yourself in?" Arthur asked, raising a skeptical brow.

"Well, *no*," Georgie said patiently. "We will be subtle. Sneaky. We're *professionals*."

"We're not, actually."

"Perhaps we could ask Constable Lexington for some tips? Although I don't expect he'd condone us breaking and entering."

Arthur laughed darkly. "I wouldn't think so, considering he's got a giant stick wedged up his arse."

Georgie blinked. "Did you have something to share, Arthur?"

He was frowning now, too, his arms crossed. "No. Just had an annoying interaction with our favorite officer of the law."

"'Favorite' might be an overly generous assessment," Georgie said. "More like, 'the only one who isn't completely useless and vaguely malicious,' perhaps?"

"Potato, potahto," Arthur said with a careless wave of the hand. "He disapproves of my perspective on the local police, and accused me of trying to discredit the entire police force with the article I'm writing about the *Dispatch*. When I told him I'd got confirmation from a second officer—off the record, naturally—that Chief Constable Humphreys was looking the other way about Detective Inspector Harriday's leaks to the *Dispatch*, however, he shut up in a hurry. Needless to say, he wasn't feeling so smug and clever after that."

"It is nice," Sebastian offered at this juncture, "to see the warmth of the bonds of community in such a wholesome, bucolic setting."

"Arthur," Georgie said, "it might be helpful if the one police officer who is remotely inclined to take us seriously didn't start despising us instead."

Arthur shot a withering glance at her. He was looking, Georgie noticed, distinctly frazzled; his dark hair looked as though his hands had been run through it repeatedly, there were ink stains on his cuffs, and his glasses were ever so slightly askew. "He doesn't *despise* me. We're simply suffering from a ... difference of opinion."

"Well." Georgie crossed her arms. "If you could perhaps see to it that you smooth his feathers a bit tomorrow, that would be brilliant. And it would be helpful if you could distract him between the hours of, say ..."

She looked at Sebastian without intending to, and he said, quite promptly, "Nine and noon. Those are the hours I've noticed Mrs. Penbaker is at the exhibition."

"Thank you," Georgie said, and glanced back at Arthur.

"Noted," Arthur said, straightening his glasses.

"I wonder, though," Sebastian said, his voice turning serious, before trailing off.

"Wonder what?" Georgie asked.

Sebastian grinned at her. "Georgie, I'm flattered. You didn't even express astonishment that I have sufficient mental capacity to wonder at anything."

"Sebastian, so help me God—"

"I wonder if we ought to let the Murder Tourists help us somehow," he finished hastily.

"Not Miss de Vere and Miss Singh?"

"It's only—well, they *were* useful yesterday, and they seem quite desperate to be involved."

"They've *been* involved," Georgie said. She was still slightly irked that Murder Tourists, of all people, had rescued them from the cellar.

"I know," he agreed. "But I ran into them after church this morning—they were lurking outside as everyone was leaving, eavesdropping and taking notes in that notebook of theirs.

After yesterday's experience, they seem absolutely desperate to uncover another crime."

"Dear God," Georgie muttered, rubbing her hands through her hair, no doubt worsening its already (always) disheveled state.

"How long are they staying for?" Arthur asked. "It's not as though there's exactly a laundry list of sights to see in Buncombe-upon-Woolly, and they've been here for days already."

"They were oddly shifty when I asked them that very question," Sebastian said thoughtfully. He shook his head. "But if we could—I don't know—tell them we need them to be our eyes and ears around the village, perhaps? Give them some sort of task? I think they'd get a thrill from it."

"And we know how much you love giving ladies thrills," Georgie said.

Arthur didn't even bother trying to disguise his laugh as a cough as he rose to his feet. "Why don't you send them to the murder exhibition?" he asked. "To ensure Mrs. Penbaker doesn't take a fancy to run home unexpectedly while you're searching her house?"

It wasn't the worst idea. If the Murder Tourists kept Mrs. Penbaker occupied, and Arthur kept Constable Lexington blissfully ignorant, then she and Sebastian could search the house in peace. "All right," she agreed.

"We can speak to them first thing in the morning," Sebastian said. "They're staying at the Sleepy Hedgehog—we can pop round there to find them."

Georgie eyed him narrowly. "You're just hoping to weasel a second breakfast out of this excursion."

He flashed that maddening, winning smile at her. "And this, dear Georgie, is how you have come to have a career that even Miss Marple would envy. Look at those powers of deduction at work!"

Georgie reached for the tin of biscuits and proceeded to lob one at Sebastian's head.

CHAPTER SEVENTEEN

Miss de Vere and Miss Singh were, unsurprisingly, exceedingly thrilled to be invited into Georgie and Sebastian's scheme.

"The Detective Devotees are at it again!" Miss Singh said as they exited the Sleepy Hedgehog, Sebastian still munching away at the final piece of toast he'd managed to sweet-talk Iris—the innkeeper's wife and an old friend of Georgie's—into giving him.

"Solving crimes and saving the day!" Miss Singh continued, brandishing her notebook like a sword. "This is our moment!"

"To be clear," Georgie said, for at least the third time, "all you are going to do is walk to the village hall and then proceed to ask exceedingly lengthy and annoying questions to ensure that Mrs. Penbaker is kept occupied. Nothing else. No crimes will be solved. No rescues will be enacted."

"You might have said the same thing before we went to

Bramble-in-the-Vale," Miss de Vere said, looking a bit smug. "And yet, if it weren't for us, you'd be starving in a dark cellar."

"I think we'd have been fine," Georgie said. "I'm a hardy sort. I could have lasted in there for days!"

Miss de Vere cast a significant look at Sebastian, who was licking a bit of melted butter off his thumb, as if to say, *And him?*

Georgie sighed. "Touché."

Once the Murder Tourists had been deposited at the village hall, Georgie and Sebastian wasted no time in heading straight for Mrs. Penbaker's house. She and Mr. Penbaker had shared a pretty, well-kept cottage directly opposite the village green; prior to moving to Buncombe-upon-Woolly and taking up local politics, Mr. Penbaker had worked as a solicitor in Bath, and had evidently done well enough for himself to ensure a quite comfortable retirement. The house was made of honey-colored Cotswold stone, featured mullioned windows that flanked the green front door, and had ivy creeping its way up its walls. A small but tidy rose garden graced the narrow space between the house and the street, and Georgie knew this must be entirely Mrs. Penbaker's doing, because Mr. Penbaker had been almost comically useless at anything to do with horticulture. The annual garden show had been a yearslong struggle in which Georgie desperately tried to convince Penbaker to stop talking about plants he knew nothing about, with limited success. (At this spring's edition, she had caught him proudly boasting about a particularly fine display of roses, which were actually peonies.)

Georgie and Sebastian ignored the front door, however, and instead cut around the corner down the narrow alley that connected the high street to one of the quieter residential streets that flanked it. A quick glance around confirmed that there was no one in sight, and they proceeded to hop nimbly over the low stone wall that bordered Mrs. Penbaker's back garden. Georgie, holding her breath, reached for the kitchen door; it turned easily in her hand.

"Shame, that," Sebastian said as he followed her through the door. "I was rather looking forward to getting to watch you do your lockpicking-with-a-hairpin trick."

"It's considerably faster if I don't have to," Georgie said over her shoulder, toeing off her shoes as soon as she walked through the door—it would be very annoying if they managed to successfully break into and search a house, but were eventually discovered because of a muddy footprint on a rug.

"I do love watching a competent woman at work, though," Sebastian said with a sad shake of his head, removing his own shoes; something about the sight of him in his stocking feet made him look oddly vulnerable, as if he were incomplete if he were not the fully, immaculately dressed Sebastian Fletcher-Ford that she had come to know.

"Well, perhaps you can get your thrills from watching me rummage through some drawers," she said, and couldn't prevent her mouth from curving into a smile when he laughed.

The Penbakers' house was small compared to Radcliffe Hall, but still fairly spacious for a childless couple—two bedrooms, plus a third, small room that it appeared Mr. Penbaker had used as a study. Every room in the house was clean to an almost obsessive degree, and Georgie's heart sank; if Mrs. Penbaker were this meticulously tidy, what were the odds that she would have left any potentially incriminating evidence lying about? Whereas Radcliffe Hall, despite Mrs. Fawcett's best efforts, was such a messy shambles that there could be a bloody knife left under a pile of shoes or a stack of post, and it might go unnoticed for weeks.

"What are we looking for, exactly?" Sebastian asked as they entered the sitting room.

"I don't know," Georgie admitted. "Just anything that might seem . . . unusual." This was, she realized, unhelpfully vague, but the truth was that she wasn't certain what she was looking for—just that she'd know it when she saw it. Hopefully.

The next half hour taught Georgie a valuable lesson: Detective work could be very *boring*.

"At least now I know that Mr. Penbaker preferred coffee to tea," Georgie said ten minutes later as they were rummaging around in the study. She brandished a grocery list, the items carefully scratched out.

"And that he spent a shocking amount on footwear," Sebastian said, staring down at a bill.

"A harrowing claim indeed, coming from you."

Sebastian grinned at her. "I think you like my shoes."

"Do I?" Georgie tried to sound waspish but wasn't sure she'd managed it.

"No woman can remain unmoved in the face of tassels." He waved his foot at her, seeming to only belatedly realize that he was in his socks. His face fell.

"I'll take your word for it," Georgie said, turning back to the desk.

A few minutes later, just as Georgie was ready to conclude

that there was nothing of interest here and suggest they move upstairs to search the bedrooms, Sebastian frowned.

"Where's the typewriter?"

Georgie blinked, looking back at the desk, which was organized within an inch of its life and—indeed—featured no typewriter.

"Maybe he didn't have one at home?" she suggested. "Surely there was one at the village council office that he could use for official council business."

"No, I think he must have—I found a spool of replacement ribbon in one of the drawers. And Miss Halifax mentioned that he was writing a novel, didn't she? Presumably he'd need a typewriter for that." Sebastian's frown deepened.

Georgie was feeling a bit impatient. "Perhaps the typewriter is being repaired or—I don't know. Are you ready to search upstairs?"

"All right," Sebastian said, still looking troubled; this was an uncommon expression for his face, and did not suit him.

They made their way up the narrow staircase and emerged into a hallway featuring a number of landscape portraits depicting flocks of fluffy sheep. Entering the first of the two bedrooms, Georgie could tell immediately that this was the spare room; it had the slightly unlived-in feeling of guest rooms everywhere. A double bed with a simple white quilt occupied one wall; against another wall, a tall bookshelf groaned with leatherbound tomes (though Georgie could not help but notice that none of the spines appeared to have been broken), and a wooden dresser with a mirror above it was situated directly opposite the bed. There was a pretty blue-and-white rug on the floor, which looked to have been recently swept. What immediately caught Georgie's attention, however, was a large wooden crate on the floor, into which Mrs. Penbaker appeared to have been packing a variety of seemingly unrelated items. There were manila envelopes stuffed to the brim with paperwork, various notebooks half filled with scribbles, but no sign of a typewriter.

Georgie sank to her knees, reaching for some of the paperwork, while Sebastian walked slowly around the room, opening and shutting drawers, sliding books off the shelf. At last, he eased himself onto his stomach, looking under the bed; Georgie glanced up at him, about to ask what he was doing, when he uttered a triumphant "Aha!" and reached forward. A few moments later, he pulled something from beneath the bed—a lumpy shape concealed in a tightly knotted burlap sack.

"What on earth is that?" she asked as he deposited the bag on the floor a few inches from her hip. Crouching down next to her, he worked away at the thrice-tied knot on the sack before finally loosening it. After a moment, he carefully lifted out a typewriter. He assessed it with an experienced eye. "An Imperial," he said approvingly. "It's clearly seen some wear, too." He gestured at the faded letters on some of the keys. "I wonder why she hid it."

"Perhaps she prefers to write by hand and didn't have any use for it."

"But hiding it in a sack beneath the bed feels like a deliberate attempt to ensure no one would find it," Sebastian pointed out. He reached for a loose piece of paper—Georgie glanced at it, and saw that it appeared to be a handwritten note from

Dr. Severin, advising Mr. Penbaker to brew a tea of nettle and willow bark to help with his joint pain—and with a practiced hand, flipped up the paper lock, slid the blank side of the paper behind the roller, and turned the cylinder knob until the paper was aligned.

Typing quickly, he wrote, *The quick brown fox jumped over the lazy dog.*

Georgie raised an eyebrow. "Having fun?"

He ripped the piece of paper from the typewriter and smiled. "With you? Always." He looked down at the paper, a frown creasing his brow.

Georgie sat back on her heels, assessing the contents of the crate. "Why do you think Mrs. Penbaker is getting rid of these?"

"I don't know," Sebastian said thoughtfully. "Not that unusual, is it? A wife clearing out after her husband's death?"

"I suppose not," Georgie admitted. "But it seems awfully... quick."

"Doesn't seem to have been the happiest marriage, does it, though?" Sebastian pointed out. "Can't imagine she's spending much time weeping over her husband's typewriter."

Georgie frowned. "Or her typewriter."

"I beg your pardon?"

"We don't know that the typewriter belonged to her husband. It could be hers—or they might have shared it."

"But then, if it was hers, why on earth would she be hiding it?"

"I don't know," Georgie said, shaking her head. She felt as though she were missing something—some detail that would clarify things. She rose to her feet somewhat gracelessly, and tried not to be annoyed when Sebastian mirrored the movement with considerably more elegance.

"Come on," she said reluctantly. "We need to keep searching."

As Sebastian turned to the master bedroom, Georgie—on an impulse she didn't entirely understand—reached out and seized one of the overstuffed manila envelopes. And, without thinking about it too hard, she tucked it under her arm and followed him from the room.

⁓

Unfortunately, the contents of the manila envelope were not nearly as thrilling as Georgie had hoped.

They had departed Mrs. Penbaker's house in furtive fashion and made for the village hall, where they found Miss de Vere and Miss Singh with Mrs. Penbaker in the poison garden, a small, walled-in plot behind the hall. Mrs. Penbaker was explaining the effects of various doses, with what Georgie thought was more or less accuracy. She was, at the very least, considerably more knowledgeable than her husband had been on the topic.

"Miss Radcliffe!" Miss Singh said, brightening, when she spotted Georgie and Sebastian. She had her Detective Devotees notebook in hand and was scribbling away but lowered her pencil to wave at them. "Mrs. Penbaker was just telling us about the lily of the valley that was used to kill the vicar." She nodded at the plant in question. "Your first case!" she added happily, as though Georgie needed reminding.

"I recall," Georgie said, gazing around at the garden. It had a warning sign on the gate advising parents to keep children out, and a rather impressive padlock kept locked when the exhibition was closed. She cleared her throat. "Erm—Mr. Fletcher-Ford was hoping to discuss tomorrow's book club with you both. I believe you've read the book?"

"We have," Miss de Vere said. "It wasn't my personal favorite, but Asha enjoyed it."

"Stella solved the mystery too quickly," Miss Singh said, with a nod at her friend. "She's very clever, you know. Often outwits the authors!"

"I'll leave you to Miss Radcliffe and Mr. Fletcher-Ford, then," Mrs. Penbaker said with a small smile, and led them from the walled garden, shutting the gate carefully behind them before vanishing back inside the village hall.

Miss de Vere rounded on Georgie. "Did you find anything?"

"Nothing of note," Georgie said, feeling the press of the manila envelope against her back, where it was tucked into the waistband of her skirt.

Miss Singh sighed, looking dejected. "Detective work is more frustrating than it seems in novels—or in *The Deathly Dispatch*." She brightened. "Perhaps another corpse will turn up and give you something more interesting to do!" She waved her notebook. "I shall be ready to take notes when that happens!"

"How . . . heartening," Georgie managed, before bidding the Murder Tourists adieu.

Now, she and Sebastian found themselves in the Shorn Sheep; she had thought it might not be busy, as it was just past noon and the pub had only just opened, but it was already shockingly overrun with Murder Tourists. They had secreted themselves away in the most private corner booth, and Georgie had gone to the bar to use the telephone; she returned to the table with drinks to find Sebastian staring at a sheaf of papers with his brow furrowed.

"Anything interesting?" she asked, setting the half-pint glasses on the scarred wood of the table and sliding into the booth next to him. He lowered the stack of papers and proceeded to spread them out on the table before her. She leaned forward eagerly, already anticipating the incriminating evidence that would be presented, and saw . . .

Bills.

Old tax records.

Copies of letters sent to Mr. Penbaker's mother.

"This is so *dull*," Georgie said despairingly, waving about an unsent letter to the editor of the *Register* on the topic of the disappointing decision not to use Ernest in the St. Drogo's Christmas pageant.

"Speak for yourself," Sebastian murmured, his attention fixed upon the letter in his hand. "Did you know that Penbaker was obsessed with Fitzgibbons's capture of the Acton Arsenic Ring? This is a draft of a fan letter."

"No, but it doesn't surprise me," Georgie said. "He has opined at length in the past about how much he admires men with bushy mustaches."

"This village is fascinating."

"I'm so glad you think so. You can't imagine how much we dream of entertaining shiny-shoed tourists from London."

"To be fair, I think that you collectively do, it's just that you personally don't."

This was not inaccurate: Georgie was a confirmed curmudgeon.

She glanced down at the letter before her, noting the fact that the letter 'O' appeared consistently filled with a small smudge of ink each time it was used. It must have been a quirk that the typewriter developed over time, she thought; a quick glance at another letter in the folder sent from Mr. Penbaker revealed the same distinctive O. "There doesn't seem to be anything interesting here," she said, trying to keep a note of frustration from her voice. They had committed a crime, and to no apparent end.

"I suppose not," he agreed, but his brow was slightly furrowed, and his tone was a bit absent. "It would be an awful lot easier to solve this case, you know, if we were certain that Penbaker *was* murdered."

"I am aware," Georgie said testily, taking a sip of her cider.

"How many poisons are there that mimic the symptoms of a heart attack?" Sebastian asked, glancing up from the papers again. "If we had a list, perhaps we could work out which the likeliest candidate was."

"A fair few," Georgie said, tipping her head to the side thoughtfully. "There's cyanide . . . and hemlock . . ."

"Perhaps we should summon Miss de Vere and Miss Singh," he said with a grin. "They're fresh off the heels of their tour of the poison garden, after all, and Miss Singh was taking copious notes."

"She was," Georgie agreed, and then paused, considering.

"Though... was she, actually? I thought she and Miss de Vere had already toured the poison garden. Multiple times, even."

Sebastian shrugged. "No doubt trying to learn as much as possible, so the next time a corpse pops up, they're ready to identify the poison that was used." He shook his head admiringly. "One has to admit, they're very passionate."

"Yes," Georgie said, her mind turning. "The next time a corpse pops up," she repeated, frowning unseeingly down into her drink. Then, she looked up at Sebastian. "Isn't that exactly what Miss Singh said?"

His brow wrinkled. "What?"

"Didn't she *just* say something about 'next time a corpse pops up'? When we saw them at the poison garden?"

"Er. Something along those lines, yes."

"And," Georgie said, growing the slightest bit agitated, "don't you think *they* would benefit, were there to suddenly be a corpse? Who here is most eager for there to be another murder?"

"The Murder Tourists," he said, comprehension dawning.

"The Murder Tourists," she agreed. "Who are frequently around, unknown to any of us, and desperate for another crime to investigate." She shook her head, excited. "Oh God, why didn't I think of it before? Some of them—like Miss de Vere and Miss Singh—have been to visit *multiple times*—and they've definitely been here when the last two murders occurred! What if they were so inspired by last year's crimes that they're willing to take matters into their own hands so that they could witness an investigation up close?"

"That's a bit of a stretch, don't you think?" Sebastian asked.

Georgie, however, was thinking, her mind churning through everything she'd learned in the past several days. "Have you noticed that Miss de Vere and Miss Singh get a bit shifty whenever we ask them how long they plan to stay? And Miss de Vere is supposed to be engaged, but I've yet to hear her mention her fiancé by name—wouldn't you think he'd eventually wonder where she's run off to?"

"They rescued us from that godforsaken cellar," Sebastian pointed out.

"All the better to make them look like the heroines in one of Mrs. Christie's novels."

"Or Miss Sayers's. I think I prefer hers—I tell you, that Harriet Vane—"

"Sebastian," Georgie asked, "do you *really* think this is the time?"

"No, I suppose not," he conceded with a regretful sigh. "Shall we convene another meeting of our little detective society—minus the newfound suspects, of course?"

"I already borrowed the telephone to ring Arthur," she said, feeling pleased with herself. "He should be here any minute." She began gathering the papers from the table, preparing to shove them back into the manila envelope. "I'm beginning to feel rather badly about stealing from Mrs. Penbaker."

"Ah, well," Sebastian said philosophically. "You know what I always say."

"No," Georgie said. "In fact, I can scarcely even imagine."

He smiled at her. "Larceny is never a wasted effort when it's a prelude to romance."

Georgie, who had just taken a sip of her cider, choked, and

glared at him when his smile widened at the sight. "I am counting the hours until you get back on that train on Thursday," she said, once her coughing had subsided.

"I *almost* think that you believe that," he replied, looking unconcerned. "Ah, there's Crawley!" He waved a hand, and Arthur, who had just entered the pub, nodded and began making his way toward them, followed—not five seconds later—by Constable Lexington.

"How did you know to meet us here?" Georgie asked Lexington as he slid into the booth across the table from her.

Lexington flushed. "I was with Crawley."

Georgie looked at Lexington, whose hair was not as neatly combed as she'd grown accustomed to, and whose clothing looked ever so slightly rumpled. Then she looked at Arthur, who appeared almost obscenely cheerful.

Georgie bit her lip and watched the color in Lexington's cheeks deepen.

Fascinating.

"So," she said, clearing her throat and resolving to focus solely on the matters relevant to the case, no matter how intriguing other developments might be. "We have grown a bit curious about the Murder Tourists."

Arthur raised his eyebrows. "Miss de Vere and Miss Singh?"

Seeing matching skeptical expressions on both Arthur's and Lexington's faces, she said, "Think about it. They're *always* around—including when a couple of the most recent crimes have been committed—and no one thinks anything of it, because we've all grown used to them."

"So . . . what?" Arthur asked, still sounding unconvinced.

"You think they learned of the first couple of murders last autumn and decided they'd quite like to commit one of their own? And visited the scene of the crime on numerous occasions, making it far more likely they'd be caught?"

Lexington cleared his throat. "Criminals *do* return to the scene of the crime, not infrequently. There are countless documented examples of this. So that aspect of Miss Radcliffe's theory isn't that far-fetched."

Arthur glanced at him, his brow furrowed in thought. "All right. But . . . Miss de Vere and Miss Singh? Have you *met* them?"

"They don't strike me as likely suspects," Lexington admitted, rubbing the back of his neck. "But I suppose we can't discount them."

"And how do you propose to test this theory?" Arthur asked. "Stroll up to one of the Murder Tourists and inform them that you've got a cunning plan for a bit of light homicide, and would they be interested in joining you? And oh, by the way, do they happen to have committed any *other* homicides recently, as well?"

Georgie sighed. "No, I suppose not. It does strike me that we don't know very much about them, though, for how often they're lurking around." She glanced around the table, and her gaze alighted on Sebastian, sitting directly next to her and currently smiling flirtatiously at a group of middle-aged women who were gossiping happily over a late lunch.

"What?" he asked, lowering his glass.

"Of course," she murmured. "It should have occurred to me at once."

"What should have?" There was a note of faint alarm creeping into his voice.

Georgie reached out and grasped his forearm. "I hope you've brought your most enticing jumper, old sport. Because it's time for you to flirt with some potential criminals."

CHAPTER EIGHTEEN

They decided that the wooing of Murder Tourists was best done by romantic candlelight, and so the group split up for the afternoon—Lexington and Arthur departed, presumably to do their actual jobs, while Sebastian and Georgie decided to head back to Radcliffe Hall in the hope of procuring sustenance from Mrs. Fawcett.

As they walked down the high street—which at the moment was fairly quiet, most villagers being at home for lunch—Georgie suddenly stumbled over an uneven cobblestone. Before she could so much as extend an arm to break her fall, however, Sebastian reached out to steady her with a hand on her arm.

She glanced sideways at him as she straightened. "Thank you."

He smiled easily at her, slipping his arm through hers. "Perilous places, these small villages."

Georgie gave him a distracted smile in return, her mind suddenly occupied by the sensation of his arm entwined with hers, the subtle pressure he was exerting to tuck her more closely against his side. Alarmingly, she rather liked it; this close, she could see the faint laugh lines at the corners of his eyes, and smell the soap he used to shave. At this intimate proximity, he seemed less like his usual figure of golden-haired, athletic perfection, and more like, simply...

A man.

A very, very handsome man—but just a man nonetheless.

He glanced down at her. "Is there something on my face?" he asked slyly, and Georgie looked away, cheeks heating.

"Impossible," she said airily. "I saw you check your reflection in a window *twice* as we were leaving the pub."

He smiled at her again—even out of the corner of her eye, she caught a bit of its blinding force. And she realized, as they walked along the high street out of the village in the afternoon sunshine, arm in arm, that they looked like...

Well, like a couple.

Which was absurd, except...

Except for the fact that she could still feel the press of his mouth to hers, like a phantom. Except for the fact that occasionally, when she glanced sideways at him, she caught him smiling at her, in a way that felt like a conversation, despite no words being spoken. She was so occupied by all these thoughts that she was barely conscious of the silence that had fallen between them, other than vaguely noting that it felt comfortable, not like the sort of silence that anyone needed to rush to fill. Like the silences she shared with Papa and Abigail and Arthur.

Not like silences she should be sharing with handsome playboys from town.

It was difficult to think of him in strictly those terms anymore, though.

"Penny for your thoughts," he said, not looking at her as he spoke; indeed, he was smiling flirtatiously at a pair of grannies who were passing them clutching paper bags of treats for Ernest.

Georgie glanced down at her feet to avoid looking at him; she certainly wasn't going to tell him what was *actually* on her mind.

"Oh, I . . ." She scrambled for an answer that was at least partly true. "I was just thinking, if the Murder Tourists have indeed been up to something suspect, it will make for an excellent article for Arthur." She tried not to sound glum as she said it.

She felt Sebastian's eyes slide back to her and looked determinedly ahead.

"Did you not know that he was interested in leaving the village?"

"I suppose I did—I mean, it's something he's mentioned often enough over the years. I just didn't think he'd actually, truly go. It's the sort of thing we've discussed in the fanciful way we talk about things we'd never actually do—like how I've talked of wanting to apprentice at Regent's Park, or study at Swanley Horticultural College."

"But why are those things that you'd never do?"

She blinked. "What do you mean?"

"I mean, just as it doesn't seem odd to me that Crawley

might want to leave the village, it doesn't seem inconceivable that you could go to Swanley or work at a garden in London."

Georgie waved an impatient hand. "Don't be ridiculous. Don't you see how I'm needed here? There are all the murders, obviously, but even before that—my father is getting older—"

"And your sister lives here."

"For *now*," Georgie stressed. "But I'm hoping to send her to stay with my aunt, and if she meets someone there—or finds some sort of work she enjoys—why, she might never come back!"

"Does your sister *wish* to go to London?" Sebastian asked, and Georgie glanced at him, startled. He was still gazing around at his surroundings with his usual expression of good-humored appreciation, but she was beginning to suspect that that expression was nothing more than a mask—and a rather sneaky one, at that.

"She is . . . coming around to the idea," Georgie said.

"Ah," he said, with far too much understanding for Georgie's liking.

"She is!" she insisted.

"If she's reluctant to go, why can't *you* go in her stead?" he asked.

"Because," she said heatedly, "in case you've not noticed, I've got my hands full with an absurd number of corpses!"

"But *we* are going to solve that problem," he reminded her. "In fact, we've only approximately two and a half days in which to resolve our current mystery before my contractually obligated departure."

"Don't tease me with the promise of happier days to come."

He grinned. "My dearest Georgie, are you *flirting* with me?"

"Does my professing to long for your departure count as flirting?" she asked him with a stony look.

"Coming from you? Absolutely."

And the worst of it, Georgie realized, was that he might well be right about that.

"My point is, I cannot possibly leave the village."

"I believe that *you* believe that," he said diplomatically. She stopped in her tracks, dropping his arm and putting her hands on her hips.

"Don't patronize me," she said, feeling heat rise in her cheeks.

He shoved his hands in his pockets and eyed her warily. "I wasn't patronizing you. I can't think of anyone I've ever known that I'd be *less* likely to patronize, frankly. You're the most intelligent, competent person I've ever met."

"I—you—" She found herself actually at a loss for words; everything about this conversation was infuriating. How dare he ask her uncomfortable questions, then raise points she'd rather not consider, then offer her what was possibly one of the loveliest compliments she'd ever received?

It was maddening.

It was maddening, too, that they were standing on the village high street, just outside the Sleepy Hedgehog, and that it was therefore unquestionably *not* the correct moment to do something as silly, as reckless, as *scandalous* (to the ladies of the St. Drogo's social club, at least) as kiss him.

And yet, despite those considerations, she somehow found herself taking two quick steps forward, reaching up to place her hands on his face, and proceeding to do exactly that.

For a split second, she caught him off guard, and could sense his hesitation in the slight delay before his hands rose to rest at her waist. After another moment, however, his mind evidently caught up to the situation, and suddenly it was no longer Georgie kissing him, but something mutual—something shared.

There was no longer any hesitation in his touch, no uncertainty—no doubt that he knew exactly what he was doing. And *of course he did*, because how many other women had he done this with before? But Georgie firmly shut that thought away, not wanting to think about it, not now—not, perhaps, ever, because it suddenly struck her as slightly unfair that she judged him harshly merely because he was handsome and liked going to bed and had done it with a number of willing women. What, truly, was the harm in that, other than the fact that she didn't like to think of him doing that with anyone other than her?

There was little room for that thought, however—or for any others—because logical reasoning was rapidly fading from her mind in the face of the relentless onslaught of sensation:

The heat of his mouth on hers.

The firm press of his hand at her jaw, tilting her mouth up to meet his at just the angle he wanted.

The smell of his skin, all around her.

The tight grip of his arm around her waist, tugging her closer to him until she was pressed flush against him in what felt like shocking intimacy, the feeling of his heart pounding against hers.

And—best, perhaps, of all—the sound of a moan working

its way up from his chest when her tongue darted out to trace the seam of his lips, deepening the kiss, and she wrapped her arms around his neck.

She didn't know how much time had passed before he pulled back. Her lips felt swollen, and she reached a hand up to touch them, unthinking, and his eyes dropped to follow the motion, darkening at the sight. He pulled her forward, placed another lingering kiss on her mouth before finally, regretfully, releasing her.

"You shouldn't compliment me like that," she said at last, after a moment of silence filled only with the sound of their ragged breathing. She became once again conscious of the fact that they were on a public road, in plain view of anyone who might have happened to be passing, but a quick glance around confirmed that they were still, mercifully, alone, and not giving the gossips of the village a story to dine out on for the next year. (Or until the next corpse materialized, at least.)

"If that's going to be your response, then I think I ought to do it more often," he said, his normally smooth voice rougher at the edges than she'd ever heard it.

"I—we can't—what are we doing?" she asked helplessly, a hand rising to touch her tingling lips. His eyes tracked the movement, gleaming with satisfaction.

"Solving crimes and kissing in the great outdoors?" he suggested, and a laugh escaped her lips before she could stop it.

A slow smile crept across his face. "I love when you do that."

"What—laugh?"

"Laugh as if you can't help it," he said simply. "Laugh against your better judgment."

She stared at him, speechless, and his smile widened. "Come, Georgie!" he said, offering her his arm once again. "Sandwiches await, and then you will have to help me pick my most alluring jumper for the evening's entertainment."

"None of your jumpers are alluring," she said, recovering sufficiently to lie through her teeth.

He smiled at her indulgently. "You know, you're a dreadful liar. Rather reassuring, really! At least I know that *you* aren't a murderer!" And with a jaunty whistle, he set off down the road once more, Georgie on his arm and wondering when, precisely, her life had become so unexpected.

∾

Several hours later—hours that Georgie had spent digging happily in the garden; hours that Sebastian had spent eating a half dozen sandwiches, a sizable portion of the bread-and-butter pudding that Abigail had made the day before, and at least three or four shortbread biscuits that remained in a tin and "looked lonely"—Georgie was curled up in the drawing room, thumbing through an old issue of *Country Life*, when she heard footsteps on the stairs. Glancing up, she was just in time to see Sebastian prance through the doorway wearing a fresh pair of trousers and a pale blue jumper that perfectly matched his eyes. The sleeves were rolled up, exposing his forearms. His blond hair was ever so slightly rumpled, in an attractive way that Georgie suspected was intentional. His face shone with a healthy glow.

Georgie leaned closer to him. "Why is your skin . . . glistening? Don't tell me you've somehow found someone to play tennis with you in the past hour?" She was nearly certain he hadn't; not an hour earlier, she'd seen him in this very room, on his back, staring at the ceiling, biscuit tin balanced carefully on his abdomen.

"No," he said, sounding pleased. "I held my face above the teakettle when it was letting off steam. Just enough to give me that delicate flush of exercise." He batted his eyelashes at her. "Although I can think of a *vastly* more pleasant way I might have worked up a healthful glow—"

"That's enough, thank you." It would be easier to stop him flirting with her, she reflected, if she could cure herself of the habit of kissing him impulsively. It would help if he could stop being so . . . (She mentally gestured at his entire physical being.)

"I am *bait*, Georgie," he explained patiently. "I have to look the part. I need to send their delicate female minds into a tizzy of unfulfilled lust. Now, are you ready to set off?" he asked, smiling charmingly at her. "Only, remember, you're to hide yourself away where the ladies won't notice you. Might put a damper on the mood if they see me with my would-be lady love."

"Your—" Georgie began, but he turned and pranced from the room again, leaving her gaping like a fish, with little option but to follow him.

Within a quarter of an hour, they'd arrived at the Fleecy Lamb, which prided itself on a (relatively) more upscale atmosphere than the Shorn Sheep. Arthur met them at the door, his mouth twitching at the sight of Sebastian, and he and Georgie proceeded to hide themselves away in the darkest corner.

"How do you propose to lure them in to have a drink with you?" Georgie asked, curious in spite of herself.

Sebastian winked at her. "That won't be difficult. Like herding sheep."

"I'd like to see you try herding Ernest, and then you might revise that turn of phrase," Georgie advised him.

Not five minutes later, however, he was back, escorting Miss de Vere and Miss Singh into the pub and proclaiming in loud, carrying tones, ". . . can't believe my good fortune in running into you ladies! And while I am unaccompanied, for once!" Georgie didn't dare crane around to look at him, but she would have bet a tidy sum that he'd dropped a wink at the end of that sentence.

"And where *is* Miss Radcliffe this evening?" came Miss de Vere's voice as he led them to a table close enough for Georgie and Arthur to easily eavesdrop.

"At home, scrutinizing clues without me, no doubt," Sebastian said, a touch mournfully. He and Georgie had spent some time discussing what angle he ought to attempt when approaching the ladies, and had landed on "man with wounded professional pride" as the one the ladies would find most plausible. Men were terribly easy to offend, after all.

"No doubt," Miss Singh agreed, sounding impressed; Georgie was tempted to laugh.

"Ladies, what can I fetch you?" Sebastian asked, and Miss Singh asked for a cider, while Miss de Vere requested a specific whisky. Next to Georgie, Arthur whistled quietly in appreciation. Sebastian left to head to the bar, and Georgie and Arthur leaned forward in their seats, listening hard.

Unfortunately for them, no confessions of misdeeds were forthcoming from the ladies; instead, they spent a few minutes debating—Georgie could not believe her ears—whether Lord Peter Wimsey and Harriet Vane should get married in Dorothy Sayers's novels.

Sebastian returned at last, and there were murmured thanks from both women, followed by a moment of silence, during which all three were presumably sipping their drinks.

"You're looking very ... healthy, this evening," Miss de Vere said after several seconds. There was a *thunk* as she evidently set her glass down on the table.

"I spent my afternoon practicing a spot of tennis," Sebastian said easily.

"Where?" This was Miss Singh's voice. "I haven't seen courts anywhere."

"Er." Sebastian was clearly thinking fast. "I practiced against the side of Radcliffe Hall. No one to play with, but want to keep the reflexes sharp." His voice dropped an octave. "For other pursuits, of course." Next to Georgie, Arthur buried his face in his drink.

"Of course," Miss Singh said, sounding a bit taken aback by this turn in tone. She quickly rallied, however. "What do you and Miss Radcliffe plan to investigate next?" She dropped her voice. "Stella and I would be more than happy to lend you our services to be a distraction once again!" She sounded as though she were about to burst with pride.

"I'm not entirely certain," Sebastian said, sounding a bit glum. "We didn't uncover anything today but a bunch of paperwork. No doubt Miss Radcliffe has plenty of ideas for what to do next, though. Not that she's shared them with me." He gave a dramatic sigh. "But we certainly won't hesitate to ask you for help again, if it's needed." A pause, and then, "I only wish I could rely on you when I return to London to work."

"What do you do for work, then, Fletcher-Ford?" Miss de Vere asked, sounding intrigued.

"Oh, it wouldn't interest you," Sebastian dismissed. "I would hate to bore two such beautiful women, when I finally have you to myself."

"But . . ." Miss Singh sounded a bit hesitant. "What about Miss Radcliffe?"

"What about her?" Georgie could practically *see* Sebastian's shrug.

"Well," Miss Singh said, sounding reproving, "you're meant to be her romantic subplot!"

"Her . . . what?"

"Romantic subplot," Miss de Vere said. "All the best detective novels have them, you know."

"Miss Radcliffe must have missed that memo," Sebastian said. "But I hardly need Miss Radcliffe, when I have two such beautiful specimens of womanhood before me."

Georgie pressed her lips together, tempted to laugh, despite worrying that this was not going precisely according to plan. When plotting this conversation, they had failed to account for the extent to which the Detective Devotees were wedded to the traditional beats of the genre.

"Mr. Fletcher-Ford," Miss de Vere said, her voice growing steely, "I really think we should focus on the case at hand. You said you and Miss Radcliffe found some paperwork?"

"There's an awful lot of paperwork in these mysteries," Miss Singh said, thoughtful now. Georgie exchanged a glance with Arthur, whose brow was furrowed in thought.

"Letters, I mean," Miss Singh clarified a moment later. Georgie frowned, a half-formed idea taking shape at the back of her mind. She considered the facts of the murder cases in Buncombe-upon-Woolly, and realized Miss Singh was right—letters did seem to connect them all. There were the blackmail letters that Mrs. Hoxton—a local housewife who'd been having an affair with a farmer—had received from the vicar, prompting her murder of him. And the anonymous letter that the bakers' son had received, informing him of his parents having changed their will to exclude him. And the letter—allegedly from an orphanage employee—alerting Lady Tunbridge's eventual murderer to her ladyship's identity as her birth mother. And the Marbles...

She wracked her brain.

There had been a draft letter uncovered by the police in Mrs. Marble's desk, supposedly to a friend, discussing her dissatisfaction with her marriage.

Georgie bit her lip, turning over these facts—and at the back of her mind a small voice reminded her of Sebastian's theory, which she had so quickly brushed aside, that the murders in the village might somehow be connected.

Sebastian, meanwhile, was silent, as Miss Singh and Miss de Vere matter-of-factly made a list of the cases, making note of the role the letter had played in each mystery. Georgie expected him, once they'd concluded, to attempt to steer the conversation back on track, toward more flirtatious territory, but there was a lengthy silence once the women had ceased speaking, and Georgie chanced another glance at Sebastian. He was staring down into his drink, deep in thought. Whatever was wrong with him?

He glanced up, and unerringly caught her eye. Georgie prepared to duck back into her hiding spot, but before she could do so, he mystifyingly raised a hand at her. "Miss Radcliffe!" he called. "Georgie!" Both Murder Tourists' heads whipped round, and their brows furrowed at the sight of Georgie, who waved weakly back by way of greeting.

"Georgie," Sebastian said, more firmly now. "Come join us. Because I've just had a thought and—" He broke off, shaking his head. "Well, old bean, I think *you* may be in possession of an absolutely corking piece of evidence."

CHAPTER NINETEEN

With such a response, there was nothing for it but to join the group at the next table.

"Hello," Georgie said, a trifle sheepishly, hovering awkwardly behind Miss de Vere's chair.

"Miss Radcliffe," Miss Singh said, her smooth brow puckering. "Mr. Fletcher-Ford said that you were at home this evening? Doing—" She glanced around, then said in a stage whisper, "—*important detective work.*"

"Er," Georgie said. "I was."

"She wasn't," Sebastian said, at exactly the same time, and Georgie gave him a scathing look, which naturally he ignored. "The fact is, ladies," he said, spreading his hands wide in a mea culpa sort of gesture, "you've been brought here under false pretenses."

"We... have?" Miss de Vere looked perplexed, and Georgie honestly couldn't blame her.

"I did not stumble across you by accident, as it seemed, but it was all part of a deliberate, forearm-forward attack."

Miss Singh blushed. "I did think that was an *awful* lot of forearm to be showing on a Monday night."

Miss de Vere looked at her inquiringly. "I'm sorry, when would be a more appropriate evening for Fletcher-Ford to be showcasing his forearms?"

"Thursday," Miss Singh said promptly. "It's the most licentious of the weekdays."

"Fair enough," Miss de Vere agreed.

"My forearms were to entice you!" Sebastian said, looking offended. "No woman can resist the sight of a man glistening appealingly with bared forearms!"

Miss de Vere and Miss Singh looked at him skeptically.

"Sebastian," Georgie said, with what she personally thought was admirable patience, "could you *please* explain why you have undone a carefully laid plan for the sake of some alleged evidence that you believe I possess?"

Sebastian, with one last disapproving shake of his head at the Murder Tourists, turned to Georgie. "Georgie, do you recall anything about the letters we saw today, at Mrs. Penbaker's?"

"Um." Georgie considered. "There were an awful lot of them?"

"No." Sebastian shook his head, frustrated. "The letters themselves. Did you notice anything about the type?"

Georgie considered; after a moment, it came to her. "The letter 'O,'" she said slowly. "There was a . . . smudge, or something. Each time it was typed."

"Exactly." Sebastian nodded. "An irregularity with the

key—it happens with typewriters, when they've been used for a while, they develop odd quirks. Fitzgibbons's typewriter has a hook on the lowercase 'g.'"

In unison, Miss Singh and Miss de Vere clapped their hands to their mouths. "Fitzgibbons?" Miss de Vere demanded. "As in, *Delacey Fitzgibbons?*"

Georgie sighed as Sebastian looked sheepishly at her. "You may as well tell them."

"He is my employer," he confessed to the Murder Tourists, who gasped again, even more dramatically.

"Then . . . you are not here on holiday at all!" Miss Singh said, looking entirely thrilled by this development. "You are here to *investigate*!" She paused to consider. "How fortunate, Miss Radcliffe, that you should have a family friend who is employed by a detective! Did he help you solve any of the previous cases?" She looked a bit disappointed at the notion that her heroine might have had outside assistance—and from a *man*, at that.

"Well," Georgie hedged.

"I did not," Sebastian said firmly. "Miss Radcliffe did all that detective work herself, with that admirable mind of hers." Georgie glanced at him, but his attention was on the Murder Tourists, and he adopted a confessional sort of tone. "And Miss Radcliffe and I might have exaggerated the extent of our family connection."

"Exaggerated . . . by how much?" Miss Singh asked.

"Er." Sebastian smiled winningly at her. "By implying that any existed whatsoever."

Miss Singh clapped a shocked hand to her mouth yet again.

"Then you are here in an official professional capacity?" Rather than looking betrayed to have been lied to, she looked—if possible—even more delighted by this development.

"Yes," Miss de Vere said, eyeing Sebastian with a discerning gleam in her eye. "Which means, when you tried to lure us into a pub using your masculine wiles, you were doing it as part of the investigation. Because—" Here, she broke off, looking more excited than Georgie had thought the sophisticated Miss de Vere was capable of looking. "Asha, *he thought we were suspects!*"

"It made sense!" Georgie said defensively. "You've been to visit multiple times, and you've been prattling on nonstop about *The Deathly Dispatch*, and you're just . . . constantly underfoot. It didn't seem outside the realm of possibility."

"It does make a certain amount of sense," Miss Singh agreed, looking absolutely elated. "This is the most exciting thing that has ever happened to me!" She clasped her hands together. "That would be a *thrilling* end to this story, I have to say. Do you mind if I steal it for my manuscript?"

"Manuscript?" Georgie said blankly.

Miss Singh nodded happily. "I've decided to try my hand at writing a novel of my own! There's so much inspiration here!"

"Is *that* why you've been to visit so often?" Arthur asked; he was leaning against the edge of a neighboring booth, arms crossed over his chest, watching this entire scene with considerable entertainment.

Miss Singh and Miss de Vere exchanged a look. "In part," Miss Singh said. "I'd been considering making the culprit *you*, Miss Radcliffe," she added, a bit apologetically. "Or not *you* you, but an intrepid lady sleuth who wears sensible jumpers.

But then I decided that it's not really playing fair, is it, to have the detective be the murderer? Agatha Christie would never."

"What was my motive going to be?" Georgie asked, curious in spite of herself.

"Continued employment!" Miss Singh said, looking pleased with herself. "Got to have a steady supply of murder victims to keep yourself earning a tidy income."

"I am not *earning* an income," Georgie pointed out.

"Oh." Miss Singh's face fell, but she rallied a moment later. "Well . . . you do it for the fame, then! The attention it brings you! You need people to continue being murdered so you don't get pushed out of the limelight!"

"I do not think your lady detective has all that much in common with me," Georgie said, feeling a headache coming on, then shook her head, looking at Sebastian. "If we could get back to the point—what's the issue with the typewriter?"

"Well," Sebastian said, "it occurred to me—that quirk on the 'O' from that typewriter looked familiar."

"Familiar how?" Georgie asked.

"That's what I've been wondering all afternoon—but Miss Singh has made me realize where I saw it: on the letter from the orphanage to the Mistletoe Murderer. It was on display at the village hall!"

Georgie stared at him, her mind racing; she dimly remembered, now, him making some sort of comment about a distinctive typewriter key on that letter, though she hadn't paid it any attention at the time, dismissing it as more of his incessant babble. But if the typewriter that produced that letter was the same typewriter that the Penbakers owned . . .

"Then either Mr. Penbaker or his wife sent that letter!" Georgie said excitedly. "And the typewriter would be evidence—and all those papers that Mrs. Penbaker was getting rid of, too!"

She and Sebastian stared at each other. Arthur had retrieved his notebook and was scribbling away feverishly, while the Murder Tourists were literally and figuratively on the edges of their seats, eyes wide.

"So the question is," Sebastian said, his eyes still locked on hers, "whether Mr. or Mrs. Penbaker was the one who sent them."

"Well, Mr. Penbaker is dead, Mr. Fletcher-Ford," Miss Singh said very gently, as though worried about offending him.

"He is," Georgie agreed. "Which doesn't necessarily mean that he *didn't* have anything to do with any of the previous cases, but which does rather beg the question—" She glanced over again at Arthur, whose pen at this point was moving so quickly it seemed in danger of levitating.

Sebastian finished her thought for her.

"Of whether his wife is the one who killed him."

CHAPTER TWENTY

*I*t was another hour before the group called it a night and the Murder Tourists—still wildly flattered to have been considered suspects, albeit briefly—retreated to the Sleepy Hedgehog, presumably to rehash the evening's developments in greater detail. Arthur informed Georgie that he would speak to Lexington about gaining access to the evidence—including the all-important letters—from the other murder investigations.

"Will you be wearing clothing for this conversation?" Georgie asked, unable to help herself, and Arthur shot her a repressive look.

"Should I ask you and Fletcher-Ford the same thing?" he asked, and Georgie, annoyingly, blushed.

"I *knew* there was a romantic subplot in this book!" Miss de Vere called over her shoulder smugly as she departed.

Sebastian glanced at Georgie, and she wondered what he saw in her face, but he said nothing more than a casual "Shall we?" and offered her his arm.

They were quiet on the walk down the high street to the edge of the village, the only sound their footsteps on the cobblestoned streets, and it was not until they reached the long gravel lane that led to Radcliffe Hall that he said, quite casually, "What are you thinking?"

Georgie glanced at him.

"You get a little wrinkle just here"—he reached out with an index finger to gently press the space between her eyebrows—"whenever you're deep in thought." They drew to a halt, the night quiet around them, the moon just peeking out from behind a cloud. He was handsome in the moonlight, but in a less shocking, golden sort of way than he was in the daylight, when he drew the eye and seemed to somehow emanate his own light. Here, the angles of his cheekbones were more pronounced, his eyes shadowed, and she could see the evening stubble on his face. He looked . . . rougher. More raw. She liked this version of him, one that felt different than the man the rest of the world saw by day.

She pushed these thoughts away and said merely, "I suppose I'm trying to come to terms with the fact that . . . you might have been right."

"It does happen once a decade or so, darling Georgie."

She rewarded him with a small smile but pressed on. "About the murders being connected, I mean." She paused, her mind still turning over the day's revelations. "Either Mr. or Mrs. Penbaker sent at least one of the letters that prompted someone to commit murder—if Arthur and Lexington find that they sent the others, too..."

"But why would they do it?" Sebastian asked, shoving a hand in his pocket as they walked. "Don't mistake me, I will cherish forever the memory of you telling me I'm right—might have it embroidered on a pillowcase, actually—"

"*Sebastian.*"

"But," he continued, undeterred, "what do the Penbakers stand to gain from turning Buncombe-upon-Woolly into a Murder Village?"

"Murder Tourists," Georgie said without missing a beat, and he blinked at her. "Think about it. Who has a perfect motive to commit all the murders in the village? The man who has spent *years* trying to draw more tourists to Buncombe-upon-Woolly, without success—until the murders started! It's precisely what he wanted. *Or*, perhaps, his wife, who has seen his fruitless struggle, and who thinks he might stop all of his unhinged schemes once and for all if the tourists actually come?"

"But wouldn't they have worried that a crime spree would have the opposite effect?"

Georgie shook her head. "I don't think so. Remember what Miss Halifax said? About how Mr. Penbaker became obsessed with Agatha Christie novels after she introduced them to him? That was about a year ago—just before the murders started. The timing makes perfect sense."

She turned and started down the drive toward Radcliffe Hall, Sebastian deep in thought beside her. They walked in silence for a few minutes, and Georgie did not break it, allowing him to catch up to the conclusion she'd arrived at.

"But," he said, as they drew close to the front door, "arrests have been made in all those cases. *You* helped solve most of them, as you pointed out to me, when I first raised this theory."

"I know," Georgie said, with a note of suppressed triumph. "Because they didn't get their hands dirty by committing the murders themselves—I think they simply gave the killers a . . . nudge, of sorts."

"With the letters," he said, comprehension dawning.

"With the letters," she confirmed.

They'd arrived at Radcliffe Hall; rather than entering through the front doors, Georgie led him around the house, through the kitchen garden, and in through the kitchen door. The kitchen was quiet and gleaming; on the counter was a plate covered with a napkin, complete with a scrap of paper labeled *Sebastian* in Mrs. Fawcett's careful script, and Sebastian whipped off the napkin with a triumphant cry to discover a few shortbread biscuits, a fat slice of Victoria sponge, and a cheese-and-pickle sandwich.

"She watched you eat a half dozen sandwiches not three hours ago," Georgie said, incredulous, as Sebastian began inhaling the biscuits.

"Mrs. Fawcett understands that I cannot work on starvation rations," he informed her.

"Come on—bring the plate and follow me," she said, leading him toward the kitchen staircase. Originally intended for the servants the Radcliffes could no longer afford, now used by the family, the kitchen staircase allowed one to ascend its narrow, rough-hewn steps to the top floor without passing through the main rooms of the house. Once they emerged on the top floor, they walked down the hallway to Georgie's room, where they were greeted by Egg, who raised her head from her tartan cushion, spotted Sebastian, and immediately commenced the sort of mournful howl masquerading as a bark that only the floppiest-eared of dogs can manage.

"Egg, for heaven's sake."

Sebastian wasted no time in sinking to a crouch, which Egg took as the invitation it was; fortunately, she was so eagerly trying to butt her head beneath his chin that she ceased her barking. Georgie pressed her ear to the door for a moment, listening intently, but did not hear the sound of any other doors opening, or footsteps on the stairs; she didn't fancy being interrupted at the moment, because she had Important Murder Business to discuss with Sebastian.

She turned back to find him still in a crouch, stroking Egg's ears and watching her with a far more guarded expression than she normally saw on his face. She suddenly realized the intimacy of their situation in a rush—in her bedroom, late at night, alone. In an attempt to dispel her own discomfort, she crossed to her desk and clicked on the electric lamp that sat there, then switched on the lamp on her bedside table as well. In the warm incandescent glow, the room lost a bit of its air of moonlit romance, though the fact still remained that they were in a literal *turret*, of all things. Georgie walked to the casement windows and eased one open, allowing cool night air to waft into the room. She stood for a moment, staring at the green hills, dark and shadowy under the night sky, which seemed to be clearing of its earlier cloud cover, a few bright stars popping into view.

She turned in time to catch Sebastian watching her, his expression unreadable, his hand on Egg's head having stilled.

"What is it?" she asked, a bit uncertain. She felt suddenly oddly conscious of her own body, in a pair of worn wool trousers and one of her oldest jumpers, her hair no doubt in disarray.

"I like watching you think," he said simply, his eyes steady on hers.

"Trying to work out how to do it yourself?" she asked, but there was no acid to it, and he smiled slowly; it was akin to watching the sun edge its way above the horizon. He climbed to his feet after one last loving pat for Egg, then walked toward her, his steps deliberate.

"What's the rest of your theory?" he asked, coming to a halt with scant inches left between them.

"My . . . theory?" Her voice was the slightest bit breathless.

He reached out for her hand and ran a thumb down her palm. She felt it like a brand on her skin.

"About Penbaker." He held her hand loosely in his. "If Mrs. Penbaker killed him, why would she have done it?"

His proximity was making it difficult to think. This was an alarming new development, since they were in the business, for two more days, of solving mysteries together, and that did require both proximity and, ideally, the ability to think clearly.

"Unless," he said thoughtfully, "Penbaker's death itself truly wasn't suspicious. He may really have died of a heart attack. After all, if he was masterminding the murders in the village, then it doesn't stand to reason that there's a separate killer out there who would wish him dead."

"I suppose," Georgie agreed reluctantly, her gaze moving restlessly around the room, landing on one of the books in a haphazard stack on her bedside table. *A Dictionary of Poisons.* There was a copy of it on display at the murder exhibition, Georgie had noticed.

The murder exhibition that Mrs. Penbaker was responsible for. The murder exhibition that featured a poison garden, no less—with ample opportunity for her to clip something from it. There were any number of poisons that could induce cardiac arrest like the council chairman had suffered, of course... but that got back to Sebastian's question: Why would Mrs. Penbaker have poisoned her husband?

Unless...

Georgie looked at Sebastian, her heart pounding in her chest.

"Unless," she said, her mind racing, still trying to consider the possible options in her head, "it was, in fact, Mr. Penbaker behind all the murders—but *without* his wife's knowledge. What if she worked it out somehow and decided to put a stop to it?"

He stared at her for a long moment, a smile spreading across his face. "I cannot *wait* to witness this particular conversation," he said, and then he leaned down and kissed her.

And Georgie, without a moment's hesitation, reached her arms up to wind around his neck, and kissed him back.

"You're extremely attractive when you're being clever," he murmured against her mouth some indeterminate amount of time later. His hand had strayed to the waistband of her trousers and slipped beneath the hem of her jumper, resting on the bare skin of her stomach, causing gooseflesh to rise on her arms.

"*You're* extremely attractive when you're not pretending *not* to be clever," she shot back, and he smiled before leaning down to kiss her throat, pulling her tighter against him. Georgie hooked a leg around his hip, keeping him pressed to her.

"If you want me to leave," he said against the skin of her neck, "we should probably stop now."

Georgie paused for a moment, her pulse pounding in her chest and between her legs, so distracted by the feeling of one of his hands straying down her back to cup her bottom that she could scarcely think straight. "And what if," she said, pulling back for a moment, just enough that he could look up to meet her eyes directly, "I don't want you to leave?"

He smiled at her—a dangerous, tempting smile.

And then his mouth was on hers once again, giving her a deep, drugging kiss before moving to trail a series of kisses down her jaw, and his hands were everywhere, somehow—tugging her jumper over her head; undoing the buttons of her blouse and helping her pull it off; and then skimming over the bare skin of her stomach, her pulse jumping beneath his touch in places that she personally thought a pulse had no business taking up residence.

She stepped back and jerked her chin at him. "It's your turn," she said, crossing her arms over her chest, the air of the room cool on her skin as she stood there in her bra and trousers. He wasted no time in reaching for the hem of his own jumper, revealing nothing but an undershirt beneath. This, too, was gone a moment later, and Georgie didn't even bother attempting not to stare at the golden skin and firm muscles of his chest and abdomen.

"Ridiculous," she muttered, feeling vaguely feverish, and took three quick steps toward him, pulling his head down to hers for a kiss rather than continue trying to resist the urge to begin mentally cataloguing his abdominal muscles. She had to preserve *some* dignity, after all.

Thoughts of dignity rapidly faded, however, under the relentless onslaught of sensation—the warmth of his hand at the base of her neck, anchoring her in place; the heat of his mouth and the taste of him, shortbread and whisky, sweet and heady; the feeling of his tongue tangling with hers; the pounding of her pulse at her core; the insistent hardness of him against her stomach, evident through his trousers, causing her to act on some wordless instinct and cant her hips at just the right angle to create some desired friction. A moan broke the silence of the room, and it took her a moment to realize that it was hers.

Without breaking the kiss, he walked her backward toward her bed and eased her onto it ever so gently, drawing back to look down at her, something soft and tender in his expression that she had never seen there before. She did not know what to do with that expression or how to respond to it, so instead she reached for the buttons keeping her bra fastened, and made short order of removing it and tossing it to the floor. His gaze tilted from tender to heated at the sight of her bare breasts, and Georgie—who apparently could not be trusted to keep her mouth shut—found herself saying, in a jesting sort of tone, "Nothing to write home about, I know, but—"

Any further speech was forestalled by his hand on her mouth. "You're beautiful," he said simply, and when he looked at her like that—when she could *see* the physical proof of the way his body responded to her—she could not even bring herself to argue with him.

After a moment, he drew his hand away so that he could direct his attention to the buttons on her trousers, undoing each one with care and then sliding her trousers down her legs, her underwear following a moment later. She should have felt embarrassed to be lying before him like this, as if she were on display, when he still had half of his clothing on—and yet, embarrassment was nowhere to be found. Nor was modesty. Instead, she bent a knee, spreading her legs a bit, and her mouth went dry at the sudden ravenous look in his eyes. He knelt on the bed, tugging her legs farther apart, and then leaned down and wasted no time at all in putting his mouth and tongue to work at her center.

Georgie arched off the bed at the first long lick of his tongue, a wordless cry escaping her lips; she might not be a virgin, but she was beginning to think that her education thus far had been shamefully limited. She felt Sebastian smiling against her, which should have annoyed her, but she could barely even remember her own name at the moment, so emotions such as annoyance were clearly far from her grasp. Instead, she reached down, slid her fingers into his hair, and proceeded to dissolve beneath his mouth. At one point, he drew back slightly from where he had a finger working inside her and his tongue busily centered on one particular spot, and asked, sounding a bit breathlessly, "Did you just start listing breeds of roses?"

Georgie glanced down at him from where she had been staring unseeingly at the ceiling. "I honestly have no idea."

"I'm going to take that as a compliment," he said with a grin, and bent his head once more, until, with a cry, Georgie shattered.

It was sometime later that she became aware of her surroundings again—the soft quilt beneath her; the cool air on her bare, heated skin; the glide of Sebastian's index finger up and down her arm. He was lying on his side next to her, his trousers having been discarded, his erection tenting his cotton shorts; he was propped on an elbow, watching her face with something that almost looked like . . . nervousness.

"Why," she asked, once she felt capable of forming words in human speech, "do you look like that?"

"Was it all right for you?" His tone was uncertain.

She reached over to still his hand, which continued to move restlessly up and down her arm. "You must know it was. You have to know how good at that you are." She hesitated, searching his face. Despite all of her previous teasing, she suddenly did not want to mention his long romantic history—did not want to think about anyone else, in the intimate quiet of this room, this bed, the small universe that seemed to contain the two of them, and only them.

"I've never received any complaints," he said, "but I've never cared this much—about making it good."

Georgie looked at him for a long moment, trying to work out the perfect words to utter—and then, ultimately, realized that she didn't need words at all. She reached for him, pulling him down atop her, relishing the feeling of his weight on her, of his bare chest against hers. Her arms wound around his neck as their lips met, the kiss slow and tender. Georgie slid a hand down his back, feeling the muscles tense beneath her touch, until she reached the waistband of his shorts.

"Do you think you might see your way to removing these?" she asked, wrenching her mouth away from his. "They're about to be very, very in the way."

"Gladly," he said, pulling away from her and shifting onto his knees, making quick work of the buttons. Before Georgie could fully appreciate the view, he was in motion, hopping off the bed and reaching for his discarded trousers. A moment later, he triumphantly brandished a packet at her—a condom, she realized.

"Prepared, were you?" she asked dryly, rising onto her elbows.

"Eternally optimistic," he said cheerfully, making his way back to the bed with record speed, and dedicating his attention to the sensitive spot where her neck met her shoulder, his hands occupied by her breasts. From there, her attention seemed to fragment, landing on small details that burned themselves like a brand into her mind:

His fingers between her legs, slipping easily through the slickness there.

The feeling of his cock, firm in her hand as her fingers slipped round it.

The hoarse, guttural sound that seemed to tear itself from his throat at her touch.

The veins in his neck as he gritted his teeth and drew back, breathing heavily, to roll on the condom.

The sudden pressure, the fullness as he entered her and

paused for a moment, their breathing ragged in each other's ears, their hearts pounding in time.

And then, suddenly: movement, friction, the feeling of sparks working their way down her spine. She wrapped her arms around his neck, braced her feet on the bed, and met his thrusts with her own.

And by the time they had finished—with his fingers once again between her legs and one of her legs hooked tightly round his hip, his face buried in her throat, words entirely beyond them both—Georgie had a sudden, ridiculous thought:

There really was something to be said for a romantic subplot in a mystery after all.

It was late—sometime well past midnight. The house was silent, and Georgie's room alternated between moonlight and shadows—she'd not drawn the curtains, having been distracted by other, more pressing concerns. She and Sebastian lay in bed, their legs tangled together. She'd thought him asleep—perhaps he had been—until a moment earlier, when he stirred and reached for her, wordlessly pulling her closer against him. She stiffened for a moment, and then, hesitantly, allowed her head to sink onto his shoulder.

She discovered that it felt rather nice.

His hand came to the tangle of hair at the nape of her neck, and slowly ran through the frizzy curls, his fingers occasionally catching in a knot. She felt her limbs grow heavy—she'd thought sleep was still out of reach, her mind too busy turning over the evening's revelations (both mystery-related and personal), but beneath his touch, she felt herself being lulled into stillness of both body and mind.

"What is your sister's name?" she asked after several minutes of this, the words coming a bit more sluggishly than they would have normally done.

His hand stilled for a brief moment, then resumed its motion. "Julia," he said, his voice quiet. A hesitation, and then he added, "My brother is Charles. Why do you ask?"

Georgie was quiet for a second or two, trying to work out how to put her thoughts into words. "It feels odd," she said at last. "To feel that I don't know anything about you, when we've just . . ." She raised a hand, sketching a vague gesture in the air. "You know."

He was silent for long enough that she began to wonder if he was going to reply at all. His hand continued its steady, rhythmic movement through her hair. At last, he said, "I think you know me better than you believe. Better than my family knows me, even after a lifetime."

Georgie felt somehow both pleased and saddened by this notion. She *wanted* to know him, and to be known by him, she realized. It was not simply that he was handsome—that he was flirtatious—that she'd wanted to go to bed with him because when he kissed her, she forgot her own name. It *was* all of that, but it, too, was the fact that each time she spoke to him, she felt that the Sebastian she thought she knew was shifting before her very eyes—his mask being slowly cast aside, the man behind it being gradually revealed.

A man that she found herself, almost against her will, liking a frightening amount.

She shifted more fully onto her side, raising her head slightly so that she could peer down into his face, illuminated by moonlight.

"Thank you," she said, and he raised a flirtatious eyebrow at her, his eyes tracking down the bare skin of her throat and shoulders. "Not for that," she amended sternly, and his mouth quirked. "I mean . . . it's been rather nice. Getting the chance to know you."

His eyes met hers, softening, and he reached a hand up to cup her cheek. "Don't say that."

Her brow furrowed. "Why not?"

"It sounds like you're saying goodbye," he said, tucking her hair behind her ear. "And I've no intention of allowing you to do any such thing."

She opened her mouth to protest—to remind him of his looming departure, of his life in London, of all the reasons that this could only ever be fleeting—but he raised his head and silenced her with a kiss. It was tender at first—the sort of kiss that felt like a conversation without words. After a few moments, however, his arm came around her waist, urging her on top of him, and all thoughts of practical concerns, of logical objections, of anything other than his mouth and his hands and his naked body against hers, were pushed to the back of her mind.

And for a blissfully long while, she didn't think about anything at all.

CHAPTER TWENTY-ONE

Tuesday dawned damp, dreary, and very, very busy.

The day commenced in less-than-relaxing fashion, with Georgie awakening warm and sleepy in her comfortable bed. Warmer than usual. *Very* warm.

Because there was a bare-chested man pressed against her back.

"Sebastian!" she hissed, scrambling to a sitting position before she was even fully conscious, belatedly grasping for a sheet to pull to her chest. "You have to leave."

"Hmmm," he mumbled, and she looked down at him, his golden hair tousled, his face oddly young in slumber. She'd been alarmed to learn the night before that the only thing more attractive than the sight of him in his expensive jumpers was the sight of him in nothing at all. She allowed herself one gratuitous look at the lean muscles of his arms and chest, then reached over, seized a pillow, and bashed him across the face with it.

That, at least, had set proceedings in motion.

He'd stumbled into his clothing—discarded in exceptionally haphazard fashion the night before—and then she'd frantically ushered him out the door so that he might return to his bedroom. With a quick glance down the hall to ensure that neither Papa nor Abigail had decided to choose that precise moment to wander around, she'd more or less shoved him out the door, and had nearly closed it behind him, giddy with the sense of having got away with something, when it was pushed open once again—

So that he could take three rapid steps toward her, seize her face in his hands, and give her a kiss so deep, so lingering, that she thought it should probably be illegal this early in the morning.

"We are going to solve a murder today," he informed her in a low voice when he drew back. "And then, once we've done that, you and I are going to talk."

He dropped his hands, swept her an absurdly courtly bow, and then was gone, leaving Georgie to slump back against the doorframe and wonder, dimly, if all her limbs were still attached.

"Ahem," came a voice from the hallway, and Georgie whirled around to find her father emerging from the kitchen stairs in his house slippers.

"Papa," she said, acutely conscious of the dressing gown she'd hastily flung herself into and of the love bite on her throat she'd caught a glimpse of in the mirror. "Good . . . morning." She feigned a coughing fit to buy herself a bit more time.

Papa looked unfazed. "Glad to see Fletcher-Ford is awake,"

he said mildly, walking past her down the corridor. "I'd like to ask him about last year's Oxford-Cambridge rugby union match at breakfast."

And with that, he was gone. It was only several long moments later that Georgie managed to wrench her jaw shut.

○○○

"It is too early for scheming," Arthur said darkly, a couple of hours later. Georgie had waited as long as she could before phoning him that morning—and had shown up at the door to his tiny flat at the not-entirely-respectable hour of half eight, Sebastian in tow.

Upon first arrival, Arthur appeared to be alone, but not five minutes after she arrived, there was a knock on the door, and Constable Lexington was revealed to be on the other side of it. "Hello," she said upon opening the door. "I brought you a scone."

"I happened to be passing," he began a bit stiffly, "and I thought—"

"Constable Lexington," Georgie interrupted, "why don't you refrain from insulting my intelligence and just . . . not bother?"

A brief, startled silence; Georgie glanced over to see Arthur suppressing a grin, and he raised an eyebrow at Lexington, who was carefully avoiding Georgie's eyes.

"All right," he said, after a long moment, and then he added, "But only because I want a scone."

And Georgie, rather startled, realized that that had been a *joke*.

Half an hour later, Arthur and Lexington had their marching orders. "I think all the files from resolved cases are in the back of some closet or other," Lexington said, draining the dregs of the cup of coffee Arthur had given him. "No one will likely even notice me digging around."

"But you can be back here by one?" Georgie pressed, a bit anxious. There were an awful lot of moving pieces to this plan.

"I don't see why not, barring some sudden murder investigation that requires my attention—and given what you've worked out, that seems unlikely."

"Has anyone at the constabulary noticed that you've been preoccupied this past week?" she asked curiously.

Lexington's mouth tightened and then eased. "I've learned, over the past few years," he said, his voice even, "that no one at the Gloucestershire constabulary cares overmuch what you get up to, so long as you don't make anyone else's job too difficult, and don't rock the boat in any way."

"How noble," Arthur muttered, his eyes on his own coffee cup, and Lexington shot a sharp look at him.

"I *told* you—"

"Not now," Arthur interrupted, his tone a bit curt. The two men looked at each other for a long moment, some sort of silent conversation taking place that made Georgie feel like a bit of a third wheel.

"Right," she said brightly, standing to take her own teacup back into Arthur's tiny, cramped kitchen. "Well, I'll leave you to it, I suppose—and we'll meet at the Shorn Sheep at one?"

"Where are you off to, then?" Arthur asked with a wary glance at her.

"To see Dr. Severin," she said.

"Why?" Arthur asked suspiciously. "If you're going to try to warn him off Abigail, then Georgie, I really think you ought to reconsider—"

"I'm not," Georgie said simply. "But I *do* have a hunch that I'd like him to confirm."

※

She might not have intended to warn Severin away from her sister, but she still was somewhat surprised—and not entirely pleased—to arrive at his cottage to find Abigail, of all people, standing on the front steps.

"Georgie!" Abigail at least had the decency to look a bit guilty. "What—er—"

"What am I doing here?" Georgie finished. "I might ask you the same."

"Well," Abigail said, creating more syllables than naturally existed in that word, "if you *must* know, I'm here to collect a packet of herbs Tom"—Georgie blinked at her sister's use of Severin's given name—"wants me to give to Mrs. Chester when I'm at the Scrumptious Scone later."

"Herbs for what?" Georgie asked.

Abigail shrugged. "Some sort of joint trouble. He has a tea he claims will help. He's quite knowledgeable about these sorts of things, you know," she added, a note of defensive pride in her voice. "He says lots of doctors think that medicinal herbs are simply something that ignorant country wives fret over, but that many of them actually work quite well."

"Does he," Georgie said. Her mind landed on that letter from Severin to Penbaker, on whose reverse side Sebastian had typed his test sentence on the typewriter. Severin had advised Penbaker to brew some sort of medicinal tea for joint pain, if she recalled correctly.

"Abigail, did you—oh!" Severin appeared at the door, a paper packet in one hand, and he looked surprised to see Georgie. "Miss Radcliffe. Hello." His voice—warm with affection when he'd uttered her sister's name—went considerably more guarded upon spotting Georgie, and she realized in a flash that she was being rather horrible about this entire thing.

"Hello," Georgie said, then paused for a moment before adding, "You might call me Georgie, if you want." She glanced at Abigail and saw her sister's face brighten. "I wanted to ask you a few questions about the day Mr. Penbaker died, if you don't mind?"

"Not at all," Dr. Severin said, handing the paper packet to Abigail. "Did you want to come in?"

"No." Georgie shook her head. "Or, rather—this won't take long. It's just a couple of questions, really. Were you still prescribing Mr. Penbaker some sort of medicinal tea for joint pain at the time of his death?"

Severin nodded. "Nettle and willow bark. It's an old remedy, but it works well. His wife had just come to pick up a new packet of herbs from me that morning."

"Had she," Georgie repeated, growing more certain by the second that her hunch was correct. "And do you recall the time you called on Mrs. Penbaker and her husband? She said it would have been just after two that she would have arrived home—does that sound correct?"

"No," Severin said slowly, his dark brows pinched in thought. "It's funny you should ask—I always keep a record in my notes of the times I attend patients, and I was just looking through them again this morning, searching for something else. It was around four that Mrs. Penbaker phoned me."

"And Abigail, you're certain that the fete planning committee meeting did not run long that day?" Georgie asked her sister.

Abigail nodded. "I remember it particularly, because *I* offered to do a dramatic recitation of 'The Lady of Shalott'—just as a trial run, so they could see how impressive it would be!—but I was told we were out of time, because it was a minute till two, and we couldn't run over."

"So you were done at two," Georgie said, "and Mrs. Penbaker did not phone Dr. Severin until after four. Leaving two hours between when her meeting ended and when she notified the doctor."

Severin and Abigail frowned. "That doesn't make any sense," Severin said. "She told me she'd just arrived home and found him in that state—I remember it particularly, because she couldn't tell me when he'd started feeling unwell."

"It *does* make sense," Georgie said, "if those hours in between were spent poisoning her husband." She met Severin's gaze directly. "And I think I know how she did it—and I'm going to get her to confess to it."

By one o'clock, their plans were in place. Mrs. Penbaker was usually at home eating lunch, after a morning spent at the village hall, giving tours of the murder exhibition. They met, as arranged, outside the Shorn Sheep, though Georgie's thoughts—of poisonous herbs and murderous plots—were derailed briefly when she caught sight of Sebastian. Or, more accurately, Sebastian's knees.

"What on earth are you wearing?" she demanded, as soon as he approached the pub; he'd returned to Radcliffe Hall to make a telephone call—and, evidently, to change his outfit.

He glanced down at his attire, his expression wounded. "These are my tennis whites."

"I see that, thank you. Is there a particular reason you're dressed for an afternoon of sport when we need to go trick a murderess into confessing?"

"Knees," he said simply, slipping a pair of sunglasses on to complete the air of glamorous-city-boy-gets-a-spot-of-exercise-in-the-country that was positively *thick* around him. A cream-colored summer-weight jumper was tossed casually over his shoulders. He looked as though he should have appeared in a catalogue.

"Knees," she repeated now, eyeing him suspiciously and determinedly *not* eyeing the joints in question.

"Yes," he said cheerfully. "Ladies love them. You cannot *imagine* the things I have got up to after the merest glimpse of my knees in my tennis attire."

"Charming," she said shrewishly.

He glanced sideways and slipped his arm through hers. "I'm not getting my hopes up for later today, but I do cherish a small dream that the pattern might continue."

"If you think that I am the sort of woman to allow you to

remove my clothing simply because you prance around looking all *golden* and *athletic*—"

"You are not doing much to discourage that small dream, Georgie," he said cheerfully, and tucked her more firmly against his side.

"Be quiet. Do you really think Mrs. Penbaker is going to take one look at your knees and confess her evil plot to us at the drop of a hat?"

"Probably not," he admitted. "But I've learned not to underestimate the allure of a pair of exposed knees on the female brain—or the male one," he added, with what he clearly considered to be admirable egalitarian spirit.

"Of course not," she agreed blandly. "I doubt you ever think about much *other* than knees, in fact."

He grinned at her and opened his mouth to reply, but at that precise moment, Arthur arrived, Lexington on his heels, preparing to go on an incredibly well-timed and not-at-all-suspicious patrol of the village.

"Hello," Arthur said, splitting a curious glance between Georgie and Sebastian, who were—she realized belatedly—looking rather cozy. "Ready to go get a confession?"

"Sebastian's knees are ready, at least," Georgie said blandly, and then set off at a march down the street, all three men trailing behind her.

⁂

Mrs. Penbaker answered the door within a few seconds of Arthur's knock, her pleasantly curious expression cooling rapidly once she realized who was on her doorstep.

"Oh. Hello."

"Good afternoon, Mrs. Penbaker," Arthur said with a nod; he and Georgie had discussed the plan at length and had determined that for their ruse to be convincing, it would be best for him to take the lead. "I hope you don't mind giving us a few minutes of your time—I've recently learned some information that I imagine you'll be interested to hear."

Mrs. Penbaker visibly paled at this, but otherwise gave no sign of distress, merely hesitating for a long moment before saying, with a bit of reluctance, "All right. Won't you come in?"

They followed her into the house, and once she'd closed the door behind them, she said, "I'll just put the kettle on, shall I? If you'd like to wait in the sitting room—"

"I'm happy to join you in the kitchen," Sebastian said, his voice entirely pleasant but a note of steel present beneath the politeness.

In a further sign that Mrs. Penbaker had some notion of what was afoot, she merely nodded and allowed them to follow her deeper into the house, which was just as obsessively tidy as it had been on Georgie and Sebastian's previous clandestine visit. The kitchen was brightly lit and cheerful; there was a blue willow teapot set on the counter, a teacup waiting next to it. Mrs. Penbaker crossed to the hob and lit it, then turned back to face Georgie, Arthur, and Sebastian, crossing her arms over her chest in a posture that looked instinctively defensive. "What brings you here today?"

Arthur cleared his throat. "We are here because I have received a tip that you are shortly to be arrested for your husband's murder."

To Arthur's credit, he managed to avoid any unnecessary melodrama while leveling this accusation; he stated it simply, without any great fanfare, and it was all the more effective as a result. Mrs. Penbaker, meanwhile, went very still; she did not move an inch from her position by the stove, her face rather paler than usual.

"Based on what evidence?" she asked, after a moment had passed in which no one said anything, as if all present were trying to gauge where the firmest ground was to place a cautious foot.

"My source did not have all the details," Arthur said, "but this source seemed very certain that you had been responsible for poisoning your husband with some herbs that he acquired from the doctor to use as pain relief. This was, evidently, a known habit of his, and it would have been easy enough to poison him by adding something toxic to the blend."

A flicker of something in Mrs. Penbaker's expression, gone before Georgie could identify it.

"If that hunch is all that the police have to go on," she said, injecting a note of forced bravado into her voice, "then I hardly think—"

As if on cue (because it more or less was), Lexington suddenly came into view outside the kitchen window, walking up the narrow lane that abutted the house on one side. The back entrance to the house, via the kitchen garden and door, was accessed through a small gate in the wall on this side of the house.

"I say," Sebastian said, sounding mildly interested, as though the events playing out in the Penbaker kitchen were merely a somewhat diverting amateur theatrical, "isn't that Lexington now?"

"By Jove, you're right!" Arthur said eagerly, reaching into his pocket for his notebook. "Well spotted, Fletcher-Ford. I just need to run and see if I can get a quote from him first...."

With that, he was out the kitchen door and hurrying through the garden. Knowing that their time was short—there was, after all, only so long that Mrs. Penbaker would believe that Arthur would delay a police officer on his way to make an arrest, before coming to realize that Lexington was not en route to any such task—Georgie turned back to Mrs. Penbaker.

"If there is anything you would wish us to know," she said carefully now, drawing Mrs. Penbaker's gaze back to her from where it was stuck, horror-struck, on the events transpiring outside the window, "now would be the time to speak. Based on my previous experience with the local constabulary, once they have a suspect in mind, they are . . . unreceptive to any information that might contradict it."

"You don't say," Mrs. Penbaker said bitterly. "I sent them an anonymous note telling them that they'd got the wrong person when they arrested Mrs. Marble for her husband's murder, but nothing came of it."

"And how," Georgie asked, trying to suppress her eagerness, "did you know that they'd arrested the wrong person?"

"Because I knew who the culprit was," Mrs. Penbaker said simply, shrugging. She eyed Georgie for a moment, her expression difficult to read. Georgie had the distinct impression that she was being sized up, her character being judged. She straightened her spine, met Mrs. Penbaker's eyes directly, and waited.

"Mrs. Marble did not kill her husband," Mrs. Penbaker said at last, still looking at Georgie with some complicated mixture of resignation, admiration, and... amusement? Georgie didn't understand it—something here did not make sense, up to and including Mrs. Penbaker's present manner. "She didn't kill her husband," she repeated, her voice firmer now, "just as I did not kill mine."

"Then who did?" Georgie asked, raising an eyebrow skeptically. She suddenly understood Fitzgibbons's fondness for his decorative monocle; she wished she had something to lift to her eye in keen speculation right now.

"My husband," Mrs. Penbaker said simply, and then turned to quickly take the kettle off the hob as it began to boil.

"Your husband... killed himself?" Georgie repeated blankly, feeling significantly less intelligent than usual.

Mrs. Penbaker nodded, as though pleased that a pupil had finally wrapped their head around a particularly tricky new concept. She spooned tea leaves into the pot, then poured the boiling water in, behaving for all the world as if this were merely an ordinary teatime visit. "Correct. It wasn't intentional—I promise you, Bertie thought far too highly of himself to ever take his own life—but he also, in a similar vein, thought he was somewhat cleverer than he actually was."

"Do you mean to say that *he* added poison to his own tea?" Georgie asked incredulously; this was too stupid to be countenanced.

Mrs. Penbaker pressed her lips together, almost as if she were suppressing a smile, which did very little to convince Georgie that she wasn't a murderess. "You might have noticed,

Miss Radcliffe, that my husband was not terribly knowledgeable about herbs and plants."

Georgie very nearly rolled her eyes at this understatement. "That's certainly true," she agreed, rather than voice her full thoughts.

"He did a bit of research, I understand—wanted an herb that would make him ill but not actually kill him... something that would prove to the police that his tea had been poisoned, but not something that would result in death."

Georgie frowned. "What did he choose?"

"Well." Mrs. Penbaker laced her hands together. "He chose foxglove, because he read an Agatha Christie book in which people at a dinner party were poisoned by foxglove but lived."

"Yes," Georgie said slowly. "The leaves will make you very ill, but it's not usually fatal unless you extract the digitalis."

"Right." Mrs. Penbaker looked at Georgie expectantly, as if waiting for her to put the pieces together.

"Ah." That was Sebastian, suddenly, looking around the room idly until his gaze at last landed on Mrs. Penbaker. "What did he mistake for foxglove, then?"

Mrs. Penbaker gave him a thin smile. "Monkshood."

Georgie's mind suddenly flicked to the poison garden at the village hall—and to the stakes she had switched so that they labeled the correct plants. "They were mislabeled!" she said excitedly, feeling the rush that came with working out a thorny knot in a case. "In the poison garden at the exhibition—foxglove and monkshood were directly next to each other, and they were mislabeled! I switched the stakes myself when I noticed last week."

Mrs. Penbaker shook her head. "His own fault—he was the one who insisted that we needed those ridiculous stakes that looked like knives in the poison garden. He switched out all the labels himself; I suppose I should have checked to ensure he'd done it correctly."

"So he clipped a bit of monkshood," Georgie said, "thinking it was foxglove, and ... added it to tea?"

Mrs. Penbaker nodded. "He didn't realize his mistake; immediately after he drank his tea, he was positively gloating about how clever his plan was. I gather in some of the detective novels he'd taken to reading, there were dramatic confessions from the villains, and he couldn't resist the opportunity to try his hand at it. He wanted to pin the poisoning on me."

Sebastian shook his head, tutting. "Usually in the novels, the confession is made to the detective—or at least to someone else while the detective is unknowingly within earshot. Seems a bit of a waste to make a dramatic confession to his wife alone."

Georgie shot him a repressive look. His eyes widened innocently. "What? I'm a man with an appreciation for dramatic flair, and I can't bear to see shoddy work."

"Why did he want you to be blamed, though?" Georgie asked, still not entirely understanding all the forces at play here. "Why did he need to poison himself at all?"

"Because," Mrs. Penbaker said matter-of-factly, "I'd figured out that he was the one orchestrating all the murders—and I knew that he'd killed Mr. Marble himself, and I confronted him."

Georgie and Sebastian exchanged a startled look. "Mr. Penbaker killed Mr. Marble?" Georgie ventured; the revelations were coming so thick and fast at this point that she could scarcely keep up with them.

"I wouldn't have thought of it if I hadn't had a conversation with Mrs. Marble the week before her husband died. She was complaining of mice in her kitchen, and how she didn't want to poison them because she was afraid to keep arsenic in her house—apparently someone died of an accidental arsenic poisoning in her village when she was a girl, and she's been nervous about it ever since." She shook her head. "So when her husband died of arsenic-laced wine, and my husband had been round to visit them the evening before, and I suddenly discovered that our bottle of arsenic was missing . . . well, it seemed obvious to me." She shrugged. "I'd already had my suspicions, over the previous months—something about all the cases seemed too convenient—and once the Murder Tourists started showing up, it just seemed to perfectly align with what my husband wanted for the village, and I started paying closer attention.

"Once I started looking more closely into his comings and goings, I learned of his affair with Miss Halifax, but at that point I wasn't going to make any sort of accusation that might put him on his guard around me, so I simply pretended to not notice. Men are terribly eager to believe that their long-suffering wives are somehow competent enough to manage an entire household and know the location of every single item they have misplaced around the house at the drop of a hat, all while simultaneously being so innocent and naive that it would never occur to them that their husbands might seek pleasure outside the marital bed. In other words, it wasn't difficult to keep him from realizing I'd worked it out."

"Bad form," Sebastian said, shaking his head. "It never does to let one's spouse know there's a bit of horizontal refreshment on the side."

Georgie regarded him stonily. "I would try not to sound like *such* an expert on the matter if I were you."

"Well," Mrs. Penbaker said, "I foolishly thought that if I confronted my husband with my suspicions, he'd . . . I don't know. Confess? Turn himself in to the police?" She shook her head again. "I just didn't want anyone else to die. I thought that if he knew that I suspected him, he'd be too frightened to continue. So I told him that I knew, the day before he died. Naturally, his reaction was simply to laugh at me—he was so convinced that no one would take me seriously, not when it was my word against his. But, just for good measure, he decided to stage a poisoning with tea that *I* would presumably have prepared for him, to ensure that I was sent to jail and he could stay here and reap the rewards." She looked more irritated than sad. "He even made sure that I was the one to collect his packet of herbs from Dr. Severin that morning, so it would look as though I'd had the perfect opportunity to poison him, and then he waited until I came home that afternoon to brew the tea. But then he gave himself a fatal dose of monkshood instead."

"And you summoned Dr. Severin," Georgie said. "But it was too late."

Mrs. Penbaker nodded, looking at Georgie directly. "He was horribly dizzy and nauseated at first—I think he planned to phone the police to pin the blame on me, but he was too ill to manage any such thing. I wasn't certain what to do, initially—I didn't ring for Dr. Severin at once, thinking Bertie would recover. But then I looked in the kitchen and spotted a few extra of the leaves that he'd used for the tea. Since I was the one who organized the planting of the poison garden, I recognized them immediately as monkshood. I rang Dr. Severin to say that my husband was unwell, but by the time he arrived, Bertie was dead. And I . . ." Here, she trailed off. "I didn't know that anyone would believe my account. So I tossed the leaves in the rubbish bin and allowed Dr. Severin to believe it was a heart attack—it just seemed easiest. I had no way to prove my suspicions regarding Mr. Marble's death, after all, and it seemed best to let things lie—I was worried that if anyone started investigating Bertie, his death might get a second look and I might be blamed after all. And then, in the village hall the other day, I heard you speaking about the distinctive key on the typewriter used for one of the letters, and realized that there *was* something linking Bertie and myself to the crimes after all, and I . . . well, I panicked a bit. As I said, I didn't think the police would believe me."

She looked, suddenly, rather exhausted—but also a bit lighter for having told her tale. "But now . . . whatever evidence the police think they have, I'm happy to tell them this entire story—though I daresay it might go easier for me if you believed me, too, and were willing to support me."

Georgie glanced quickly at Sebastian as Mrs. Penbaker turned back to the counter, pouring cups of tea, then asking, casually, over her shoulder, "Milk? Sugar?"

Georgie held Sebastian's eyes for a second longer, a quick, silent conversation passing between them, before Sebastian broke her gaze, turned back to Mrs. Penbaker, and said, "Both, if you please."

He accepted his cup from her, and—despite the fact that, not five minutes earlier, they'd more or less accused her of killing her husband with a poisoned cup of tea—took a long, deliberate sip.

So Georgie supposed that answered her question. "The police know nothing," she said frankly, laying all her cards on the table as she reached out to accept her teacup from Mrs. Penbaker. "We were bluffing—hoping to trick you into making a confession."

Mrs. Penbaker's eyebrows rose slightly. She glanced back out the window. "Then Constable Lexington—"

"A coincidence," Georgie said hastily, not wanting any word of Lexington's role in this to make it back to his superiors and somehow get him in trouble. She could see that he and Arthur were now standing very close together in the shadow of Mrs. Penbaker's kitchen wall, nearly out of sight, their heads bent toward each other, deep in conversation. Georgie watched them for a moment, then shook her head and looked away. "But we've not told anyone of our suspicions, so you won't be in any trouble. And since no one thought there was anything suspicious about your husband's death in the first place, I suppose we could let things lie ... except there's the matter of Mrs. Marble."

"I wonder," Sebastian said, his brow slightly furrowed, "if we could perhaps ... plant a bit of evidence."

Georgie crossed her arms and leaned against the kitchen counter, considering. "The typewriter," she said, snapping her fingers. "If we could forge a note from Mr. Penbaker, some sort of confession..."

"Do you think that would work?" Mrs. Penbaker asked uncertainly.

"Perhaps," Georgie said, exchanging a glance with Sebastian. "It's worth a shot, though. I mean, unless he kept a journal where he confessed all his crimes, which would obviously be the most—"

Here, Georgie broke off, her mind racing.

"You're very lovely when you're thinking," Sebastian said, his eyes on her, and she refused to find this romantic, despite the fact that a small voice was informing her that this might be the most romantic thing anyone had ever said—to her, or anyone else.

Instead, she turned to Mrs. Penbaker, her eyes wide. "Can we use your telephone? We need to ring Miss Halifax."

Mrs. Penbaker's eyebrows rose. "Miss Halifax," she repeated. "The woman who was having an affair with my husband."

"The woman," Georgie corrected, "who introduced your husband to Mrs. Christie's novels in the first place—and the woman to whom he gave a draft of a novel he was writing."

"You don't think... he based it on the truth?" Sebastian said, a smile playing at the corner of his mouth.

"Surely even Bertie wasn't that stupid," Mrs. Penbaker said.

"Oh," Georgie said, growing more confident by the moment, "I think he was *exactly* that stupid, actually." She lifted her chin. "Your telephone, please? I think we'll find that Miss Halifax is in possession of just the evidence we need."

CHAPTER TWENTY-TWO

"You know," Georgie said the following evening, "I never thought I'd say this, but thank goodness for a man who wanted to write a novel."

"Excuse me," Arthur objected, taking a sip of his ginger beer.

"I'm sorry," Georgie said, "but have you ever read a man's attempts to describe a woman's inner life? You can hardly blame me for preferring novels written by women." She allowed herself an eye roll. "But I think I'll have to reconsider this stance, now that a man's literary ambitions have led to the clearing of an innocent woman's name."

"And also to a murder," Lexington pointed out.

"I don't think we can blame that on his dreams of literary glory," Georgie said, shaking her head. "The obsession with tourism came before the attempt to write a novel." She took a small sip of her whisky, then leaned back against the fabric of the booth.

It was fairly late; the various Murder Tourists who had descended upon the Shorn Sheep had been nearly impossible to be rid of that evening, hanging onto every single detail of Georgie, Arthur, and Sebastian's explanations of the twisted plot of Mr. Penbaker that had gripped Buncombe-upon-Woolly for the past year.

"I can't believe a distinctive key on a typewriter got him caught," Miss de Vere had said with a disapproving sniff. "How *amateur*. A Detective Devotee would never."

"Ahem," Georgie said, extremely dryly. "I hope that a Detective Devotee would never commit a crime in the first place."

"And yet, you thought just that, only two days ago," Miss de Vere said, with a cheeky smile. "I've never been a red herring before!" She sighed a bit despondently. "London will seem so dull after this."

"Won't you have a wedding to plan?" Georgie asked, curious.

Miss de Vere and Miss Singh exchanged a look. "Well. No, actually."

Georgie blinked. "What do you mean?"

"I mean," Miss de Vere said patiently, "that I haven't got a fiancé."

"But," Georgie said. "But."

"I come into my inheritance when I turn twenty-five next year," she explained. "I convinced a friend of mine to propose to me, because my parents were driving me mad. He was about to set off on a two-year trip to conduct field research in Peru. By the time he's back and we call off the wedding, I'll have my inheritance and be able to buy my own house." She looked vaguely smug as she explained all this.

"But why," Georgie began, then trailed off when her gaze landed on Miss Singh. "Oh. I see."

"It is helpful to have such a *close friend* who is a fellow Detective Devotee," Miss Singh said innocently. "All our Murder Tourism seems just a harmless bit of holiday-making for two young ladies." She blinked, wide-eyed.

Georgie was beginning to think she'd rather underestimated the Murder Tourists.

Now, however, she was alone with her friends—Arthur, and Lexington, and . . . Sebastian.

Friend didn't feel like quite the right word to describe him.

Events had proceeded rapidly since yesterday afternoon; Miss Halifax had quite willingly produced the incriminating novel draft in question. ("I only read the first two pages," she'd confessed. "It was dreadful. But apparently I should have stuck with it.") Constable Lexington's investigations at police headquarters had revealed that the false will in the second murder, the letter revealing Lady Tunbridge's secret in the third, and the forged letter allegedly from Mrs. Marble had all been produced by Mr. Penbaker's typewriter, with its distinctive "O."

"But not the blackmail letters from the vicar?" Georgie asked, citing the first of the village's murders.

Lexington had shaken his head. "No. It would seem that Penbaker had nothing to do with that."

"I suppose it's where he got the idea in the first place," Georgie said thoughtfully. "Is this enough evidence to prove his guilt?"

"I don't know how a trial would shake out, if he were still alive," Lexington replied, "but combined with Mrs. Penbaker's evidence about their missing arsenic, and her husband's visit to the Marbles the night before the murder, it should certainly be enough to see Mrs. Marble released." He sighed. "This has been an utter shambles of an investigation from start to finish." He was looking somewhat grim about the mouth; evidently, he'd had a conversation with Chief Constable Humphreys about Detective Inspector Harriday having leaked information to Miss Lettercross, only to be told that it was none of his concern. He did not seem terribly enamored of his profession at the moment, for all that the day overall had been a success.

Lexington's professional woes aside, however, they were all in a somewhat celebratory mood that evening—Harry had produced a bottle of particularly fine whisky that he saved for special occasions, and they were now sipping their drinks in the cozy glow of the fire, the atmosphere affectionate and relaxed.

"I'm rather going to miss this," Sebastian said, leaning back in his seat in the booth next to Georgie. He was even more handsome by firelight, his hair gleaming like a new coin. He'd loosened the top couple of buttons of his collared shirt, and Georgie could see the golden column of his throat.

She swallowed—and then, like a dash of cold water, his words belatedly registered. "You're . . . leaving tomorrow, then." She tried to play off this observation as light and casual, but didn't think she'd remotely managed it. If the way everyone else was suddenly looking into their drink was any indication, she *definitely* hadn't.

"I've a bit of business to attend to in London," Sebastian

said, and then, before he—or Georgie—could say anything else, Arthur added, "Speaking of London."

"You've accepted the position with *The Times?*" Georgie guessed.

"I have," Arthur agreed. "I'll start next month. Should give me time to sort out a flat. And . . . other arrangements." He stole a glance at Lexington.

"Well," Georgie said, draining the last of her whisky with a bit of a grimace and standing. "That's lovely. But it's been a long day, and I think I'd like to get to bed."

Sebastian was on his feet immediately. "I'll walk you."

Georgie waved him off. "I'll be fine. You should stay here—no reason for you to come home early, too."

"Georgie—"

"I have my bicycle," she said curtly. "I don't think you can keep up."

And then, before anyone could offer any further objections—or even much in the way of a goodbye—she was gone, out the front door and down the steps to where her bicycle leaned against the front gate, waiting for her.

"Georgie."

Sebastian's voice was quiet, but it startled her nonetheless; she hadn't heard his footsteps. She turned and found him a half dozen feet away, hands in his pockets, watching her with an unreadable expression on his face.

"I told you I didn't need an escort home," she said, the words sounding more clipped than she'd intended. "You're leaving tomorrow, anyway—it's not as though I need you to walk with me."

"I wanted to speak to you about that, actually," he said, his voice still quiet, more serious than she'd ever heard it.

And, suddenly, she was gripped by a desperate desire to avoid whatever conversation he was about to attempt with her. She didn't want to hear his pretty words about how much he "appreciated their time together," or something along those lines. She didn't want to think about the feeling of his mouth on hers, or of how the muscles of his bare back had felt beneath her hands, or of how peculiarly safe she had felt tucked in his arms with her back pressed to his chest. And, somehow, most of all, she didn't want to think of the moment last night—after they'd returned home, triumphant from the success of their meeting with Miss Halifax, and they were having celebratory cocktails with Papa and Abigail—when, as they sat next to each other on the sofa, listening to Abigail discuss her plans for the new desserts she was going to introduce at the Scrumptious Scone, Sebastian had reached his hand over, just enough to hook his little finger around Georgie's. And she'd thought, in that moment, that she had never felt less alone.

"I don't think there's anything to discuss," she said now, keeping her tone brisk. "You're going home tomorrow—I know you're fond of me, but once you're back in London, I'm sure you'll have moved on to someone new before twenty-four hours have passed. Soon, I'll be nothing but a happy memory."

"Is that what you think of me?" he asked. His voice was still low and quiet, and he took a couple of steps toward her as he spoke. "After the past week of working together, of talking, of—after the other night, do you still think of me as someone who cares for nothing except luring every woman I meet into bed?"

She reached out a hand, then yanked it back just as quickly. It was best not to touch him now. "Do you think I would have gone to bed with you if I thought that?"

"I don't know," he said, and there was the slightest bit of uncertainty in his voice, completely alien in this man who always seemed so self-assured, so *unbothered*. "You told me afterward—you said that you'd done that. Before. Which I don't care about," he added hurriedly, seeing the no-doubt-dangerous look that crossed her face at that. "Of course I don't—I'd be a raging hypocrite if I did. I don't *care* what you've done in your past, or with whom. But . . . well, I'm starting to wonder if *you* care. About me, and my past."

"You prattle on to anyone who will listen about your romantic exploits, all your conquests in town. It took me *days* to realize that it was just—"

"Just what?" he asked, more quietly still.

"Just a shield," she said simply. "A defense tactic. If no one knows the real Sebastian—not those women you slept with, not anyone you meet who sees you only as some sort of playboy—then you can't be hurt when they underestimate you. If you set their expectations low yourself, then you avoid any chance of disappointing anyone."

He was silent for a long moment, then abruptly stepped closer to her still—close enough that she had to tilt her head back to look him in the eyes.

"And if *you* convince yourself that no one in this village

could possibly do without you, then you don't have to find the courage to chase after what you really want."

Georgie took a step back. "I didn't ask for your opinion—the opinion of someone who's leaving on a train to London tomorrow, who will prance away without another thought for me."

"Why don't you ever pay attention?" he asked, reaching out to take both of her hands in his, his grip firm without being painful, strong enough that it would have taken some effort for her to wriggle herself free. "What have I done for the past week, other than try to show you how much I cannot stop thinking of you—how brilliant I think you are? How clever? How impressive, and beautiful, and maddening, and . . ." He trailed off, searching for something that seemed to evade him. "How perfect I think you are," he finished, and she blinked as if she'd been struck.

"No," she said, her cheeks flushing from his words, which in turn somewhat contrarily made her feel a bit angry, because there were few things on earth she despised more than blushing. She refused to stand here and let this man call her *perfect*, of all things—not when he wasn't going to stay. Not when he couldn't be hers.

"You were flirting, and being charming—the same as you do with everyone else. And you kissed me, and—and all the rest—because you're—well, you're bored, I suppose, since there are no other ladies in the village to romance."

"No, Georgie." He laughed then, a sharp laugh that was not at all similar to the usual winsome sound of his chuckle. "I kissed you, and all the rest, because I am falling in love with you, and I don't know how to tell you." He shook his head. "Except I suppose I just did. And I suppose it doesn't matter, if you're never going to take me seriously." He loosened his grip and raked a hand through his golden hair, mussing it just as her fingers had two nights earlier.

Georgie stood as though rooted to the spot, unable to make the words he had just uttered come together in her mind in an arrangement that made the slightest bit of sense.

I am falling in love with you.

He couldn't be.

"You can't be in love with me," she said definitively, placing her hands on her hips.

"I do think I have the right to make that decision for myself," he shot back, looking more frustrated by the moment, and if the situation hadn't been so serious, Georgie would have found herself badly tempted to laugh. Naturally they couldn't even manage a declaration of love without quarreling.

"I—you—this is absurd!" She threw her hands in the air. "You live in London!"

"You could move to London."

"No, I couldn't." She laughed incredulously. "Have you not listened to anything I've told you since you arrived? I'm needed here."

"No." He shook his head, crossing his arms over his chest. "You've made yourself needed here. You're frightened to admit that you want something more than life in Buncombe-upon-Woolly, and telling yourself that you can't possibly leave because no one could survive without you is the easiest way to avoid facing the truth."

"And what truth is that?" she shot back.

"That you want to move to London—that you want to see more of the world—that you have dreams that lie beyond this village, but you're too frightened to reach for them."

"You know nothing about my life," she said sharply, his words prickling at her skin like nettles. "You think that you can waltz into the countryside and that we'll all immediately take your word as the most important, simply because you live in London and work for a famous detective—you think that you can charm me, and that I'll suddenly fall in love with you and listen to whatever you say, believe that you are right—"

"I promise you," he said evenly, color in his cheeks to match her own, "I rarely think I am right. I've been reminded plenty of times that the opposite is usually true." There was no hint of hurt or wounded pride in his voice, and yet Georgie felt a pang in her chest at the words all the same. "And, to be clear, I think you are the cleverest woman I've ever met, and it's a privilege to be in your company, to watch you think, to watch how you work. You are brilliant, Georgie," he said, more fervent now, reaching out to take one of her hands in his once again. "And I want you to see it. To realize that you deserve your own dreams."

"I have dreams," she said, more quietly now. Admitting this aloud made her feel small, vulnerable, soft in a way that she tried to protect herself from ever feeling. A week ago, she would have laughed in the face of anyone who suggested that Sebastian Fletcher-Ford, of all people, could make her feel this way. But much had changed in the past week, somehow without her fully realizing it.

"I know you do," he agreed. "But you've convinced yourself that they're not as important as ensuring that everyone else in your life is well cared for."

"What would you know of it?" she snapped.

Rather than recoiling at her tone, he smiled. "You're trying to drive me away, and it won't work," he said. His hand was still holding hers. "You told me not three minutes ago that you saw through me. Well, I see through you, too, Georgiana Radcliffe."

"No, you don't," she said stupidly, because she couldn't think of anything else to say, when it felt as though his words had pierced her to her very core. She turned, fumbling a bit with her bicycle, and flung one leg over the seat. "And, for the last time, I told you I don't need any help getting home."

And with that, and a quick, somewhat clumsy kick of the pedals, she was off, cycling down the high street, leaving him alone in the warm glow of light that spilled from the doorway of the Shorn Sheep. She allowed herself one last glance at him, standing there looking golden and a bit rumpled and frustrated and so handsome that, truly, it ought to be illegal, and then she wrenched her gaze forward again.

Leaving him behind her, where he belonged.

CHAPTER TWENTY-THREE

The next morning, Georgie slept late. This was unlike her—she was an early riser, despite how often she stayed up late; it was a joke in the family that she needed less sleep than the average person. But this morning, she was in bed until half nine—hours later than usual—and did not, in fact, awaken until she became dimly aware of a pounding at her bedroom door.

"What?" she called, not bothering to attempt to sound anything other than peevish, and a moment later Abigail poked her head through the door.

"Are you dead?" her sister asked bluntly. "Dying? Ill? Having some sort of personal crisis?" Her expression turned canny. "I expect it's the latter."

"Go away."

From her spot on the floor, Egg whined fretfully, and Georgie cast her an apologetic look. Wonderful. Now she was even worrying the *dog*.

Abigail rolled her eyes. "I need to be off. I'm taking Papa to purchase a new hat—he got sunburned on his head yesterday when we were on a walk—and then I'm going to the Scrumptious Scone to help Mrs. Chester for a few hours."

Georgie blinked at her sister—wide awake and fully dressed before ten in the morning—and wondered, in a wild moment, where the sister she'd spent her entire life with had gone. When had Abigail grown up and how had Georgie failed to notice?

Something of her thoughts must have shown on her face, because Abigail's smile turned a bit smug. "It's rather enjoyable, seeing you at a loss for words, you know. By the way," she added, as she turned to leave, "Sebastian's downstairs waiting for you. He's been lurking around the breakfast room ever since he came downstairs, more than an hour ago. He seems rather . . . agitated." She lowered her voice to a stage whisper. "He's *refusing to eat*."

And then, after imparting that astonishing bit of information, she was gone.

Georgie was downstairs five minutes later, Egg at her heels; she'd pulled on her pair of gardening dungarees, thinking that she might work in the garden for much of the day—and thinking, too, that she wanted to look as shabby and horrible as possible, if Sebastian thought that they were going to have some sort of romantic farewell before he caught his train. *Men!*

When she reached the base of the stairs, she found Sebastian deep in conversation with Papa; he said something that made Papa laugh, and something within Georgie softened at the sound. She cleared her throat, and Sebastian and Papa turned to watch as she descended the last couple of steps.

"Hello," she said warily.

Papa frowned. "Georgie, love, are you unwell? It's not like you to sleep this late."

Georgie matched his frown. "No. I'm merely tired, Papa." She paused, and wondered, startled, when had been the last time she'd admitted even the slightest bit of weakness to her father. She spent so much of her time ensuring that her family was well, that the wheels of Radcliffe Hall turned smoothly. For once, it was rather nice to not pretend to be all right, when she was feeling anything but.

Papa opened his mouth, but Abigail was there all of a sudden, seizing him by the elbow and practically pulling him out the door. "We'll see you later, Georgie," she called over her shoulder. With considerably more warmth she added, "Sebastian," and dimpled at him. He grinned at her in return. Georgie watched all this with exceedingly bad humor.

"Don't you have a train to catch?" she asked, the second the door shut behind her family.

"That depends," he said casually.

"Depends," Georgie repeated. "Depends on what, exactly?"

"Depends on whether you'll come with me."

Everything around Georgie seemed to go still and silent. Her focus was solely fixed on Sebastian, wearing . . .

She blinked. His trousers weren't perfectly pressed. His hair was a bit disheveled. She leaned closer. His jumper was on inside out.

"What is happening?" she said aloud, wondering if she was having a stroke.

"Not permanently," he said, taking a step closer to her.

"Just for a visit, for a couple of nights. I thought you might... well—" Here he broke off, looking a bit sheepish. "I thought you might need the reminder that London isn't so far from Buncombe-upon-Woolly, after all."

She'd never thought of his gaze as *piercing* before. It wasn't normally, surely? Perhaps a piercing gaze was a weapon he kept tucked up his sleeve, like a murderer with a knife. (Oh dear. Perhaps she *did* need to get out of Buncombe-upon-Woolly for a bit.)

"You don't have to come with me—*with* me, with me, I mean," he continued. "You can stay with your aunt, and I thought we could—or you could—I just thought, you could visit a few of the gardens in town and see if they're hiring apprentices. If you wanted, I mean." He fell silent, looking suddenly uncertain, but then, seemingly unable to stop himself, added in a rush, "But if none of that sounds appealing—if you truly don't want to ever move to London, if you want to stay here forever, I understand. It's not my job to tell you what to do. And I'll be back."

"You'll be back?" she asked, trying to make sense of his words.

"I've bought a return ticket," he said, as though that explained things.

"A return ticket," she said slowly. Stupidly.

"Yes."

"To come back... here," she added, her mind still not processing.

"Indeed." He gave an encouraging nod.

"To... see me?" she ventured, feeling her way in the dark.

"I wanted to explain this to you last night," he said, raising an eyebrow at her. "But you were rather intent on picking a fight with me, so I wasn't able to get around to it. You see," he continued, ignoring Georgie's indignant huff, "I intend to give my notice to Fitzgibbons—that's why it's so urgent that I return to London today—and I'd like to strike out on my own, set up my own agency. The past week has taught me that I rather like detective work—when it's actually being conducted properly. When we're actually helping people. And, well, it's the sort of work that doesn't *require* that I live any particular place. So I could set up shop in Buncombe-upon-Woolly," he said airily. "Even if your crime spree has come to an end, there are bound to be other rural murders—I even considered the fact that a notorious Murder Village on the business cards might add to my appeal with a prospective clientele. And I can't help but wonder if your friend Lexington might be interested in private detective work—though," he added, eyes twinkling, "I do think that in his case, the offer might actually be more appealing if the job were in London, near a certain reporter."

Georgie felt as though her brain were no longer functioning properly. "You would move to the Cotswolds . . . to be with me?"

"Georgie." His smile was gone now, his legendary charm suddenly entirely absent, his expression serious and his gaze on her direct. "I would move to Timbuktu if that were required to be with you."

"I don't think I'm the adventurous travel sort," she said, fighting a losing battle against the smile tugging at her mouth.

"All the better for me—I'd never keep my trousers properly pressed in that sort of environment."

"They're not pressed *now*," she pointed out, and he grinned at her.

"I know. I slept horribly last night—your fault—and I've been awake for hours. I was so rattled I seized the first pair of trousers at hand. The whole experience has been deeply shocking, as you can imagine, and I expect I'll need weeks to recover from this blow to my sleep regimen. Can't imagine what impact it will have on my stamina."

"Stamina, is it?" She smiled at him.

It was his turn to raise an eyebrow. "My dear Georgie. Are you flirting with me?"

"You see flirtation everywhere," she said, affecting coolness but not quite managing it with the smile that kept wanting to spread over her face.

"That," he said, pulling her toward him, "is not an answer to my question."

She reached out to rest her free hand on his chest and tilted her head back so that their eyes could meet. "Isn't it?"

She stood on her tiptoes to kiss him, and his arm snaked around her waist, pulling her flush with his chest. He tasted of sugar from his tea, and he smelled like whatever horribly expensive soap it was he used to shave. She wanted to sniff his skin. She wanted to *bite* him.

She pulled back, pressing her face to his neck. His breath was in her ears and was the slightest bit unsteady.

"I'll come with you," she said, and then her teeth grazed his throat.

"You will?" he asked, breathless. "Did you just bite me?"

"Of course not," she said, tilting her head back slightly so that she could look at him. "What sort of woman do you take me for?"

"My very favorite sort," he said, and the hint of color in his cheeks and the hungry look in his eyes as he regarded her meant that she did not doubt the truth of that response. "Do you mean it? You'll come to London?"

"I do," she said. "I think . . ." Here, she hesitated, feeling somehow frightened to voice the thought that had crossed her mind more than once in the past week. It felt so vulnerable to admit—and yet, she realized in a flash, there was no one she'd rather be vulnerable with than Sebastian. When had that happened? "I think that the reason I got sucked into solving murders—"

"Is because you're a genius?"

"Hush." She couldn't prevent the smile tugging at the corners of her mouth. "Is because I'm . . . bored. And I didn't know how to admit it. And so solving the mysteries, it gave me—a sense of purpose, I suppose. I didn't realize how much I'd needed that. And it's not—it's not an insult to this place to admit it. It doesn't mean I love the village, or the people, any less, to want to go away for a while. Not forever—this is home; I know it's where I'm meant to be."

"That botanic garden won't create itself," he agreed with a smile against her hair, and something in her chest tightened at the knowledge that he considered her dreams no less important than his own.

"It won't," she agreed. "But . . . it won't hurt to go with you for a couple of days, just . . . to see." She laughed a bit uncertainly. "But Sebastian, I don't—I don't want you to throw your career away and move to the middle of nowhere, just for me, if I get to London and decide I don't like it after all."

"But it's not throwing my career away," he said, and she frowned up at him. "It's doing something I should have done long ago; it's just that you've helped me see it."

"But still," she pressed; it would be so easy to relent here, so tempting to yield to the rosy view of the future he painted. But just as he wanted more for her, so she, too, wanted more for him. "Everyone underestimates you," she continued now, more quietly. "You underestimate *yourself*, but I think you're actually rather smart, despite your best attempts to convince me otherwise, and I want you to make a proper go at this. You deserve to have a job you love—one that will show everyone in your family how wrong they've been about you all these years. And if I return to the Cotswolds, and it would be better for you to remain in London—"

"No." He gave a quick, decisive shake of his head. "It's as I said—I can do this work anywhere. If I'm good enough at it—and I think I might be," he added, his voice uncharacteristically uncertain, nearly shy, "then the clients will follow. I just want . . ." He looked at her with an expression of naked yearning. "I just want to be with you." He searched her face, then added, "But there's no rush, Georgie. With you and me, I mean. I'll—" Here, he broke off, seeming to weigh his words carefully.

"You'll?" she asked, her heart kicking up an irregular rhythm in her chest.

"I'll be waiting," he said, "for as long as it takes for you to realize that we belong together. I love you, Georgie."

She blinked rapidly, staring at him, so handsome and rumpled and golden and perfect and, improbably, *hers*. If she wanted.

"I love you too," she said, stumbling over the words in her rush to get them out. She glanced down ruefully at her worn, stained dungarees. "If you don't mind..."

"Mind what?" he asked, his brow wrinkling.

"Mind the fact that I'm nothing like the women you must have known in London," she burst out, waving a hand before her face. "I'm not—not *polished*."

"No," he agreed, pulling her close. "You're perfect."

And before she could object, he kissed her again.

"How long will your father and sister be gone?" he asked, drawing back some indeterminate amount of time later. His hair was now looking even more tousled. She thought she rather liked it that way.

"A couple of hours, I should think," she said, a bit breathless.

"Well," he said, a sudden gleam in his eye, "if you need help packing, here in this large, empty house—"

"Mrs. Fawcett is in the kitchen," she informed him, before adding thoughtfully, "Which is ideal, really, as I'm sure you'll work up an appetite."

"Doing what, precisely?" he asked, the gleam in his eye even more pronounced.

"Helping me change my clothing," she said innocently. "I can hardly travel to London in my gardening dungarees."

"You can travel to London in an old sack, as far as I'm concerned," he said, looking as happy as she'd ever seen him.

She reached a hand up to feel his forehead. "If you no longer care about clothing, then we'd better go upstairs in a hurry—this might be our last chance, as you're surely feverish and will undoubtedly be dead soon. Besides," she added, "your jumper is inside out."

He glanced down, startled. "Good God almighty, perhaps I *am* dying."

"Well, at least you'll die a happy man," she said cheerfully, pulling at his hand and leading him back toward the stairs. He tugged her to a halt and kissed her, fierce and hard.

"The very, very happiest."

Later, there would be time to sort the details—of their journey to London, of whatever Georgie was going to do once she got there, and of what a future with Sebastian might look like—but for now, the house was quiet, Egg's tail was wagging, there was a handsome, posh man with hair to be rumpled and clothing to be removed, and, most importantly of all, no one at all was being murdered.

Acknowledgments

This book would not exist without my friend Meg Everist. Several years ago—before we both, in a weird twist of fate, moved to Maine within six months of each other and became close friends—we were coworkers at the Chapel Hill Public Library, and had a joking conversation at work one day about murder villages in mysteries, and the idea of a mystery novel about *why*, precisely, there were so many murders in a quaint village. Meg: Here, at long last, is the book I promised you.

With each successive book I write, I grow increasingly astonished at the good luck I have to get to work with my agent, Taylor Haggerty, and my editor, Kaitlin Olson. I wasn't sure how they'd feel when I floated the idea of a silly, spoofy mystery/rom-com mash-up, a definite departure from my Regency books, but they were both incredibly enthusiastic about the idea from the very beginning, and I am so appreciative. Kaitlin—I am grateful for your insight with every book, but honestly, given the state of

ACKNOWLEDGMENTS

my brain as I was writing this one, I am particularly grateful for it this time. Thank you for helping me turn this into the book I'd been dreaming of.

Endless thanks also to Gabrielle Greenstein, Jasmine Brown, Holly Root, and the rest of the astonishingly wonderful Root Literary team. At Atria, I'm so grateful to Zakiya Jamal, Megan Rudloff, Ifeoma Anyoku, Morgan Pager, and the copyeditor, sales team, art department (and Katie Smith for the beautiful cover art!), subrights team, and everyone else who makes my books as successful as possible. Getting to see so many of you in person at Book Bonanza last summer was an absolute joy (despite my jet lag).

Thank you to Sarah Hogle, who went on the emotional roller coaster of writing this book right along with me, and to the many author friends (Leah Stecher, Laura Sebastian, Alwyn Hamilton, Rosie Danan, Kaitlyn Hill, Sarah Adler, Emma Theriault, Tirzah Price, Sarah Chamberlain, Rachel Lynn Solomon, Marisa Kanter, Alicia Thompson, and Jen DeLuca, to name but a few) who—whether in person over a meal, sitting next to each other in a café on our laptops, or at the other end of a text message—made the act of writing a book feel less lonely.

Thank you to the booksellers, librarians, bloggers, and book influencers who spread the word about books they love, and to the readers who continue to pick up my work.

And, as always, thank you to my family, and my friends who are like family—most of you are an ocean away from me at present, but you're still the only reason I am able to write anything at all.

About the Author

Martha Waters is the author of *Christmas Is All Around* and the Regency Vows series, which includes *To Have and to Hoax*, *To Love and to Loathe*, *To Marry and to Meddle*, *To Swoon and to Spar*, and *To Woo and to Wed*. Originally from South Florida, she is a graduate of the University of North Carolina at Chapel Hill and currently lives in London.